LITTLE
LOST
DOLLS

BOOKS BY M.M. CHOUINARD

Detective Jo Fournier

The Dancing Girls

Taken to the Grave

Her Daughter's Cry

The Other Mothers

Her Silent Prayer

What They Saw

The Vacation

LITTLE
LOST
DOLLS

M.M. CHOUINARD

bookouture

Published by Bookouture in 2023

An imprint of Storyfire Ltd.
Carmelite House
50 Victoria Embankment
London EC4Y 0DZ

www.bookouture.com

ISBN: 978-1-83790-070-1
eBook ISBN: 978-1-83790-069-5

For Bianca

CHAPTER ONE

Madison Coelho cranked up the heat in her mother's beat-up Camry and stared out through the darkness, eyes glued to the house's lit windows.

She tried to shrink down into the seat but grunted when her belly wouldn't let her—she still wasn't used to the ever-growing bump. But they couldn't see her anyway, she was pretty sure; even if they glanced out of the wide-open curtains they'd only see their own reflections.

She clenched her teeth at the cozy tableau shining out through the cold fall evening—such a pretty domestic picture. *He* sat in the living room, watching some sitcom on the huge TV, sipping whiskey from a tumbler. *She* set the dining room table beyond him, periodically disappearing into the kitchen. Dripping gold and designer clothes, gliding in and out with plates and silverware and food, mouth moving as she sang some song through it all.

Of course she was singing—why wouldn't she be? *She* had all the comfort and peace and security that money could buy.

Madison's eyes narrowed as she imagined blowing up their illusion of perfection. Sauntering up and ringing the doorbell, drinking in *her* confused politeness. Seeing the panic on his face as he realized what was happening and raced to stop it.

"Your husband is my baby's father," she'd proclaim, watching his face.

What would he do? Call her a liar and slam the door? Or start begging for forgiveness, promising Madison meant nothing to him?

Yeah, well. That much was true, at least.

He needed to pay for what he'd done. But was calling him out the answer? It would only have the desired effect if *she* didn't already know what sort of man he was—but how could she not when it all paid for the fancy clothes and the big house and the bling? She'd probably just laugh and call the cops.

And if Madison did do that, he'd know the baby was his. With her luck, his one redeeming feature would be some deep desire to be a father, and he'd sue to be involved—maybe even try to take the baby away from her. And she didn't have money to pay the fees for small claims court, let alone fight that kind of legal battle.

He got up, refreshed his drink, and sat back down on the leather sofa. The sight of his profile sent a bundle of emotions Madison couldn't even label swirling up from her stomach, and suddenly the car was sweltering. It was all so jacked up—not only what he'd done to her, but that she'd been in that situation in the first place. She'd busted her ass in high school to get her scholarship, kept straight A's despite being on the debate team *and* in French club *and* working at McDonald's to save for the expenses the scholarship didn't cover. But then—

"Stop," she said aloud. There was no point going over it again and again. Life wasn't fair and crying about it wasn't going to change anything. Soon she'd have yet another person to take care of when she could barely hold it together as things were. She needed money and solutions, and she needed them fast.

As he laughed at whatever zany half-hour problem the

sitcom players were navigating, she gripped the steering wheel so hard her knuckles turned white, trying to convince herself to just walk away. She needed every bit of energy she had to continue putting one foot in front of the other.

But there was only so much any one person could take.

CHAPTER TWO

"Madison was late again tonight."

Naomie Alexander watched Madison's navy jacket disappear into the bistro's bathroom before she responded to the comment. "It's just an exercise class, Julia. Give her a little grace."

"I have." Julia Gagnon's dark eyes followed Naomie's gaze. "She was late to one session last week and missed another completely."

"She has so much on her plate, and our Friday klatch should be a safe space. Don't get on her about it." Keeping one hand on her belly, Naomie braced herself with the other as she slid onto the ice-cream-parlor-style chair, hoping the little flutter she'd just felt would repeat.

"Everything okay?" Julia's razor-sharp professional gaze bounced between Naomie's face and belly.

Naomie pulled her mahogany waves up to let the cool air brush her neck. "The baby's just kicking. It's getting more distinct now, like she's trying to say hi."

Julia's face eased, and she picked up the menu. "Right on track for twenty-three weeks."

Naomie stroked her bump. In addition to being a certified nurse midwife who worked with Naomie at Beautiful Bouncing Babies—Naomie's maternal-and-infant-health non-profit that served Oakhurst on a sliding-scale basis—Julia was her aunt-in-law and friend. Julia was married to her uncle Pete, the youngest of her father's brothers, and was only ten years older than Naomie's thirty. Naomie had been ten when they'd married, and she'd adored her aunt as long as she could remember. Julia had taught her how to apply make-up, style outfits, and speak Puerto-Rican Spanish like a native. Now she was guiding Naomie through her first pregnancy.

One of Julia's phones buzzed and she dipped into her omnipresent black tote to check the notification. "Should we just order for Madison and Chelsea? They always get the same thing."

Naomie glanced toward the restroom, then the entrance. "No, let's wait in case they want something different. I'm sure they won't be long."

Julia glanced at her watch, then poked at her braided black topknot, absently ensuring it was in place.

Naomie studied her face. Even at Julia's most relaxed, she could never be called easy-going, but something seemed off tonight. "Everything okay?"

Julia grimaced and flicked the question away with her hand. "Just a few things I need to take care of. I'll do the Mango Madness this time." She set the menu down and glanced back toward the entrance.

"Something to do with Triple-B?" While Naomie ran the administrative side of Beautiful Bouncing Babies with her cofounder, Julia was the hands-on medical professional who saw clients and taught classes to expectant mothers.

"Partly. I have two people in my Birthing From Within class who are getting close to delivery, and I want to check in on them." Her purse buzzed again, but after a quick glance in it, Julia lasered back in on Naomie's abdomen. "So, no problems?"

"Not really. I've been having trouble sleeping and I could do without the hot flashes, but I'm just glad I'm not getting morning sickness anymore. You were right, the prenatal exercise class is helping," Naomie said. "Thanks for talking me into it."

"You need to set a good example for the clients." Julia glanced around the room again.

"True." Naomie laughed.

Julia's posture relaxed slightly as Madison reappeared and wove her way through the tables. All the women in the exercise class were lovely, but from the moment Naomie met Madison they'd had a special connection. Naomie had always longed for a younger sister, and at nearly a decade younger than Naomie, Madison slipped right into that space. Probably because Madison had a slightly lost quality to her that resonated with Naomie's maternal instincts—instincts she'd had since cradling her first Do-It-All Dolly, and that were currently in hormonal overdrive searching for an outlet.

Naomie stood and carefully hugged her around both their bumps. "I haven't had a real chance to say hi yet today."

Madison's round cheeks flushed, and her eyes dropped to the floor. "I'm so sorry I was late to session. I, um, had to run an errand right before." She hung her jacket over the back of her chair and eased herself down.

"No need to apologize." Naomie smiled. "I hope all is well."

Madison shot a glance at Julia. "I don't want you to think I'm not taking it seriously. I know the spots for people who can't afford to pay are limited."

Naomie waved her off. "How you ever make it on time between your day job and night classes and taking care of your mother I'll never know."

Madison smiled her gratitude, then her brows popped up. "Oh, I got your email. You said you needed to talk to me?"

"You. Guys. I am *so sorry*." Chelsea Whitens appeared at the table breathless and hurricane-frenetic, messy blonde bangs bouncing around her face and hot-pink tunic flapping as she navigated her swollen abdomen under the table. "I got caught up talking to the others after class and they *would not stop* talking about breast pumps. I'm in such deep denial about breast pumps I can't even tell you. So horrifying—just keep that whole topic *far* away from me."

Naomie smiled indulgently. If Madison was like a little sister to her, Chelsea was like a sorority sister. Ironic, given they were fairly different. Chelsea was petite and blonde to Naomie's tall and auburn, and had cheerleading and Insta-obsessed energy rather than Naomie's more quiet career focus. And while Naomie was happily married, Chelsea was single, her pregnancy an accident from a boyfriend who turned out to have a wife and children. But Chelsea was only a year younger than Naomie, and they instinctively under-stood the core of each other's Ivy League, wealthy-family backgrounds.

"You can't put off getting your breast pump much longer," Julia said, expression pointed.

Chelsea scrunched her nose and laughed. "I have *three whole weeks* before my due date. Plenty of time, Miss Teacher."

A shadow passed over Madison's face. "I don't know how you do it, Chels. I wake up in a panic every day about being a single mother, but you're so confident and effortless. Too bad you can't lay hands on me or something and transfer some of that calm."

Chelsea reached over and squeezed her hand. "Oh, stop. I've just had two more months to prepare for it, that's all."

Both Madison's and Chelsea's faces flickered. Naomie understood Madison's expression: Chelsea hadn't had all that much more time, but she definitely had more money. And no matter what people tried to claim, money bought a fair amount of peace. But Chelsea's reaction confused her—for a reason she didn't understand, it felt disingenuous.

Julia's purse buzzed again. As she checked it, she gestured the waitress over. "Should we order?"

"I'd like the Caribbean Craze smoothie with extra coconut and a vitamin boost, please," Chelsea said when the waitress arrived.

"I'm in full fall mode, so I'll take the Cranberry Pumpkin, also with the vitamin boost," Madison said when the waitress's gaze shifted to her.

"We're so predictable." Julia laughed but her jaw tightened, and after she ordered she glanced at her watch again.

Surely Julia couldn't be annoyed just because Naomie hadn't wanted to order for the others ahead of time? No, something odd must be happening with her clients for her to be this on edge. But she wouldn't respond well if Naomie pressed her about it in front of the others, no matter how close their group was becoming.

"But seriously, though, Chels," Madison said once the waitress gathered up the menus. "At the risk of getting gooshy, I admire you. When you found out David was married, you didn't hesitate, you just kicked him to the curb. That couldn't have been easy."

Chelsea beamed. "I'm a firm believer that you have to know what you deserve in life, and *demand* it." She punctuated the point with a bubblegum-pink acrylic nail. "You can't spend your life with someone that doesn't make you happy. That's not good for you *or* your child."

Julia cleared her throat. "Speaking of which. Pete and I are getting a divorce."

Naomie's gaze dropped to the table. She'd known there were problems, but had respected Julia's privacy by keeping quiet. And, if she were honest with herself, because she'd been hoping Julia and Uncle Pete would work out their issues.

"You're sure?" Madison asked.

"He filed last week." Julia stared toward the open kitchen where various fruits were blending into liquid oblivion.

"Damn," Chelsea said. "I'm sorry."

"Don't be." Julia's smile was tight and brisk. "Didn't some comedian say no happy marriage ever ended in divorce?"

Naomie shook her head. "What happens now?"

The waitress returned and distributed their rainbow of smoothies.

Julia lifted hers in a toast, and smiled for the first time since they'd arrived. "I'll tell you what happens now. We all go on a shopping spree tomorrow afternoon. There's an adorable new baby-slash-maternity-wear boutique I spotted in Oakhurst the last time I visited my son, right next to where I get my favorite dresses. I need something to cheer myself up."

Chelsea's eyes lit up over the straw in her mouth, and she hurried to swallow. "Yes, yes, *yes*! Nothing like a little retail therapy. I need a pick-me-up."

A shadow settled on Madison's face. "I should probably study."

Naomie wasn't fooled. "Study after. I have no idea what to get for your shower, so you need to come pick something out." Pleased when relieved excitement crept over Madison's face, Naomie turned to Chelsea. "You need a pick-me-up? Is everything okay?"

Another odd something flashed over Chelsea's face, but she covered it with a grimace and a wave. "Just my back, all that. The only place I'm comfortable these days is in the pool."

Naomie kept her skepticism hidden—a shopping trip would make the backache worse, not better. Should she push to find out what the real issue was? No—a text later would be more discreet.

"Good, that's settled, then. One o'clock tomorrow at

Maman et Bébé in Oakhurst." Julia stood. "In the meantime, I have to visit the ladies' room. Be right back."

Naomie watched Julia wend her way toward the bathroom, trying to sort out what was happening. Everyone had warned her about 'pregnancy brain,' that she'd become forgetful, but nobody told her it would interfere with her ability to read people. Her normally spot-on instincts had turned oversensitive and indiscriminate. All her friends seemed off tonight—out of sorts and evasive. But they couldn't *all* be hiding something.

Could they?

———

Julia slid quickly into the bathroom stall and shot the bolt into place, grateful for the moment of silence. Everything was getting on her last nerve today, from Madison's tardiness to Chelsea's normally endearing chatter.

She winced at the word *tardiness*. When had she turned into an elderly school marm? Between the moodiness and the gray hair she'd spotted that morning in her eyebrow, she'd think she was going through early menopause if she didn't know better. But no, this was just the stress of everything hitting the fan, and it would pass as soon as she got a handle on things. But if she had to hear Chelsea chirp for one minute longer she'd drown the girl in her Caribbean Craze.

Julia pulled out her phones. Eight unread messages between them, some from Pete. She winced at the prospect of whatever he had to say—if only there were a filter that only sent through the messages you wanted to see, while stashing the others out of sight until you had the emotional bandwidth to deal with them. Until that day, she had no choice but to get on with it.

But she could soften it all by checking Rick's first. She tapped the first chain of three.

Missing you, babe.

Then, twenty minutes later:

We need to celebrate.

And ten minutes after that:

Swing by tonight?

Temptation pulled at her. Rick was five years younger, with the energetic fitness of a cyclist and the Italian good looks of Raoul Bova. Nobody could sand off her rough edges better, and right now she needed to feel wanted. But it wasn't safe.

Not tonight, love. Long day.

She picked up the other phone, then tapped on Pete's messages. The first three had come in quick succession:

I just got off the phone with Simon.

This is fucking ridiculous.

Five thousand dollars last month?

Then, after a fifteen-minute delay:

I told you, this is NOT how this is going to go down.

I warned you.

She burst out a sarcastic laugh, and her thumbs shot over

the screen, typing a response. *What are you going to do, divorce me?*

She stared down at it, itching to hit Send. *He* was the one who'd pulled the trigger on all of this. *He* was the one who'd fallen out of love with her and wanted the marriage to end, not her. Did he think she was going to make it easy for him to dump her? After all these years? After she bore and reared his son, nearly dying in the process?

But she was walking a very, *very* fine line. One misstep would send her over the edge into oblivion, and she couldn't allow that to happen. If she could stay the course for a few months, everything would be okay.

She deleted the message.

After a push that slammed the stall door into the wall, she washed her hands out of habit, then strode back to the table.

Chelsea swiped at her bottle bangs. "We were starting to get worried about you."

"Everything okay?" Naomie's hazel eyes held hers.

"Just fine." Julia forced herself to smile. Naomie would see through the lie, but she'd also be sensitive enough not to say anything in front of the others. Julia raised her hand to signal their bored-looking server.

The waitress hurried over and set the check down in the middle of the table. Julia reached for it.

Chelsea's bubble-gum clad arm shot out to intercept her. "We can't let you pay on the day your husband filed for divorce. It's not right."

Madison chimed in agreement, but Naomie kept quiet. She knew better than to poke that particular wound.

"It's my turn, and that's that." Julia plunked her credit card into the little black folder. No way was she going to allow Pete's choices to define her life.

"I was just looking at that shop you mentioned." Chelsea held up her phone, now prominently displaying the Maman et

Bébé website. "Look at all the adorable stuff! Seriously, a toddler tuxedo? How did I not know about this place?"

Julia smiled as the others fussed and cooed, swiping and pinching and pointing at outfits. Shopping may not be able to buy true happiness, but it sure as hell smoothed over the cracks.

The waitress sidled up to her, and Julia reached automatically to take her credit card and slip.

The woman leaned in, looking embarrassed, and lowered her voice. "I'm so sorry, but the card was rejected."

A hush fell over the other ladies.

"Please try it again," Julia asked.

"I, um." The waitress cleared her throat. "I did. The card has been reported stolen."

The world froze for a moment as Julia stared at the woman, trying to make sense of what she was saying, while the other women looked anywhere but at her.

The son of a bitch.

Heat rushed up her neck as the realization hit, but she pinned a delightfully confused look onto her face and reached into her purse. "How strange! Not a problem, I have another one here." She extracted a second card and sent the waitress off to process it.

Thank goodness she'd listened to her mother. *Never go out on a date without money for a cab*, she'd said when Julia started dating at fifteen. *You never know when a man will leave you high and dry, or you'll have to make a quick getaway.* Julia had extended that wisdom as soon as she realized her marriage was in danger, channeling whatever small sums she could manage into a checking and savings account Pete didn't know about and securing a set of emergency credit cards. But despite knowing this was coming, she hadn't realized how painful it would be to have the man who'd once loved her and promised to care for her now declare war on her.

The other women were back to chatting. She sat straighter,

lifted her chin, and joined back in. Because she'd faced far worse than this before and always managed to survive.

If this was how he wanted it, this was how it would be.

———

Chelsea twisted and turned her way into the front seat of her silver Lexus, then started it up. As she waited for Julia to pull out of the parking spot next to her, a strange motion in one of the nearby parked cars caught her eye. She peered through the darkness, trying to make anything out. A man in a baseball cap sat in one, staring down like something was in his lap, and didn't look up as she watched. But something about it gave her the creeps.

She shook her head and rolled her eyes. She was just being paranoid because of all the time she spent driving past Sophie and David's house, and David's new place. She didn't like being *that* girl, but David was her baby's father and she needed his help. She had to know the truth about him and his wife.

She followed Julia out of the parking lot, fixating on the horrific braided bun that made Julia look like a guard in some 1960s prison movie. Try as she might, Chelsea's subtle hints about how sexy Julia would look in a messy bun went nowhere. Such a shame, because Julia really had a decent figure—for a forty-something—though she had to hide it under nurse's scrubs most of the time. But even when she wore her black hair down, she kept it pin straight—*so* two-thousand-and-ten. Such a shame she refused to try a little harder.

Ugh, that scene with the waitress and the credit card—absolutely humiliating. Julia had tried to play it off, but the flush on her neck said it all. Thank the Lord above Chelsea had her own money, and wouldn't ever need a man financially. But then— she glanced at the phone sticking out of her purse—money wasn't the only way a man could screw you over.

As Chelsea turned out of the lot, she threw a goodbye wave to Naomie in the car behind her, then watched until she and Madison turned off onto their respective routes. Once they were out of sight, her hand dropped to her stomach. She spoke to the car. "Call David."

The call rang. Then again. Three times—each a stab in her heart. Back in the day he'd pick up the second she called, at least when he wasn't home with his wife and the girls. Even then, he'd text right away.

He finally picked up. "Chelsea. Is everything okay?"

"Hi, David. Yeah, I'm okay. I mean, I'm *okay* okay. But I'm feeling a little strange, and I'm not quite sure what to do. I'm sorry to bug you."

Whatever chair he was in creaked. "What do you mean, strange?"

"It's probably totally fine but I'm having some pains. Not bad, just little stabs. Is that normal? Did that happen with your girls?"

"Not that I remember. When was the last time you felt the baby move?" he asked.

"Just a few minutes ago. That's why I think it's okay, just maybe like Braxton Hicks or something. I shouldn't have bothered you, it's just I'm never quite sure—"

"Don't be silly." Something rustled in the background. "Go to the ER and I'll meet you there."

"Oh, no," she said. "I don't think it's bad enough for that. But if it gets any worse I will."

"It sounds like you're in the car right now," he said.

"I am, but I'm almost home. It's okay, I think maybe I just ate something that didn't agree with me."

"I don't like the idea of you being alone." He sounded concerned, and unsure what to do. "Make sure you keep the phone right next to you in case you need to call an ambulance."

"Okay, I will." She pursed her brow. "I'll ask Sienna to come over. That way somebody's here if something happens."

He paused for a long moment. "No, don't do that, we don't need her raising your blood pressure. I'll come sleep on the couch."

She had to push back. "No, David, it's okay. Sienna and I can manage for short periods. I know my sister well enough to know she won't be happy but it's late enough she'll just bury herself in the guest bedroom anyway."

His voice took on a scornful edge. "If she even says yes. When was the last time you talked to her?"

"Now you're upset. I shouldn't have called you, but I wasn't—"

"Of course you should have called me. It's my responsibility to see you through this. I'm coming over now, and I don't want to argue." He hung up the phone.

She hit End Call on the steering wheel, and stared out into the darkness, the car silent around her, carefully navigating each stop and turn.

CHAPTER THREE

"Aunty Jo, look at this one!"

Josette Fournier turned to where Emily and Isabelle, her nieces, waved from amid the sprawling tangles of the pumpkin patch. She burst out laughing when she saw the huge, convoluted orange monstrosity they were hovering over.

"Come look, come look, come look!" six-year-old Emily called as nine-year-old Isabelle thrust her hand on her hips.

Jo glanced up at Matt Soltero and gave a gentle they're-so-crazy shake of her head. Matt squeezed her hand. "We have to humor them."

"Do we though?" She laughed.

As they headed toward the girls, he snaked his arm around her. She leaned into his side, etching every bit of the moment into her memory: the cool, crisp fall air biting into her cheeks; the slashes of brown and green and orange framing the earthy smells of the dying pumpkin vines; the soft glow of the late-afternoon Saturday sun; her niece's elfin laughter. But most of all, the warmth of Matt's body pressing through her jacket, ensuring that whenever she thought back to this day, Matt would be an integral part of it all.

Her heart soared with appreciation for him. Handsome with dark hair and eyes, warm brown skin crinkled with wisps of middle-aged wrinkles, and a tall musculature he kept fit, he was also smart, gentle, and kind. Just about the ideal partner, yet she'd almost managed to ruin the relationship right out of the gate—when he'd moved in a few weeks back, the wounded part of her psyche had rejected the infringement on her personal and psychological space. She still battled moments of claustrophobia, but they were fading against the glimmers of security growing within her.

"See, Aunty Jo! It's perfect!" Emily cried.

"What are you going to do with that, *mes chères*? It's almost as big as you are!" Jo said.

"Not for us, for you! For your porch! You can give it triangle eyes and fangs for teeth and paint it with green stripes and it'll be a monster!" Emily did a little jumping dance, pointing to various parts of the gnarled gourd.

"But I don't put out a jack-o'-lantern," Jo said. "And you're supposed to be picking out pumpkins for yourselves."

"But you have to put one out this year. You and Uncle Matt have to do *something* to celebrate Halloween," Isabelle said, her tone telegraphing how ridiculous Jo was to not have considered this.

Jo hid her smile and looked up at Matt. "What do you think? I have no idea how to even go about carving something that big. I think it weighs more than I do."

He playfully puffed out his chest and flexed his biceps. "I haven't met a pumpkin I couldn't bend to my will. Wrap it up!"

The girls cheered, and Isabelle said, "We should take a selfie with it."

A small corner of Jo's heart tugged. Isabelle was hurtling toward that tween phase where selfies and Instagram would take over her life, and the little girl she'd been would disappear.

Jo pulled Matt into a squat in front of the pumpkin and the

girls pressed in on either side of them. She snapped three pictures, and marveled as she showed them to the girls how much more Emily looked like her each day—Emily's chestnut hair was now below her shoulders just like Jo's, and her green eyes glowed out from the same heart-shaped face.

The girls chimed approval, then ran back out into the field in search of their own pumpkins.

"I can't believe you fell for that," David, her brother-in-law, said as he and her sister Sophie appeared next to them. "That thing'll take over your porch."

"That's what aunts are for. To be indulgent." Jo took the cider Sophie handed to her, then removed the lid and blew on the contents to cover the annoyance she didn't want to show.

Several months before, David had been caught cheating on Sophie with a much-younger woman, Chelsea Whitens. A bad enough mistake on its own, but he'd also gotten her pregnant, which meant Sophie and the girls would have to deal with the fallout of that mistake for the rest of their lives. Sophie had been struggling with whether to get a divorce or give David a second chance; he claimed Sophie was the woman he truly loved and had asked her to take him back. This trip to the pumpkin patch, buffered by the presence of Jo and Matt, was a first tentative step to see how it felt to bring him back into the fold. She'd support Sophie in whatever decision she made —but even if Sophie could forgive him, Jo wasn't sure she ever could.

"I want this one!" Emily hopped up and down next to a squat fairy-tale pumpkin.

"That one's too short, you won't be able to carve it," David answered.

"I can, too! It will have a small face, like a dolly," Emily said.

"Fine, but I don't want to see a single tear later if it goes wrong," Sophie said.

Emily crossed her heart. "I promise."

"I want this one," Isabelle said, standing a few yards away next to a perfect, round orange globe.

Jo smiled. Not only did Emily favor Jo in looks while Isabelle was the spitting image of Sophie, their personalities had the same parallels. Emily was fearless and spirited while Isabelle was traditional and staid.

"Looks like we're done, then," David said, cutting off Isabelle's pumpkin.

"Time for the corn maze!" Emily did another little dance.

As the girls ran ahead with their pumpkins and David and Matt struggled with the mutant monstrosity, Jo leaned over to Sophie. "How's it going?"

Sophie pushed her light-brown bob behind both ears and shrugged. "Very strange. On the one hand, it's familiar and comfortable, like nothing ever happened. On the other, it's alien and bizarre, like everything's different. Like that bodysnatcher movie you loved when we were kids."

Jo understood—she'd been having a similar reaction. "Do you think you're going to let him come home?"

Sophie glanced back at David. "I think so. If I take him back and he cheats again, our marriage will be over, but I know now I'm strong enough to make it through that pain. But if I don't give him a second chance, I'd spend the rest of my life wondering if I gave up too easily on my marriage."

"And you've got your boundaries in place?" Jo asked.

"I have a list of topics we need to agree on before he comes back. Mom said if today goes well, she'll take the kids tomorrow so he and I can have a little chat about it all."

"Sounds very organized and well-thought out." Jo bumped her shoulder into Sophie's. "I'd expect no less from you."

They paid for the pumpkins and put them into their respective trunks, then strolled over to the entrance to the corn maze.

"I think we should do teams, and see who finishes first," Isabelle said.

Emily ran to Jo and grabbed her hand. "Then I want to go with Aunty Jo and Uncle Matt."

"So what are the rules?" Jo asked.

"At the first branch, we go right and you go left."

"And no running," Sophie said. "The adults set the pace."

As they lined up for tickets, Jo's phone rang, displaying a number she didn't recognize. She considered not answering it, but visions of her ill-tempered lieutenant flashed through her mind. She tossed her empty cider cup into the nearby trash can and tapped the phone to answer. "Josette Fournier."

"Jo, this is Chelsea Whitens. I need your help. My friend Madison is missing."

CHAPTER FOUR

Chelsea Whitens? Was this some sort of sick joke? She must have misheard, because why the hell would David's mistress be calling her?

Jo held up a finger to signal she needed a minute, then turned her back and strode far enough away from the group to be out of earshot. "Who did you say this is?"

"Chelsea Whitens. It's weird I know, but please don't hang up. We need your help." Her voice trembled.

Jo's hand flew up to the bridge of her nose. "How did you get my number?"

"It was on the list of emergency numbers David gave me for when the baby comes," Chelsea said.

Waves of red-hot anger flew up the sides of Jo's head. What the hell was David thinking? She made a mental note to punch him directly in his face as soon as he was out of sight of the girls. "Call the local police, Ch—" She cut herself off—the last thing she needed was for Sophie to hear her say that name. "Call the local police."

"We did, but they won't help us. They said they can't do anything but 'put her in the system' because she probably just forgot about our shopping date. But she definitely didn't and you're the only person I know in law enforcement."

You don't know me. Jo's eyes squeezed together with the effort to bite back the response. "Is Madison an adult?"

"Of course. She's twenty. Or twenty-one."

"Then they're right, there's nothing they can—"

Chelsea's tone rose. "She's not a flake. She's late sometimes but she would have called us and she didn't and she's not picking up her phone and her mother said she hasn't seen her or the dog since this morning when she went for a walk, and—"

"Stop," Jo sliced through the jumble of pronouns. "Breathe. Count to ten."

As Chelsea counted her way through a series of deep breaths, Jo glanced back over her shoulder to where Sophie was staring impatiently at her. She'd had nightmares like this—quite literally. Despite recent improvements, her relationship with her sister was fraught with hidden sibling traps and fault lines; if Sophie had even the slightest reason to think Jo was on even cordial terms with her nemesis, a black hole would open up and spaghettify their relationship in seconds flat. But at the same time, she couldn't turn her back on a missing girl who might need help.

When Chelsea finished her count, Jo said, "Okay, start from the beginning. Why do you think Madison is missing?"

"We were all supposed to meet at one this afternoon for a shopping trip, but she didn't show. We spent over an hour inside the boutique shopping, figuring she'd turn up. But when we finished and she still hadn't shown up or called or texted, we called her. Her phone just went to voice mail, so we called her mother, but—"

"Aunty Jo. Come ooooooooon!" Emily's voice rang out behind her.

"Hold on." Jo turned and made eye contact with Sophie, mouthed the word "work," then flapped her hand toward the maze to indicate they should start without her. She shifted her eyes to Matt, and mouthed "sorry." Matt smiled and winked, then turned and said something to the girls. They ran to him, then into the rows of corn.

"Where are you right now?" Jo asked Chelsea.

"At Know What I Bean in Oakhurst."

Know What I Bean was a café in the fancier part of Oakhurst, surrounded by upscale boutiques. "I'm not far away. I'll be there as soon as I can."

———

After hanging up, Jo sent a text to Matt and Sophie explaining that a girl had gone missing. She'd have to miss the maze, but would meet up with them for dinner after they finished.

Sophie's response came quickly: *If anybody can find her, you can. See you soon.*

Bile bit into Jo's throat as she stared at the message. This felt like a betrayal, like she was some sort of cheating wife sneaking off to see a lover. She wanted to be upfront right now, from the start, but dumping that on Sophie while she was with Matt and the girls would ruin the outing. So, stomach churning, she shoved her phone away and strode to her Chevy Volt.

Ten minutes later Jo pushed into the brick-wall-and-brass interior of the café and, amid the rich coffee aroma swirling around her, scanned for Chelsea. She'd only seen David's mistress once before—in a picture of them kissing—but that image was burned into her memory, and she spotted the butter-blonde curls immediately. Dressed in a pink maternity top dotted with sunflowers, Chelsea sat at a table with two other women, all three gripping their cups with worried expressions. One, also pregnant, was white with auburn waves and bright hazel eyes; clad in sophisticated neutrals, her easy, casual grace sent an image of Jackie O flashing through Jo's mind. The other woman, a brown-eyed Latina with straight raven hair, kept an eye on the other two without seeming to.

Chelsea spotted her as she approached and started to rise, bracing her back with one hand. "Jo?"

The too-casual use of her nickname was nails on her mental chalkboard. But she'd decided the best way to handle the situation was to treat Chelsea like any other witness she was meeting for the first time. As for how she'd deal with Sophie, well, she was still praying for divine inspiration before dinner.

"Please, don't get up." Jo met Chelsea's eyes, then turned to the other two women. "I'm Detective Josette Fournier of the Oakhurst County State Police Detective Unit. You're friends of Madison?"

"We are." Jackie O pointed to the free chair. "Please sit. I'm Naomie Alexander, and this is my aunt-in-law, Julia Gagnon."

Jo shook each woman's hand, then sat. "How do you know Madison?"

"Primarily through our prenatal exercise class." Naomie nodded across the table. "Julia teaches the class. But I've known Madison a little longer, since I'm the head of administration at Beautiful Bouncing Babies, the non-profit that holds the class."

Jo kept her tone neutral. "So, you've only known her for a few months?"

Chelsea jumped in. "We've become close quickly. Pregnancy is such an *intense* experience. We have three evening classes every week, and we hang out after our Friday class. Like happy hour with juice instead of alcohol."

"Got it." Jo refrained from pointing out that, no matter how many exercise classes were involved, there was a limit to how deep a friendship could run in such a short time. "Ms. Whitens gave me a quick version of why you're all concerned. Ms. Alexander, can you walk me through the day again?"

"Naomie, please." Once Jo nodded acknowledgment, Naomie recapped essentially the same story Chelsea had told

Jo. "So we called her mother, but Madison had already taken the dog for a walk when she woke up. She assumed Madison had just stayed at the park to study, because she does that sometimes."

Jo pulled out her notepad and pen. "Her mother lives with her?"

"Yes, in an apartment in Phelpston. Her mother's sick, so she moved in with Madison." Chelsea tapped at her phone. "I'm texting you a recent picture of her."

Naomie sent Chelsea a quick, wary glance. "I'm sure it doesn't matter, but Madison never moved out. They live in the apartment Madison grew up in."

"Oh, right, sorry." A slash of pink flushed Chelsea's cheeks.

Naomie laid a gentle, brief hand on Chelsea's forearm. "I only know because I took down all her financial details at Triple-B."

Jo pulled up the picture. Madison was younger than Naomie and Chelsea by about a decade, with a girl-next-door type of prettiness telegraphed with brown hair and eyes over an infectious dimpled smile. "Her mother's sick?"

Julia answered. "COPD that recently progressed into emphysema. She's now on continual oxygen."

Jo nodded. Her uncle Hebert, a life-long two-pack-a-day smoker, had recently been diagnosed with emphysema and put on oxygen. "So when Madison didn't return from her walk, her mother assumed she was studying. Are you sure that isn't the case?"

Naomie's hands rubbed the sides of her coffee cup. "She'd have picked up when we called. She always had her phone on at least vibrate in case her mother needed her."

"And there's just no way she would have missed shopping with us." Chelsea's head thrashed back and forth. "Naomie was going to pick out Madison's shower gift at the boutique, so she'd have been insane to—" She stopped abruptly.

Jo's antennae went up, and she quickly scanned the women's expressions. Naomie's: slight distress. Julia's: distaste directed at Chelsea. "Insane to what?"

Chelsea cleared her throat. "I normally wouldn't say something so rude, but Madison was... struggling financially. The chance to pick out something at such a high-end store was a big deal."

A new understanding fell over Jo. Madison wasn't like these women, who each wore hundreds of dollars of designer clothing and jewelry. She recalibrated the group dynamics, tailoring her image of Madison, then resumed. "Does she have a romantic partner? Someone she might be with and forgotten the time?"

The women glanced at each other; Naomie answered. "She's single and not dating."

Something in their expressions pulled at her. "She's not with her baby's father, then?"

"She's not," Naomie answered. "He doesn't know about the baby."

A thousand unpleasant possibilities sprung up in Jo's head, and her fragile hope that Madison was okay began to crack. "What's his name?"

Naomie glanced at the others, who shook their heads. "We don't know. She didn't like to talk about it, and we didn't want to push."

So much for the deeply close friendship. "So she was caring for her mother while also dealing with a pregnancy on her own. And she's in school?"

"She takes evening classes." Naomie's hands resumed rubbing her cup. "And she's a part-time receptionist at a chiropractic office."

Jo jotted down the company name Naomie gave her. "That's a lot for one person to handle, especially a twenty-year-old. Has she been depressed, anything like that?"

"She's been late recently, and missed a class session," Julia said.

"But she's been in a good mood," Chelsea said. "I don't think she would hurt herself."

"Do you know of anybody she was on bad terms with?" Jo asked.

"No, nobody," the women chorused.

Jo switched gears. "Where does Madison normally walk?"

"Crone Ridge Woods. She lives right next to the back end of it," Naomie said.

Jo nodded. "Who did you talk to at Phelpston PD?"

Naomie slid a card across the table. "Officer Garaffolo. He said we could reach him at this number."

Jo snapped a picture of the card, asked for Madison's home address, then closed the notebook and met each of the women's eyes in turn. "Unfortunately, what Officer Garaffolo told you is correct. Without evidence of foul play, we can't do much more than put her in the database and check to be sure nobody matching her description has shown up at any area hospitals or such." No need to use the word 'morgue' if she could avoid it.

"Can't you send out a search party into Crone Ridge Woods or something?" Chelsea asked.

"Not with what you've told me so far. Adults have the right to disappear if they choose. But I'll talk to Officer Garaffolo and Madison's mother and see if there are any leads we can pursue. With as much as Madison has on her plate, it's very possible she just got overwhelmed and needed some time to herself."

Chelsea's face tightened. "Then I think the three of us should go look there ourselves. If she did fall asleep or something, she might still be there."

"If you do, stay together and keep to populated areas," Jo said. "I'll be in touch as soon as I talk to Phelpston PD and Madison's mother."

CHAPTER FIVE

Phelpston was the sort of small town that had ebbed and flowed over the years. In the early 1900s it housed the men who ran the nearby mills, giving them a place close enough to be hands-on with their businesses while being far enough away that they weren't rubbing noses with the workers they employed. As time and technology forged forward, cars replaced carriages and the few miles' distance became irrelevant; the wealthy escaped to farther enclaves, taking their money and leaving a gradual decline only briefly interrupted by a burst of post-war prosperity. Artists and entrepreneurs looking for cheap rents inadvertently brought the town a cultural, if not fiscal, renaissance during the seventies by attracting hippies, who, when it came time to rear their broods, departed for climes less bohemian and more yuppie-focused. By the turn of the new millennium, meth and oxy rooted themselves into the counterculture cracks, leaving abandoned psychedelic murals to peek through gang tags and section-eight housing havens dominating the original, ancient Victorians. Just a few months before, the roof of one decrepit apartment building collapsed, nearly killing several tenants.

Jo stared up at the gray-beige concrete monstrosity in front of her and wondered, based on the furiously peeling paint, how likely *this* roof was to stay put.

She shook her head and pushed into the internal hallway, then found her way to apartment 1B. Madison's mother took a long moment to answer the door; she clutched a cane and stooped under a gray, purse-like oxygen tank draped over her shoulder that trailed a tube up her chest, around her ears, and to her nose. Her face, an older version of Madison's, was pinched and wide-eyed.

"Susan Coelho?" Jo asked.

"Yes. Are you with the police?"

Jo introduced herself and explained why she'd come. "You haven't seen Madison since last night?"

"Please come in." Susan stepped back and gestured to a couch swathed in an ill-fitting gray fabric cover, then lowered herself into a matching armchair. "Last night when I went to bed around midnight. She was already gone when I woke up. She walks Ginger every morning first thing."

Jo took in the room as she sat. Sparse, except for two plastic-framed art prints that bookended a wall decal exhorting 'Give thanks with a grateful heart' in flowery script. "What time did you wake up?"

"Around eight, but I read in bed until ten. I just assumed she decided to study up at the ridge so the house would be quiet for me. But then her friend said Madison was supposed to meet them and she didn't answer the phone when I called. She always answers when I call, even when I forget she's in class, because of my condition. And she doesn't have any Saturday classes this term anyway."

"Saturday classes? Isn't that unusual?"

Pink spots bloomed on Susan's face, and she wrung her hands. "She goes to Phelpston Community College. They schedule classes for people with jobs. She's working her way through school so she can be a veterinarian. She always loved animals since she was a little girl."

Confused by Susan's distress, Jo chose her next comment carefully. "She must be very smart."

Susan's pride shone across her face. "Straight-A student. She was her class valedictorian."

The claim twanged in Jo's head—something didn't fit. "With those grades, I'm surprised she didn't get a scholarship to a four-year school."

The cloud settled back on Susan's face. "She earned a full scholarship to UC Davis. But... it didn't work out." Her eyes dropped to the portable oxygen tank.

The pieces slipped into place. "She didn't want to leave you."

Susan's eyes filled with tears. "I told her I could take care of myself, but like you said, she's smart. When I was diagnosed with COPD, she knew it was only gonna get worse. And when I couldn't waitress anymore and had to go on disability, I couldn't pay my rent let alone pay for some sort of caretaker. And since April I can't be separated from this thing." She flicked her fingers toward the oxygen bag.

Jo's heart panged. "Well. Madison is obviously hardworking and bright. It may take her a little longer, but she'll get there. What classes is she taking this term?"

"They change so often I can't keep them straight." Susan wrung her hands again. "But she's probably just off studying at the park, right?"

Jo kept her expression neutral. "If she's done that before, it's possible she's there now. Madison's friends went over to look for her. Does she normally walk or drive to the park?"

"Walk, so I'll have the car if I have an emergency. I checked, the car's in the lot outside." Panic filled her eyes. "I figured she'd be safe with the dog..."

"What sort of dog is Ginger?"

"Golden retriever."

Not the most stranger-wary of breeds. Jo forced herself to smile. "Could she be out on some sort of date?"

She shook her head. "She hasn't dated anybody since she broke up with Kiernan."

"Kiernan? Is that her baby's father?"

Frustration flashed across Susan's face. "She wouldn't say. But I'm pretty sure."

Another clang—Madison and her mother were clearly close. "Why wouldn't she tell you?"

Susan raised a hand only to let it drop back onto her lap. "No idea. All I can think is they broke up before she found out she was pregnant and she didn't want to get back together with him, so she didn't want him to know."

"Forgive me, but I have to ask. Was she dating Kiernan exclusively?"

Her head nodded vigorously. "She's only had two boys she's been interested in her whole life."

"What's Kiernan's last name? Do you have contact information for him?" Jo asked.

"Kiernan Wendiss." Susan's eyes flicked around the room and landed on the counter that separated the living room from the kitchen, and she started to get up. "I have his number in my phone."

"Please, let me." Jo rose and retrieved the phone for her.

"Thank you." She tapped and scrolled and produced a number that Jo copied down.

"Could she possibly be with Kiernan?" Jo asked.

Susan sighed. "I wish. Kiernan really cared about her."

"Why did they break up?"

Frustrated skepticism screwed up her face. "She said she wasn't in love with him anymore."

"But you don't believe that."

"No, I don't. She wouldn't look me in the eye and when I pushed her, she shut me down."

"What about other friends she might be with?"

"It takes her a long time to let people in. I had to push her to make friends in high school, and she lost touch with the two she had when they went off to college." She paused to draw in a breath. "Between work and school, she doesn't have much time for friends. Since she got pregnant, she's felt like people are judging her. It was a load off my mind when she met those nice girls at the baby classes."

"Do you know of anybody who has a problem with her, anything like that?"

Susan flinched like she'd been slapped. "Everybody loves Madison."

Whether that was true or not, Susan certainly believed it. "Where else does she go to study, or spend time? Cafés, anything like that?"

"We don't have extra money to throw away. She usually just studies here." A sudden hope lit up Susan's face. "Or on campus? She likes the library there. That's probably it, right?"

Jo stood, biting back the urge to give false assurances. "I've seen many cases where a missing person lost track of time or needed some space to themselves. I'll check the campus and let you know what I find."

"Thank you." Her eyes filled with tears. "I don't know what I'd do without her."

———

Jo hurried back to her car. The light was fading quickly, and her nieces would be finishing up the maze soon. Sophie would make sure of it, because she wouldn't risk Emily especially becoming frightened of the shadows that would transform the maze once the sun went down.

But the conversation with Susan had alarmed her—it was odd that Madison wouldn't return her mother's call when she'd sacrificed so much for her—and she couldn't just walk away. If she hurried, she could fit one more stop in, and the campus was on her way.

The administrative building of Phelpston Community College intrigued her—one half was a traditional, ivy-league red-brick architecture, while the other was three-tiered floor-to-ceiling glass that exposed everyone and everything inside. A long-forgotten memory of the hamster condo she had as a girl in New Orleans flashed back; after watching Gomez, her hamster, repeatedly bury himself under the wood chips that lined the spaces, she'd taped a piece of binder paper over one of the sections so he could have privacy.

She was in luck, barely—only ten more minutes until the offices closed. She hurried into the vast lobby and crossed to the main information desk, where two honey-blonde middle-aged white women were chatting about their plans for the next day.

"Can I help you?" one asked, her smile broad and welcoming.

Jo produced her badge, explained why she was there. "Can you direct me to the library? Also, it would help me know where to look if I could get a list of the classes Madison's taking. Maybe she's studying somewhere nearby them."

The woman's face dropped. "You said Madison Coelho?"

Jo pulled Madison's picture up on her phone and slid it toward the woman. "You know her?"

"Of course, one of our all-time best students. And always so sweet." She nodded down at the picture, then met Jo's eyes. "You think something happened to her?"

"I'm doing a check for her mother and friends."

The second woman chimed in. "I'm so sorry, but I'm afraid we can't be much help."

Jo had anticipated that—technically the school wouldn't be

allowed to release information about a student without permis-sion or a warrant. "I understand, I don't want you to violate your privacy policy. But maybe you can just direct me to some areas besides the library she's likely to be?"

The woman's brow creased. "Oh, no, I don't mean that. I mean, you're right, I couldn't give you her schedule information. But what I mean is, you won't find her here. She's not enrolled in classes this quarter."

CHAPTER SIX

Jo stared dumbly at the administrator's face, a chill stabbing down her arms and legs. "You're sure? Both Madison's friends and her mother seemed certain she's currently taking classes. Maybe it was last quarter she took off?"

The woman shifted to a computer terminal and tapped something into the keyboard. She scanned the screen, then shook her head. "No, I'm sorry. She's not currently enrolled."

"But she did like to study in the library. Maybe she stopped by for some reason?" Administrator Two said.

"Can she get in if she's not enrolled?" Jo asked.

"Our library is open to the public, that's part of our mission. You just can't check out books unless you're enrolled," Admin One said.

Jo thanked them, then checked the library. But neither the librarians nor any of the students camped out inside had seen Madison anytime recently.

As Jo strode back to her car, she tried to fit this new troubling piece into the puzzle. Madison wouldn't be the first girl who seemed uncomplicated on the surface only to be hiding a swamp of secrets underneath. Maybe Madison hadn't been able to handle everything, but couldn't bear disappointing her mother further by telling her she'd stopped taking classes? But then why lie to her friends? No matter what, the development was ominous given Madison was missing.

Jo's phone buzzed as she climbed back into the Volt. When she checked, she found a text from Matt: *Is everything okay? We're done with the maze and are heading over to Pizza Palace.*

She tapped out a reply. *I'm about twenty minutes away. Go ahead and order the food and I'll be there as soon as I can.*

He replied immediately. *See you soon. Drive safely.*

She smiled, then sent a text to Chelsea. *Any luck?*

Chelsea's response came through as Jo started the car. *None. Naomie is supposed to meet her husband for dinner, and Julia doesn't want me out here in the dark with the temperature dropping.*

Dread pulled at her. The innocent explanations about where Madison might be were dying with the daylight—if she'd simply forgotten the time, sunset would have reminded her. And Jo didn't like the idea of the three women, two pregnant, wandering around in the dark.

She fired back a reply. *Julia's right. Go home and stay safe, and I'll call you as soon as I can.*

She did a quick calculation. She was about twenty minutes away from the Pizza Palace, and Kiernan's apartment was just off the pike into Oakhurst. If she fudged the timing a little, she could stop by on her way to the restaurant. Because the sad truth was, if something unpleasant had happened to Madison, her ex was the most likely suspect.

———

Praying for green lights, Jo drove as quickly as she could without breaking any laws, and pulled up to Oakhurst Garden

Apartments ten minutes later. The complex, a series of colonial-esque duplexes with red brick and cream clapboard, made a stark contrast with Madison's. While not fancy, it was clean and well tended, surrounded by a healthy, mowed lawn scattered with falling oak leaves.

The six-foot, early-twenties white man who opened the door had short, dark-brown hair, a clean-shaven face, blue eyes, and a swimmer's build. His black T-shirt and olive cargo pants hung well on him, and he exuded a relaxed confidence unusual in someone so young.

"Kiernan Wendiss?" Jo asked.

"That's me." He smiled. "Can I help you?"

Jo introduced herself. "I understand you used to date Madison Coelho. Have you seen her today, or recently?"

His brow creased. "No. I haven't seen her since we broke up back at the end of March. Is everything okay?"

Jo weighed her approach, and how much to tell him. She made a show of glancing toward the right half of the duplex. "Can I come inside? I have a few questions I'd like to ask you."

"Sure—I—come in." He stepped back.

A huge television dominated the room, across from a shabby brown futon and a beanbag chair. A can of Coke sat amid a scatter of books and notebooks on the coffee table, and Panic! at the Disco wafted out of a Bluetooth speaker perched on an anemic bookshelf.

He gestured to the futon and sank into the beanbag chair. "Is Madison okay?"

Jo sat. "Madison didn't show up to an appointment with her friends today, and she's not picking up her mother's calls."

Kiernan went pale. "That's not like her."

"Do you have any idea where she might be?"

He tugged at the pocket just above his right knee. "No. I mean, I don't think I'm the right person to ask."

"Back when you were dating, where would you have told me to look? Did she have any spots she liked to hang out?"

He gave a bewildered head shake. "Not really. If I wanted to go somewhere, she was always down. But mostly we hung here or at her place."

"Do you know of anybody who might have a grudge against her?"

"Madison gets along with everybody." He waved both his hands out to encompass the world. "She was a good person, and fun once she opened up."

Jo paused, considering whether or not to bring up Madison's baby. If Madison was fine, she was entitled to her secrets. But if she wasn't, time was of the essence.

"If it helps, I know she's pregnant," he said. "My sister goes to PCC. When she saw Madison was pregnant, she was worried the baby was mine, but the timing's off."

Jo hid her surprise. Very few people were able to guess what she was thinking when she had her professionally passive face on. "Madison was six months pregnant according to her friends, and you broke up six months ago. Very possible if she wasn't sure about the date of conception."

He shook his head vigorously. "A little more than six months, and we didn't have sex for a few weeks before we broke up. She'd been distant and didn't want to see me."

Too long, if he was telling the truth. "Do you have any idea who the father is, then? Was she seeing someone else?"

His jaw flexed, and red splotches appeared on his neck. "Nah. And my sister never saw her with anyone."

Jo decided to play a hunch. "So that's not why you broke up with her?"

His brows popped and his index finger flew to his chest. "*I* broke up with *her*? Who told you that?"

"You didn't?"

The splotches made their way up to his ears. "I loved her. *She* broke up with *me*."

"Why?"

"She said she'd fallen out of love with me. But I don't believe her."

"Why not?"

"Because of the timing. Right after her mother's diagnosis was upgraded."

"But she was already taking care of her mother. Why would that matter?"

"It jacked up the copayments and medications and oxygen. She had to work full-time."

Pieces shifted around in Jo's mind. A switch to full-time work explained why Madison wasn't enrolled at the college. Getting hired full-time also would have provided her far better medical insurance than a student plan, and would have qualified her for maternity leave. And since it would have delayed her education for the foreseeable future, she would have kept the switch to herself, to keep her mother from self-flagellating even more.

But—if she wasn't taking classes, what had made her late for her evening prenatal sessions?

Kiernan broke into her thoughts. "I told her I'd help. We'd talked about getting married when I was done with school, and the three of us moving in together—I told her we could do that sooner. Then the next thing I knew, she was breaking up with me."

"Maybe she didn't want to hamstring your future," Jo said, then softened her tone. "Do you think she would have run off, or hurt herself?"

He searched the wall again. "She would never have left her mother alone and sick. And she *never* would have hurt her baby."

Jo nodded, thanked him for his time, and left.

No, she thought as she strode back to the car, what she'd learned about Madison didn't fit with self-harm or abandoning her loved ones—but that meant few hopeful possibilities remained.

CHAPTER SEVEN

Welcoming scents of basil and red sauce pulled her into Pizza Palace, and the rumbling of her stomach reminded her she hadn't eaten anything since a handful of kettle corn at the pumpkin patch. She glanced around the exposed-brick interior and spotted Sophie, David and Matt at a round wooden table with three coat-covered empty seats. The food hadn't come yet and Isabelle and Emily were playing Skee-Ball in the attached arcade, leaving Jo no excuse to put off explaining why she'd left so abruptly. She sighed—best not to keep it from Sophie longer than necessary, regardless.

As she approached the table, David said something to Matt, his smile casual and easy as if he were anything other than a continual purveyor of chaos in their lives. Anger burst through her—his bad choices had put her in this impossible situation, tiptoeing between fracturing her own relationship with her sister or the fledgling reunion of her sister's marriage. He was the one who should be in the hot seat, not her, and she'd had enough of him tossing around manure and being the only one left smelling of roses.

Matt rose to kiss her and pull out her chair. As she slid into it, she met Sophie's eyes, then David's, and started without preamble. "What I have to say isn't going to be pleasant. Do you want to hear it now, or wait until the kids are asleep?"

Sophie followed Jo's glance to David and narrowed her eyes at him. "Out with it."

Jo checked to be sure the girls were still out of earshot, then leaned toward David. "You gave your girlfriend my phone number for her emergency call list?"

Sophie's eyes blazed. "You *what?*"

David leaned away from Jo despite the table separating them. "She's not my girlfriend."

Jo glared at him. "My apologies. We can go with *baby mama* if you prefer."

David shook his head with disgust. "Very nice."

Jo clenched her teeth against her rising anger—she wasn't going to let him bait her. "No, sorry. You don't get to be offended when you're the one who created this situation."

David's disgust dropped and he held up an apologetic hand. "No, you're right, I have zero moral high ground here." He turned to Sophie. "But my understanding is you want the girls to know their brother. That means civil communication, and since she's having a difficult pregnancy, I figured you'd rather have her call Jo than you if she couldn't reach me."

"Doesn't she have her *own* family?" Sophie said.

"Just a sister, and they don't get along. And that's no help if she needs to reach me." He pointed at himself.

Sophie's gaze dove to David's phone and back. "So why didn't she just call *you?*"

David threw up his hands. "I have no idea. This is the first I'm hearing about any of this."

Jo cut in. "She called me because a friend of hers is missing and she knows I'm a detective."

Sophie's eyes widened briefly, then narrowed again. "Why didn't she just call the police?"

"She did," Jo said. "They can't do much when an adult woman misses an appointment. But Chelsea doesn't respond well to hearing 'no.'"

"Oh, I'm sure." Sophie laughed sarcastically and crossed her arms over her chest. "She's been doing whatever she can to keep her claws in David. She calls constantly. And now you're playing right into it."

Jo started to object, but Matt preempted her. "Wasn't she the one who broke things off with David? And what was Jo supposed to do? Just ignore a woman who may need help?"

Sophie's arms clenched tighter around her chest. "She could have had *another* detective handle it."

Jo forced her voice to remain steady. "I can't just call another detective and ask them to look into something for my brother-in-law's pregnant ex-mistress."

Sophie flinched, and checked that the girls were still happily throwing wooden balls. She watched them for a long moment, then finally answered. "No, I suppose you couldn't. But it's bad enough she has to be in contact with David because of the baby. I don't need her wiggling her way into my only sister's life, too. Please tell me you found her friend and this is over."

"No." Jo put a pin in her sister's surprising possessiveness and briefly recapped the situation, leaving out as many details as possible. "I don't have a good feeling about Madison and I won't be able to get her off my mind until she turns up. So, as awkward as this is, I need you to be okay with it. But rest assured I've made it clear to Chelsea she shouldn't be calling me."

Sophie's face and posture softened as Jo described the situation. "Of course Madison needs your help. I apologize for reacting so badly."

"No need," Jo said, pointedly avoiding David's eyes. "This is a difficult situation for us all."

Matt wisely diverted the subject. "What do you do now in a case like this? Isn't time of the essence?"

Jo took a frustrated deep breath. "There's not much else I can do. Without clear evidence of foul play, she's not considered a critical missing person. It's far more likely a young woman her age took off for the weekend with someone she met and didn't think to tell anyone. There's no way I'll get authorization for a search party."

Sophie's face screwed up in annoyance. "That's ridiculous. What do we pay taxes for?"

"Hundreds of people are reported missing every day, and we don't have the resources to send out search parties for all of them, especially when the vast majority show up on their own. And, this is Phelpston PD's jurisdiction. The SPDU doesn't usually work missing persons cases unless there's extenuating circumstances or they turn into homicides." Jo reached for Matt's beer and took a swig. "If she doesn't show up tonight, I'll go out to Crone Ridge Woods in the morning. And if she doesn't show up to work Monday, I'll be able to make an argument for a possible homicide."

"Hopefully she'll turn up safe and sound." David turned as the waitress approached with their extra-large combo.

Spotting the pizza's arrival, Emily and Isabelle ran back to the table. Jo pinned a smile carefully in place as they enveloped her in hugs and jumped onto their chairs.

But her mind was elsewhere. Because in her experience, when just a cursory look into a missing person's life turned up secrets and inconsistencies, it wasn't at all likely they'd turn up safe and sound.

CHAPTER EIGHT

Jo slept soundly but lightly, and the first rays of the sun pulled her out of bed and into the kitchen. After filling two travel mugs with coffee, she crept back into the bedroom to leave one on Matt's nightstand, but he was no longer in bed.

He appeared in the bathroom doorway, toweling fat droplets of water off his hips. "Morning, beautiful."

She handed him the mug and reached up to kiss him. "You're up early on a Sunday."

He took a long sip before responding. "I haven't been getting enough weight-bearing exercise lately, so I figured a hike around Crone Ridge Woods would do me good. Plus, two pairs of eyes are better than one, and it gives me a chance to see you in action." He wiggled his eyebrows at her. "Very sexy."

She laughed. "Whatever works."

———

Zipping her parka against the crisp, dewy fall air, Jo surveyed the back entrance to Crone Ridge Woods half an hour later. A small parking lot ran along the edge of the park, ending at a spacious clearing dotted with picnic tables. Periodic birdsong and spurts of rustling broke the silence as the woods' inhabitants started their day, sending red and orange leaves fluttering in gentle arcs toward the ground. Jo snapped a series of pictures with her phone, analyzing the terrain.

"And so it begins," Matt said. "Your expression just shifted into your work mode."

Jo half-smiled, and gestured across the clearing. "I'm making educated guesses about the best use of our time. The trees lining the edge of the clearing and the trail head are sparse, with no large boulders or fat trees to hide behind, so any attack here would be in full view of the clearing and the parking lot. If something nefarious happened to Madison, it was deeper inside the park."

Matt raised his brows and shook his head.

"What?" Jo started toward the trail.

He gestured to the trees. "I see a canopy of fall colors over a romantic forest. You see degrees of danger. Please tell me you're able to switch it off."

She wagged her head. "I can appreciate the beauty, and I can shift my focus. But there'll always be a part of my brain calculating risks and danger, even if I'm not consciously aware of it. An unavoidable side-effect of police work." As they reached the trail, Jo bent to take pictures of the path's gravel and the foliage lining it.

"Something important?" Matt asked.

"Just tracking environmental composition in case it becomes relevant."

"Gravel in the tread of a suspect's running shoes, leaves in a girl's hair?" he asked.

The half-smile returned. "Exactly. Even the act of documenting it can make sure whatever's important is present in my mind."

"Focused encoding of information for multiple retrieval cues, plus memory aids. Excellent strategy," Matt said.

"Now who's being all memory-doctor sexy." Jo laughed.

Matt wiggled his brows.

Jo shook her head at him and continued down the path. After about a quarter mile, the gravel switched to packed dirt before branching off in three directions; Jo took another series of pictures, then considered the options.

"If you were a twenty-year-old girl walking your dog, which of these paths would you take?" she asked.

He pointed to the left. "This one, definitely."

Jo turned, startled. "Why?"

"No idea." He shrugged. "I just picked one at random."

Jo laughed, and her phone buzzed. "Susan Coelho." She tapped to connect the call. "Jo Fournier."

"Detective?" Frantic sobbing came over the line. "I just got a call from animal control. Someone found Ginger. Alone, without Madison."

CHAPTER NINE

The trees seemed to close in around Jo. "Someone found Madison's dog? Is she okay?"

"Animal control said she's fine, she was tied up to a maple tree, and they want me to come get her." She choked on another sob. "But—why isn't she with Madison?"

Jo shifted into her crisis-mode calming voice and reassured Susan as best she could as she walked her through the details. "It's possible she's injured somewhere, and we need to act quickly. I'm going to send my partner, Detective Bob Arnett, to you for an article of Madison's clothing, that way we can get search and rescue dogs looking for her. Then I'll call you back as soon as we know anything, okay?"

"Okay. Please hurry."

"Well," Matt said as Jo ended the call, "that sounds like evidence of foul play."

She nodded and tapped in the number for animal control. They gave her the name and number of the couple who'd found Ginger, Trey and Stacia Williams. She immediately called them in turn to ask if they'd be able to lead her to the location where they found the dog. Once they were on their way, she called the State Police Special Operations Section for a team to search the area. Then she called Arnett, as she and Matt hurried back to the park entrance to wait.

———

Twenty minutes later, a thirty-something black couple hurried toward them. Both lean and tall, they wore exercise clothes; hers, a navy jogging outfit, his, jeans with a North Face puffer jacket and hiking boots.

Jo stepped forward. "Are you the Williamses?"

"We are," Trey Williams said.

Jo introduced herself as Arnett's car screeched into a parking spot nearby. "And here's my partner, Detective Bob Arnett."

Jo gaped at him as he exited the car. She'd never seen him in jeans before, and the glimpse of brown flannel at the neck of his fleece jacket was a decidedly rural departure from his typical urban twill chinos and sports coat. He ran a self-conscious hand through his slightly-too-long salt-and-pepper hair, then greeted her and Matt.

"I'm so sorry to have to interrupt your Sunday," Jo said, still taking him in.

He held up an evidence bag with what looked like a shirt inside. "Not a problem. I'm not a big fan of apple picking."

That explained the outfit, at least. Arnett and his wife Laura had come close to divorcing close to a decade before, and had agreed to dedicated date-night and date-weekend extracurriculars. Laura had cycled through a wide variety of activities to broaden their horizons while bringing them together.

"*She* tried to get me out to do that once." Mr. Williams jerked a thumb at his wife. "So I drove to the grocery store and *picked* up a bag of Granny Smiths."

Stacia shot him a nasty glare. "A girl's in trouble, Trey. This is no time for jokes."

Jo gestured them down the trail. "The State Police Special Operations Section has a search team on their way. But since Madison could be alive and injured, time is crucial, and we need you to take us immediately to the spot where you found the dog. What time did you find her?"

"About four-thirty?" Stacia glanced at Trey, who nodded confirmation. "We were on our way back because we had a dinner we couldn't be late to. We called the humane society, but they were closed for the weekend. The dog seemed really sweet and we didn't know how long animal control would take, so we put her in our garage for the night with some water and some canned chicken. We didn't get home 'til after midnight, so we called animal control first thing this morning."

"Susan said the dog was tied to a tree. Do you mean literally tied, or was her leash just caught on it?" Jo asked as they approached the trail split.

Stacia took the right-most path. "Literally knotted around the trunk of the tree. No way it happened by accident."

Exactly what Jo was hoping not to hear. The only reason to purposefully tie Ginger to the tree was to make sure she didn't follow and interfere. Still, Susan said Madison was an animal lover who wanted to be a vet, so possibly she'd stumbled on an injured animal and restrained Ginger so she wouldn't attack or be attacked. And maybe, as she tried to help the animal, she'd slipped and injured herself. It was possible—but not likely.

"Did you search the area for the dog's owner?"

"We called out in case someone was nearby, and Trey took a quick look around. But looking for the dog had already made us late, and we didn't have a lot of time." Her eyes pleaded with Jo for understanding.

Jo nodded reassuringly. "You did more than most people

would have done." She turned to Trey. "How far away did you search?"

He shook his head apologetically. "Not far. Maybe a few hundred feet?"

"What made you decide you needed to take the dog, that the owner wasn't coming back?" Arnett asked. "Did you see some evidence of a problem?"

"No." Trey's posture tightened. "But it isn't right to leave a dog tied up alone in the woods like that. I've heard of bears out here."

"You did the right thing." Noticing the growing defensiveness, Jo switched to small talk about the recent influx of leaf peepers. She kept one eye on the terrain surrounding the path, searching for any unusual flashes of color or damage to the greenery. As the topic shifted to trail safety, Stacia slowed slightly.

"Are we close?" Jo asked.

"We turned off somewhere around here, I remember that twisted maple in the distance. I was careful to keep track of landmarks so we wouldn't get lost, and I remember a big rock that looked like a whale—there." She pointed into the distance.

Jo spotted the boulder, and reached out to stop Stacia. "We'll need to take care where we walk, and stay single file as much as possible. Follow me."

Stacia nodded and Jo reset the pace, with Matt and Arnett trailing behind the Williamses. Light struggled to filter through the now-dense trees, breaking the forest into alternating patches of shifting shadow and blinding sun. Jo turned on her flashlight and scanned carefully in a one-eighty arc as she trudged forward, searching for evidence of footprints or disrupted foliage hiding in the pools of darkness.

When they reached the rock, she turned back to Stacia. "Where to now?"

Stacia frowned, then pointed a forty-five-degree angle. "We walked from the head side of the whale, that way."

Keeping Stacia close, Jo continued her visual sweep in front of them. After a few hundred yards, she asked, "Is anything else familiar?"

Stacia squinted into the distance. "That tree that looks like conjoined twins. It was just a little past that."

Once they passed it, Trey pointed to another. "The one with the Lion's Mane mushrooms. That's where she was tied."

Jo instructed them to stand back and approached the tree with Arnett. "The ground is dry enough I'm not seeing any tracks, not even yours. There's some damage to the bark. Is that about the height where she was tied?"

"That's about right," Trey said.

Jo swiveled at the waist, surveying the forest around them. "Odds are the search and rescue team will want to radiate out from here."

She pulled out her phone and called the number she'd been given for the search and rescue team's incident commander, Ethan Roscoe. When he answered, she advised him of their GPS location, and listened to his instructions.

She hung up, sent a quick text, then addressed the group. "Massachusetts Environmental Police are on their way, as well. They have topo maps and ATVs that will allow them to get to us quickly. IMAT, the Incident Management Assistance Team," she clarified for the Williamses and Matt, "will direct us what needs to be done from there. In the meantime, I've asked our crime-scene investigators to send out some techs, because we'll need to analyze this scene as soon as possible. We need to cordon off this tree, and the area around it." She paused to check everyone was following her. "Stacia and Trey, since you almost certainly touched the tree when you were untying the dog, we'll need to get DNA samples and fingerprints from you so we can exclude you from the evidence we collect. After our techs take the samples, Matt, will you escort them back out to the park entrance?"

"Not a problem," Matt replied.

"Thank you." She handed Stacia and Trey one of her cards. "And thank *you*. Hopefully you've saved a second life today."

CHAPTER TEN

By the time Incident Commander Roscoe of the State Police Special Operations Section, a six-foot-three, broad-shouldered tree of a man, arrived with his team, Jo and Arnett had cordoned off the area with crime-scene tape. After a brief conversation with Jo and Arnett, he turned to his team.

"Listen up. We're looking for a missing young woman, Madison Coelho. Twenty, average height, brown hair and brown eyes, six months pregnant. She may still be alive, so our first priority is to locate her, but we'll also need to preserve any potential evidence. As IMAT begins organizing the grid search for the Special Emergency Response Team, we're going to send in our K-9 unit as well as the Airwing's helicopters and drones. Between the infrared technology and Rocket's nose, hopefully we'll find Madison quickly and have everyone back home warming up in front of their fireplaces by lunch. As always, we have a dedicated radio frequency for the search, so tune to it and use it. Any questions?"

Everyone shook their heads.

Roscoe nodded grimly. "Then we all know our roles. Let's do this."

A tense focus took over as the team members shifted into action. Within minutes, the whirring of the helicopter's rotor blades lifted into the air, followed by the higher-pitched whine of the drones. A subset of the team began to search the immediate area, probing shrubs and underbrush for evidence occluded from immediate view. Even the birds seemed to understand the gravity of the search; their songs hushed and their rustling stilled.

Jo crossed quickly to the familiar K-9 team, a tall, white man in a bright orange jacket next to a white-and-tan pit bull with a matching harness.

"Ivan Geary," Jo said, extending her hand. "Good to see you again."

"Excellent memory, Detective," Ivan said. "Fournier, right?"

"Jo." She squatted and extended her hand to the dog. "Good to see you, Rocket."

Geary extended his hand. "Detective Arnett."

Arnett shook, then held up Madison's shirt. "We're hoping Madison went off to help an injured animal and sustained some sort of injury that left her unconscious."

Geary ran a hand through his buzz-cut hair, subconsciously acknowledging the unspoken alternative, then took the evidence bag. "If I'm not mistaken, the last time I worked with you, the missing woman in question turned up alive. Let's hope we can keep that streak going."

Jo mentally knocked on wood. "We'd like to accompany you as Rocket searches, if that's possible."

Geary nodded, then opened the front of the evidence bag and held it out to the dog to allow her a several-second sniff. "Rocket, find it!"

The dog's head swung back and forth, and she moved forward in a zigzag motion. Hesitantly at first—then she bolted northeast.

Jo took care to follow Geary's steps as closely as possible as

Rocket swerved them uphill through trees and boulders, away from the main path. Strafing the shadows with her mini MagLite, Jo ticked off criteria with each sweep—no prints, no crushed foliage, no human artifacts, no blood.

After several minutes Rocket slowed, wavering between two possible directions. Jo's chest tightened and she prayed desperately Rocket wasn't losing the trail.

Then the dog bolted again. The trees grew still denser, like a crowd closing in on them, forcing Jo's attention to the branches and bushes stabbing and swiping her. Time slowed as she twisted and tugged, touching as little as possible while keeping up.

After another quarter mile, Rocket veered abruptly and disappeared behind a large trio of moss-covered boulders. Geary followed, then reappeared from behind them imme-diately.

"Good job, Rocket." Geary offered a handful of treats with an artificially positive voice. "Good girl. Good girl."

Jo's stomach clenched. She carefully circled around the boulders into a small, flat clearing protected by a canopy of outstretched tree branches.

Madison Coelho lay naked atop the forest-floor detritus, her milky-white skin contrasting sharply with the greens and blacks of the forest floor beneath her—and with the brown-red of the symbols drawn in blood around the knife jutting from her abdomen.

CHAPTER ELEVEN

Jo and Arnett secured the crime scene while Incident Commander Roscoe redirected the teams to the new goal of searching the area for further evidence. They left Officer Scott Rankin, a squat, fifty-something white male with a perpetually bored expression, to guard the perimeter as they hurried into new PPE and approached Madison for a closer look.

Despite the intervening time to come to terms with what she'd just witnessed, Jo struggled to coalesce the scene. Two competing tableaux constructed themselves in her mind, as though she were staring at a holographic picture that flipped between two images when she shifted it. On the one hand, Madison called up the essence of a forest fairy lain down mid-frolic for a nap—eyes closed peacefully as though enjoying a dream, brown hair radiating a crown around her head, legs crossed straight over each other and hands clasped in repose over her breast. Beautiful and resplendent—if not for her neck, slashed open and gaping side to side, and the knife stuck nearly to its hilt out of her pregnant belly, dead center amid strange symbols painted across her abdomen in her own dried blood.

Try as Jo might, she couldn't bring the two aspects together in a way that made sense.

She squeezed her eyes shut and tried not to picture the baby inside that abdomen—tried not to think about how at six months it would have fingers and toes and eyelids and ears. Had it felt the pain of the knife slicing through? Had Madison been alive when the knife plunged into her, forced to watch, feeling the tiny life inside her drain away? Jo had lost her own baby when she'd miscarried earlier in the year, a horrible enough experience when it was an accidental occurrence. The stone-cold evil of someone purposefully ripping away a growing soul bruised something deep in her own.

When she reopened her eyes, she snapped a picture of the convoluted lines on Madison's abdomen. She shifted forward and back, trying to make sense of the symbol—it felt both complete and incomplete, like several separate items merged together. At the top, an inverted triangle dropped two lines down from its top corners, resembling the two points of an upside-down pentagram with a line drawn across the top. But instead of the bottom of a pentagram, the two bottom sides of the triangle extended beyond where they crossed, ending in half-circle curlicues. A large 'V' cut through and below those curves.

Jo leaned in for a closer look at the strokes themselves. They were uneven, like finger painting, with blood concentrated on the edges and next to none in the centers. She studied them inch by inch, hoping to find a smear that revealed a partial print —but the killer, or killers, had used gloves. At the end of several strokes she could detect the faint stippled texture of nitrile.

As she straightened, a strange distortion between two of Madison's clasped fingers caught her eye. She snapped several pictures before calling Arnett over. "Can you record this for me? Right here?"

As he pointed his camera at Madison's hands, Jo tried to lift the topmost. It resisted; she gripped the arm and carefully broke the rigor. As the two hands separated, a small figurine of a naked infant dropped out.

"A king cake baby," she blurted.

"A what now?" Arnett asked.

"A baby you put inside a king cake," she said.

He squinted at her. "I realize you think that explanation helped, but it didn't."

"Right, sorry." She placed the figurine into an evidence bag, and then straightened up. "A king cake is a Mardi Gras tradition. Well, technically, it's an Epiphany tradition."

"Epiphany?" Arnett asked. "Why does that sound familiar?"

"It's one of the feasts we don't celebrate much anymore, at least not here. It's the end of Christmas and the beginning of the Pre-Lenten Mardi Gras season. The twelfth day of Christmas, actually, like in the song, the day the three kings visited the Baby Jesus. So, on Epiphany, party hosts serve a king cake, named for the three kings, with a porcelain or plastic figurine of a baby symbolizing Jesus inside the cake. If you get the baby in your slice you'll have good luck in the next year."

Arnett waved his arm across the scene. "Just bizarre enough to fit with whatever twisted deal we have going on here."

Jo followed his gesture. The trio of boulders took on a new significance; the middle boulder's face was flat, and shaped generally like a revolutionary-era gravestone. The two smaller rocks beside it were short and squat, with flat tops dotted with candle stubs; the candles, all red or black, had melted down, some completely, some with an inch or two left.

"Like a makeshift altar," she said. But the same sense of discordance she'd felt when looking at Madison washed over her. Something about it felt wrong, like a note sung off-key.

"Satanic panic," Arnett said, voice framing sarcastic quotes around the words. "Hit-you-over-the-head subtle."

Yes, the scene felt staged—but that wasn't what was bothering her. "How well do you remember all that? It was dying out by the time I hit my teens."

"I missed the heyday, but the tail-end was when I was at the academy." Arnett squatted down to examine the gash on Madison's neck. "People running scared of devil worshipers. Made it a 'cool' bandwagon for teenaged rebels-without-a-cause. But nothing real."

Jo snapped several pictures of the candles; the configuration could have been the points of a pentagram. "That fits with what I remember. So I see two possibilities. Someone wants us to think this was some Satanic ritual sacrifice, or we have a serial killer whose particular brand of psychopathy was influenced by the trend."

"Or," Officer Rankin interjected from across the crime-scene tape, "it's that new group popped up 'round here not that long ago. Lucifer something."

Jo's head snapped up. "New group?"

He pointed vaguely into the distance. "Property owner over in Scoby caught a group of punks out on his land. Wearing all black, animal skulls and pentacles, the whole nine. Built a fire on his land. And, what, twice now park rangers here at Crone Ridge have found ashes from bonfires with similar items left behind."

"Three possibilities, then. We'll look into it. One way or another, that group must be relevant, either because they're involved directly or because they inspired what happened here." Jo carefully examined the forest floor. "No footprints or other markings, or trodden underbrush."

"There wouldn't be if she went missing yesterday afternoon. Any vegetation would've righted itself again by now," Rankin said.

The comment brought one of the shadows tugging at her mind into focus. "The timing—it's off. Madison left to walk the dog no later than ten. She was supposed to meet her friends in Oakhurst at one that afternoon, so she would've headed back no later than twelve-fifteen to make it to the baby boutique. So whoever abducted her did it not only in broad daylight, but in the middle of the day. But you said the other incidents happened at night."

"Could've stumbled on a pregnant woman, snatched her, then kept her alive until it was time for the ritual." Rankin pointed at the knife. "And who knows what sick shit they did to her while they waited."

Jo pushed down the images that sprung into her mind. "So we need to know if she's been dead twelve hours or twenty-four." Jo glanced toward the path. "Is the CSI team close?"

Rankin spoke into his radio, then relayed the answer. "They're making their way through the park as we speak, and the ME is en route."

Arnett straightened, stretching his back. "So, next steps. We need to find anyone in the area yesterday or this morning," he said. "See if anybody recognizes Madison or saw anything strange. And we need to find this Lucifer group."

"That'll get us started on the serial killer line of inquiry." Jo chewed on her lip. "In terms of personal suspects, given what I learned yesterday, I think the strongest possibility is the baby's father. Since Madison was in such dire financial straits, she may have approached the father for child support, and he may not have responded well to the request. I'll ask Lopez to get started looking into Madison's phone and email records, to see if we can get a sense of who that is. Right now the only lead we have is the ex-boyfriend, so I'll have her see if she can get a warrant for his records, too." Jo turned and stared into the distance, expression grim. "But first we need to break the news to her friends and her mother."

CHAPTER TWELVE

Chelsea squinted down at the phone, not seeing the screen.

She'd relayed the news about Madison to Naomie, but wasn't sure what to do now. No matter how she'd tried, Jo had refused to tell her anything other than they'd found Madison dead—even though Chelsea had been the one who'd reported the whole thing to her. Surely the person who filed the complaint was owed at least a few answers?

She needed to know what was going on.

She stabbed at the phone, connecting a call to David. He sounded distracted and annoyed at first, but when she told him Madison had been found dead, either the news itself or her hysterical tears had snapped him to attention. He promised to call Jo and find out what was happening, and told her it was important that she stay calm in the meantime.

Easy for him to say. But he was right, she couldn't afford to let herself get worked up. She cradled her belly and tried to come up with a way to distract herself while she waited. A year ago, she'd have called Sienna or her ex-bestie Pierce, but both of those relationships had been severely dented by her choice to date David. Sienna, always judgmental and holier-than-thou, lost it when Chelsea revealed she was dating a married man. Not that they'd ever been exactly close, but after their parents were killed in the car crash, they'd become clos*e*r, and had been able to at least hang out and chat now and then—until David. Pierce hadn't cared about that so much, he'd always said if a man leaves he was never yours, but—well, it didn't really matter. She couldn't call him, and that was that.

That was that, but it hurt. She'd been friends with Pierce since they were in elementary school. He'd been her shield against loneliness, because no matter how hard she tried to form friendships with girls, they'd always been jealous of her—her looks, her money, her boyfriends, her good grades, everything. No matter how many fancy slumber parties she held, awesome birthday gifts she gave, or random girl-grudges she stayed loyal to, the jealousy always surfaced and the only thing she got for her efforts was an advanced degree in feminine relational aggression and manipulation.

She shot a resentful glance at the sorority yearbooks on her bookshelves. That was the whole point of sororities, wasn't it? To have an automatic, have-your-back sisterhood of friends to support you? But no, her 'sisters' were exactly the same as all the other girls had been. Jealous, spiteful, manipulative.

She'd become resigned to it long ago, the tightrope dance she had to do when it came to relationships with women. That's why all this was so important.

The phone shrilled, and she snatched it up.

"I'm so sorry, Chelsea," David said, tone soft and concerned. "But Jo couldn't tell me much. They have to be careful about what they release to the public."

The room turned to ice. "But family's different."

"I'm not on her list of favorite people right now. And she's smart enough to know what she tells me goes straight back to you."

The ice instantly transformed to flame, and her fingers

clenched around the phone. "I—I can't—I need to know. Who could do such a thing to Madison? Who could do such a thing to a *pregnant* woman?"

"They probably didn't realize she was pregnant," David said. "I'm sure sickos like this just abduct whatever defenseless woman they can snatch."

Chelsea made a choking sound. "Oh, God."

"Damn, I shouldn't have said that." His voice rose a notch. "Are you okay, Chelsea?"

"No, I'm not," she blurted, voice shaking. "I can't believe she's gone. She was such a sweet person, and I just keep imagining it, seeing someone hurting her. Even the fear on her face—I can't get it out of my mind."

"You need to distract yourself, otherwise you'll make yourself sick. Read a book, or watch a movie you love. We'll know more soon, I'm sure. Jo's very good at her job."

"I feel like I'm going to vomit." Her mind raced, and she scrambled to keep control. "Are they sure it's a random killing, not someone she knew?"

He paused. "I assumed so. She didn't say."

"She must have given you some sense," she pressed.

"Do you have reason to think it was someone Madison knew?"

"No... but something's been up with her lately. She's been late and distracted. But the thing is, as horrible as this sounds—"

"What?" he asked when she didn't finish her thought.

"It's just that—if it was someone she knew, there was a reason for it. But if it's some random psycho killing pregnant women, they might do it again—"

"Stop," he interrupted. "There's no reason to think that. You said yourself Madison has been acting strange lately. Whatever's going on, Jo will figure it out quickly."

"No, of course, you're right." She cleared her throat. "And

you're right I should distract myself. Maybe I should go over to Madison's mother's house, make sure she's okay—"

"No, don't do that," he interrupted. "Your doctor said you're supposed to stay away from stress." His footsteps echoed over the phone—he was pacing. "Can you call your therapist? She'll be able to help you process all this."

"She retired, that's why I stopped going to her." She gasped. "The other night when we were leaving the juice bar—there was a weird guy in his car. I had the strangest feeling he was watching us all leave. What if that's the guy who killed her?"

"Did you tell Jo about that?" His tone tightened—he was worried now, too.

"I—I think I did. But even so, there's no way they could have tracked him down this quickly if so. And that latch on the one guest bedroom window never got fixed. If there's a killer following us, he knows where I live—"

"Right," David said, voice firm. "I'll come over now and fix the window. I'll spend the night on your couch so you don't have to worry about being alone. Tomorrow we'll call an alarm company and have them put in some security cameras."

"I don't want to put you in an awkward situation," she said, sniffling. "Sophie won't like it."

"Let me deal with that. I'll see you soon."

CHAPTER THIRTEEN

Naomie sank onto the couch, stunned, tears pouring down her cheeks.

Madison was dead. Murdered.

Chelsea hadn't been able to tell her much, and her soul screamed for answers. But at the same time, she knew the details didn't make much difference—all that mattered was the sweet, kind girl whose life was just beginning was dead. She and her baby both snuffed out in a horrible act of wasteful cruelty.

Oh, God—Madison's mother must be inconsolable. Losing her daughter and future grandson all in one fell swoop? And who would take care of Susan now? Naomie pulled up the contact to call her, see if she needed anything. The call went to voice mail.

Reaching past her stack of work papers—so important just moments ago, but now pallid and pointless—she grabbed her Pellegrino with a shaking hand and gulped most of it down. Her eyes wandered across the living room, over the yellow accents and paintings of flowered fields, seeing only Madison's face.

She took a deep breath and reached for her phone. Word

would spread through Beautiful Bouncing Babies quickly, and everyone would look to her to lead them through it. There were details to be seen to, and with Chelsea half-hysterical and Susan Coelho unwell, someone had to step up.

First on the list—she'd promised Chelsea she'd deliver the news to Julia so Chelsea wouldn't have to go through it again.

Just as the call was about to beep over to voice mail, Julia answered amid the static of background objects shuffling. "Hello?"

Julia wouldn't want her to beat around the bush, so she dove straight in. "The police found Madison murdered out in the woods."

"Damn," Julia said, and the background noise stopped. "Her poor mother."

Naomie's front door opened and closed; her husband Chris had returned from his round of golf. "She must be devastated. I tried calling her, but she's not picking up. I'm going to drop by later and make sure she's okay and has something to eat. We can take turns checking in on her until the worst is over."

Julia hesitated. "She barely knows us. Will she be okay with that?"

Naomie pulled over her day planner and jotted down a quick rotation. "I'll feel her out. But Madison was her only family, and she's not well. If she won't accept our help, I'll have to contact EOEA to make sure she's taken care of."

"No, right. I can go over there tomorrow morning, but if she looks like she's struggling medically, call me immediately."

"Perfect. Then Chelsea, then me again." Naomi scanned her scheduled events for the next few days. "I doubt Madison had life insurance, so there won't be money for a funeral. I'm fairly certain the state will pay for cremation, but not for returning the ashes. If so, I'll pay for that and a decent urn."

Chris strode into the room. He stopped short as he registered the expression on her face, then mouthed, "What's going on?"

She held up a finger to let him know she'd be a minute, ducking eye contact. "And I think we should offer to host some sort of memorial. A celebration of life or whatever she feels is appropriate."

Chris perched on the armchair directly across from her. She kept her eyes on the day planner.

"Right," Julia said tentatively. "There's something I should probably come clean about."

Naomie braced herself. "What's that?"

"The other night at the juice bar. There wasn't a mistake with the credit card. Pete canceled it. I didn't tell you before because I didn't want to put you in the middle."

Naomie stroked her brow. As upsetting as it was, she wasn't surprised. Her family was insular in an old-fashioned way—when you were part of the family, they'd do anything for you. The heads of household provided a warm cocoon for family members—spouses, children, siblings—in the form of a lifestyle that reflected the Gagnons' power and position. But once that connection was severed, you were worse than an outsider, ejected and abandoned to the cold.

Julia continued, voice tight. "So I can't really contribute financially to the memorial. But I'll help any other way I can."

"Not a problem. Chelsea and I will take care of it." She glanced at the clock on the mantle. "Chris just got home, so I'm going to start dinner and get something over to Susan. I'll update you when I get back."

After she and Julia said their goodbyes, she told Chris about Madison.

"Oh, God." His face dropped. "She's the young one, right? Unmarried, with some sort of medical bills?"

She nodded, brushing away new tears.

He dropped onto the couch next to her and grabbed her hand. "I'm so, so sorry. That's awful."

"It is." She braced herself for the reaction to what she was about to say. "Her mother is struggling with emphysema and has no money, and now she's alone in the world. And I know what you're going to say about our finances, but I can't stand by and do nothing. Madison deserves a decent memorial service, and Chelsea and I are the only ones who can provide it."

He nodded, his face blank. "No, I understand. She was important to you. We'll find a way to make it work."

Surprise and relief flooded her, and she squeezed his hand. "I promise, nothing extravagant."

He kissed her forehead and rose from the couch. "How about I make dinner? I can whip up a quick Bolognese, a double batch so you can take some to Madison's mother. That way you can get started on the planning."

"You don't have—"

He held up a hand. "Of course I'm going to do what I can to help. Now let me go get started."

———

As she watched him walk out of the room, guilt stabbed at her. She'd assumed the worst of him and had been ready for a fight, and that wasn't fair. He was trying, and this was a significant concession. Just last month she'd agreed to cut her spending dramatically, and now she was springing the cost of a memorial service on him on top of all the impending expenses of the baby. No matter how tragic the circumstances, he had a right to protest.

She sighed, and stared over at the stack of work papers. Her work at Beautiful Bouncing Babies wasn't just an interest or a passion, it was her very core. At the impressionable age of twelve she'd watched Julia almost die due to preeclampsia complications when she gave birth to her only son Ethan; as she got older and discovered the paucity of information and resources available to lower-SES women, particularly women of color, the work had become her life's mission. But it paid next to nothing.

Chris's job as an insurance agent wasn't much better, and their relatively low paired income had been an adjustment for Naomie. No matter how much she cut back, it wasn't enough. When her parents noticed the changes in her lifestyle, they tried to compensate. Her mother insisted on shopping trips, her father bought her a new Lexus for Christmas, and they both insisted Naomie and Chris join them for family vacations. In retrospect, Naomie should have realized allowing that generosity wasn't a good idea. She'd seen enough of how her father and uncles ran their families to realize their respect for Chris would be dinged if he couldn't give Naomie the life she was accustomed to without their help. So when he'd objected, she'd put a stop to it—mostly. Her mother still managed to slip money into Naomie's purse and to find beautiful brand-new dresses in her closet that she suddenly 'changed her mind about.'

Most notably, a gorgeous Versace her mother produced before last year's Christmas party. Naomie *had* to wear the dress, her mother insisted, because Naomie's appearance reflected on the family. The Gagnons ran multiple high-end venues throughout New England with associated party-planning and catering branches, institutions people used for their poshest occasions: weddings, business gatherings, even political events. The main purpose of the party, and other occasions like it through the year, was to dazzle existing and potential clients, make them want what only Gagnon events could give to them. Having their daughter show up in anything less than a show-stopper wasn't good for business.

Naomi had peered down at the dress, trying to ignore the

part of her that very much wanted to take it. And not just the one dress, but the loophole that would allow her to have at least a few of the things she wanted. After all, the family's money was her money, too—she'd worked hard her whole life helping build the business and still did, pitching in whenever they needed her. And what Chris didn't know wouldn't hurt him. That wasn't deception—it was making a marriage work.

She ran her finger across the datebook in her lap, down the notes she'd started jotting about the memorial, and Madison's face sprung up before her. The shadow of it fell cold over her guilt and struggles. Dresses and parties and whether her mother bought her a dress or her family gave them a car—it was petty and small. Life was short, and what mattered was the people you loved and living every day while you could.

She pressed her empty hand onto her abdomen, hoping to feel a kick.

CHAPTER FOURTEEN

Julia slid her phone onto the counter after talking to Naomie and shook her head at the box she was unpacking in her new, cramped duplex. She was surprised at how surprised Naomie and Chelsea were—how had they not seen this coming? When a pregnant woman and her dog disappear overnight, they aren't gonna show up in the morning with a box of donuts and a tray of Starbucks.

Maybe it was because she was a decade older than both of them, or because she was a nurse—she'd seen more of life, and certainly more death. But no, she'd known more at fourteen, navigating the rougher parts of Boston's South End, than they knew at thirty. Money and privilege had sheltered them from the world's ugliness and struggle their whole lives.

She swore out loud when she reached up to put away a glass —the cabinet was full. She'd stripped down to essentials, but the duplex was tiny. She'd have to shove the extra boxes in the spare bedroom, which would get in Ethan's way when he visited from the dorms.

She laughed at herself—who was she kidding? Why would Ethan spend the night here when his father's mansion was just a few miles up the road? This would be the first Christmas morning she'd wake up without him.

Pete was well aware of that.

Fucking prenuptial agreement. Pete wasn't going to show an ounce of mercy, which was complete bullshit. She'd given him a son despite almost dying from complications, put her own career on hold until his branch of Gagnon Events had taken off, and spent countless hours helping the Gagnons build their upscale-event empire. She'd earned every damned cent of split assets and alimony.

Stop being such a victim, her mother's voice said in her head. *You knew what the prenup said when you signed it. You made your choices.*

Of course she had, in response to Pete's choices. He'd turned into a phantom, his time divided between work, golf, and car-racing. Sure, she'd taken a man as a lover, but his Titleist driver and his Formula-whatever race car were *his* lovers. They took all his time, money, and affection, and if she hadn't been so damned lonely she'd never have cheated in the first place. A prenup was one thing when she was an unproven twenty-something who might just want his money. But after all these years and everything she'd contributed, how could that prenup possibly still be relevant?

Her lawyer assured her it was.

Thank goodness Pete had jumped the gun. He'd had her followed, but his private eye had snapped pictures of the wrong man; she'd been consoling the husband of a client who, due to horrendous preeclampsia complications, had lost her baby and had a stroke. The incident left Pete without the proof he needed to enforce the prenuptial agreement, while alerting Julia that he was trying to obtain it.

But it still left her in this awkward situation, with hidden credit cards and borrowing from Peter to pay Paul.

Her other phone buzzed. A text from Rick: *How's the unpacking going?*

Her mood lifted, and she leaned playfully against the counter. *Slow, but getting there. How's your day going?*

Missing you. About to head out to the gym, thinking it'd be great to christen your new place after.

Warmth swept through her hips. A bottle of wine and an evening of lovemaking would be a defibrillator to her flagging energies.

Not yet, she replied with a longing sigh.

She watched for his dancing dots, but they didn't come; his anger and frustration were palpable in the delay.

When it came, the response was simple and searing. *When?*

Fear stabbed at her stomach. She was walking a line uncomfortably close to the fire. He was rapidly approaching his limit, and a text wouldn't cut it. She put through a call.

He picked up immediately and she spoke without preamble. "Not until it's safe."

The familiar sounds of his café murmured and hissed behind him. "It *is* safe. You're separated, and he asked for a divorce."

"He's still looking for proof."

"So what?" An employee called out a pumpkin spice latte. "Separated means you can do what you want."

Her temple throbbed. "He's not stupid. If he finds out who you are, he'll dig and find out we've known each other for months. His lawyer will check your phone records and my burner number will show up. Then they'll track *that*." And once they found her burner, they'd find her other affair, too.

"Come live with me. You won't have to pay rent, and I'll be able to take care of you. You don't need him or his money."

Another call beeped over the line. She ignored it.

She put on her soothing, sexy voice, the one that'd been getting her what she wanted since puberty. "Someday we'll live together, and it'll be amazing. But right now, there's a lot more I have to pay than just rent."

"I can't buy you designer dresses, no. But I can take care of you."

She winced—his pride was hurt. But at the end of the day, Rick barely made enough money for the *insurance* on her Mercedes S-Class, let alone the payment. She could do without designer dresses, but there was a limit to how far backward she was willing to go. She wasn't getting any younger, and there were other complicating factors. "I need a space where Ethan can come see me without him having to show up to another man's territory. Remember how you felt when your mother started dating after your parents divorced?"

He blew out a frustrated sigh. "I get that. But I need a timeline."

"Once the judge grants the divorce, we should be fine. So, a couple of months?" She crossed her mental fingers. "By then the SMS data from the old burner phone won't be recoverable anymore, so they'll have no way to trace it back to me."

Something metal clanged. "Maybe we can use the trick we used before?"

Six months ago he'd moved into the same apartment complex her friend Celia lived in; that way if a private investigator followed her, she appeared to be innocently visiting her friend. But Celia had moved recently because she got engaged. "Her new complex doesn't have any apartments, and you have six months left on your lease."

"I could get out of it," he said. "Maybe we should look for another complex we could both move in to."

Why couldn't he understand it was too complicated? Because he didn't know Pete, that's why. "I'll try to think of something else."

"I'll see what I can come up with, too. I love you."

"I love you, too." She disconnected.

But as she set the phone back down, it rang—and her entire body went cold. She sank into the nearby kitchen chair, staring at the number she'd hoped never to see again.

Of all the mistakes she'd made in her life, *he* was the biggest. In fact, that was how she'd come to think of him—as The Mistake. He'd been forbidden, with stolen sessions snatched in dangerous locations laced with excitement, all at the height of her heartbreak when she needed to feel alive and attractive again. But when the novelty wore off, so did the excitement, and only the danger was left.

But not for him. When she started pulling away, he gripped harder. Nothing overt—no physical abuse, not even any name-calling. But an underlying intensity she could never put her finger fully on, and that left her unsettled.

So she'd made him think the breakup was his decision—or, at least, made him think it benefited him. Convinced him that with Pete's vicious jealousy, he'd use his money and power to destroy them both.

They'd agreed to end it. So why was he calling?

She hit the ignore button.

Because the problem was now gone, she realized. Since Pete had filed for divorce, the gossip had splashed and rippled through every corner of Oakhurst and the surrounding area.

"Fucking hell," she said aloud, hoping she was wrong. Because how could she get rid of him now? And if he found out about Rick—Oh, God.

She slipped into problem-solving mode, the controlled state she used when dealing with dangerous births and other emergencies: one step at a time, handling whatever came. She tapped the corner of the phone as she thought.

A voice mail notification chimed, followed by a text: *Hey beautiful. Miss you. Let's meet up.*

On the surface it was simple enough, something she could take or leave. But she knew better. He wouldn't settle for a no.

And because she'd told him about the prenup when justifying the end of the affair, he knew her weak point—now one phone call offering to testify to the affair would give Pete all the evidence he needed.

She slammed the phone onto the table in frustration. She needed this like another hole in her head on top of everything else, trying to keep Pete from finding out about Rick, and trying to keep Rick from losing patience with the situation—

That was it. She'd put him off the same way she was putting off Rick.

She sent the response, direct, truthful, but with no details: *Life is too complicated right now. Hope you're well.*

He didn't respond right away, and she hunched over the phone, praying for some version of "no biggie, just wanted to say hi, take care."

I'll call tomorrow so we can talk.

Ice burrowed through her. He wasn't going to let it go.

Her thumbs flew into position, about to tell him not to call. But—if she could juggle it rather than swatting him down right away, maybe something else would catch his attention and he'd move on. She'd let him call, but wouldn't pick up. She'd send another text delaying gently.

By the time he got the message, she'd have something else figured out.

CHAPTER FIFTEEN

As Arnett drove back to Crone Ridge from Madison's mother's apartment, Jo texted Sophie to let her know what was happening, then dove into a search for the purported Pagans in Scoby.

"Found something," she said, skimming. "Pretty much what Rankin said. Trespassing, kids wearing black, all the typical Satanic Panic accoutrements. But wait—here's a more in-depth article about the group responsible, from our old friend Lacey Bernard." Bernard was a journalist who'd recently helped Jo and Arnett solve a case. "They call themselves Lucifer Lost."

"Very poetic."

"Mmm. The article includes an image of the symbol we saw on Madison's abdomen. Apparently it's called Lucifer's Sigil. And the group's not just from around here, there are several chapters across the country. Including a physical location in Boston."

"Tell me we don't have to make that drive."

"The group's name reflects their underlying philosophy. 'Lucifer' was a figure in Greek and Roman mythology before he was the fallen-angel devil. The name translates to 'light-bringer,' and he's associated with dawn and the planet Venus.

The argument is that when Christianity subsumed the figure into its teachings—"

"But isn't the fallen angel in the Old Testament? Would that make it a Jewish change?"

"He was called something else in Hebrew, and later translators switched the name to Lucifer. The point is, the members of Lucifer Lost feel the name 'Lucifer' has been inappropriately commandeered and his 'light' extinguished. They're against any religious strictures that limit freedom and try to control people. For them, a return to Lucifer isn't about the devil, it's about a rejection of controlling dogma."

"While replacing it with a different dogma?" Arnett asked.

Jo shrugged. "I'd have to know more to say. And Bernard identifies the member of the Scoby crew she talked to, Brad Pratt, aged twenty-one."

"Sounds like it'll be worth paying Mr. Pratt a visit once we talk to the CSIs."

"Agreed."

―――――

The team was well under way by the time Jo and Arnett returned to Crone Ridge. Jo spotted Janet Marzillo, who oversaw the Oakhurst lab, from the familiar brown eyes and hints of her curly black hair peeping out from the few visible portions of her PPE. Marzillo squatted next to Madison while Hakeem Peterson, Marzillo's right-hand man, processed the twin altars.

"Jo, Bob." Marzillo nodded to them. "We've been here about forty-five minutes, so I have a general sense of what we're looking at."

"Catch us up," Jo said.

"Cause of death is almost certainly the slashed throat, based on the amount of blood coming from that site versus the abdomen. The incision is long and deep, most likely caused by a right-handed person kneeling behind her head while she was already lying down."

"So not when she was still standing up?" Arnett asked.

"See the slight upwards angle at the right end of the wound? If Madison had been standing, her killer would have had to raise the knife up toward the sky at the end of the slash, which would be a very awkward angle and the opposite of what you'd normally do." She mimicked the sharp direction the killer's arm would have to take. "And if you look at the blood, gravity pulled it to the sides right from the start, and the pooling is contained. If she'd been standing, I'd expect to see blood spatter elsewhere on the ground. We checked with luminol, and that's not the case."

"No signs that she was restrained, unless we missed them?" Arnett said.

"I've found no evidence of that, either in terms of abrasions or bruising. In fact, there's no bruising anywhere I can see, and no signs of a struggle or sexual assault. She may have been drugged, so I'll have the tox screen double-check for that."

"So our killer could easily have been a woman." Jo gestured toward the knife in Madison's abdomen. "Please tell me the killer did that after she was dead."

"He—or she—did. But if you're asking if the baby was already dead by the time it was stabbed, there's no way to know without an autopsy. Most likely not even then. As soon as Madison was killed, oxygen would have stopped flowing to the baby, but the baby would have been alive for five to ten minutes after that."

Bile rose in Jo's throat, but she forced herself to push down the images flashing through her mind. "Do you have an estimate on time of death?"

Marzillo's brow creased. "A very general one. She's in full rigor, except for where you broke it to examine the baby figurine, which, generally speaking, would mean she's been dead at least six hours. But given how cold it was last night, I'd expect it to take a little longer, maybe minimum eight hours." She bent down and motioned around the face and throat. "But—and keep in mind I'm no expert here—blowflies lay their eggs on open wounds and cavities, and it takes twelve hours for those first eggs to hatch. You can see that's well under way, with both eggs and maggots around the neck incision, the eyes, nose, and mouth. But the ones that have hatched are only about three millimeters in length; by twenty-four hours they'd be in their second instar, which would put them at about six millimeters. So the best we can narrow down time of death to is between twelve and twenty-four hours. You'd have to talk to a forensic entomologist to be sure, but I'd put it closer to twenty-four."

"Damn." Jo tapped a nail on the side of her leg. "That puts us right back where we were. She could have been killed last night after dark, or shortly after she left to take Ginger for a walk."

Marzillo stood back up. "I've taken samples from the blood used to draw on her in case our killer was stupid or unhinged enough to use his own."

"Can we tell anything about the knife?" Arnett asked.

"We'll do a search; Hakeem is good with weapons. We're doing a spiral search out from the scene for any evidence, and I sent a tech out with a park ranger to check all of the trash cans throughout the park."

"On top of it as always." Jo gazed out past the boulders, then back at Madison. "Hard to tell at this point if we're looking at a serial killer or something more personal. If it is personal, my main suspect is the baby's father, but we need to figure out who that is. Can you be sure to take a DNA sample from the baby?"

"Not a problem," Marzillo said over her shoulder.

A voice crackled over Officer Rankin's radio. He responded,

then called out to them. "Detectives. One of the CSIs found something else in the woods."

———

The CSI in question was Alicia Sweeney, a red-haired early-thirties recent addition to the lab. They found her several hundred yards from the gravestone boulders, guarding a handful of evidence markers.

"Alicia. This is the second time you've helped us find crucial evidence in the woods," Jo said.

Sweeney's smile lifted her eyes, the only thing visible through her PPE. "When my father told me I'd come to appreciate the time we spent camping as a family, I don't think this is what he meant."

Jo half-smiled as she followed the markers. On a small boulder the height of a chair lay a pile of neatly folded clothes, along with a cell phone and a small keychain both attached to a wristlet case. A pair of trainers were neatly settled at the base of the rock, with socks stuffed inside. "You found them like this?"

"Yup. I marked them and photographed them, but that's it. I figured you'd want to see them before I dug in."

"Please, carry on," Jo said.

"Some people use those kinds of cell-phone cases as mini purses, so there may be some identification inside. I'll start there." She fingerprinted the outside, then swabbed it for DNA. She opened it, did the same, then held up the windowed ID for Jo and Arnett to see.

"Madison Coelho." Jo pulled out her own phone. "I'll let Lopez know. She'll want to get her hands on the device as soon as possible."

As Alicia finished processing the phone, she ran a finger over the side buttons. The display sprung to life.

Jo's eyes snapped up. "The phone's on?"

Alicia peered closely at it. "It's down to five percent battery, but yeah, it's on. Guess our killer forgot to deactivate it."

Jo's hand flew to her necklace. Given all the other precision here, that was a strange detail to overlook.

Alicia moved on to the other items. A red maternity tunic. Black leggings with an expansive maternity waist. White underwear and bra. Socks that, when she pulled them out of the shoes, had little red strawberries on the ankles. For some reason, that detail cut through Jo, and she had to look away.

Arnett tilted his head at the display. "You think he forced her to undress, or undressed her once she was out?"

Jo cleared her throat. "Hard to say."

"My guess is she did it herself," Alicia said. "Because why bother to fold it all and assemble it so neatly so far away from the body?"

"Might have been part of his constructed ritual sacrifice," Arnett answered.

"Either way, let's hope he undressed her, because he might have left us some evidence that way." A text buzzed Jo's phone; she looked down at it. "Lopez is on her way. Doesn't want to wait until the phone is back at HQ to get a start looking at it."

"I'll make sure it's ready for her," Alicia said.

"Thank you," Jo said. "Because I agree with her that time is of the essence. It's one thing if this is someone who knew Madison, and this was personal to her. But if this was a random abduction and murder, people who do things like this"—Jo swept an arm around to indicate the items in front of them and the direction of the makeshift altar—"don't just do them once. We need to figure out who's behind this before they kill again."

CHAPTER SIXTEEN

"So, our next steps," Jo said as they made their way back to the cars. "Since Madison's friends began and ended with her prenatal-class group, we need to check out her job. She must have at least talked with someone there, and I'd like to verify the exact hours she worked. Her friends claimed she's been showing up late to the class, but we now know she's not enrolled in any classes."

"We also need to follow up on this Lucifer Lost cabal." Arnett gestured broadly back toward the scene. "Even if it doesn't have anything to do with this, whoever did this wants us to think it does."

"And I've learned not to underestimate how obsessed humans can get about any range of things," Jo added.

"Especially teenaged ones with overactive hormones and underdeveloped frontal lobes," Arnett agreed. "Madison's job'll be closed today, so I say we chat with Lucifer Lost."

"You drive," Jo said. "I should be able to track down the doctors Madison worked for even though it's Sunday."

As Arnett pulled out of the parking lot Jo put through a call to the chiropractor's office. As she waited on hold for the after-hours message line, she stared up at the sun setting behind the tree line, setting off a blaze of red, orange, and yellow in the dying light. A reminder they were racing time, and needed to move as fast as possible. Jo caught her nails drumming impatiently on her phone as she waited, and Matt's earlier words flooded her mind—he was right, even the beginnings of a stunning sunset was sinister if she allowed it to be.

A bored young woman's voice droned over the line. "Blue Bay Chiropractic you've reached the after-hour answering service my name is Tayla name and date of birth please."

Jo blinked at the flood of words, then introduced herself. "I need you to put through an emergency message to whatever doctor is on call."

"Patient name and date of birth?"

"This isn't regarding a patient, it's regarding one of their employees," Jo answered.

"Is the employee in their patient system?"

Jo shot Arnett a questioning look. "Possibly, but it's not relevant. I just need you to get an emergency message to whichever doctor is on call."

"I'm sorry, ma'am, but I can't help you if this isn't about a patient. I've been instructed not to bother the doctor on call unless there's a legitimate emergency. Any other messages will be received Monday morning when they reopen."

Something slammed shut in Jo's brain. "Tayla, let me explain the situation to you in a different way. One of Blue Bay's employees was abducted and brutally stabbed to death. As part of our investigation, we need to talk to her employer. That means if you don't put this message through to the on-call doctor, you're officially obstructing a murder investigation. And *that* means we can arrest you and put you in jail."

There was a brief moment of silence before a burst of typing erupted. "I'll page Doctor Huang with your message. You should receive a call back within half an hour."

"Thank you, Tayla. Your help has been invaluable." Jo dictated her number, then hung up the phone.

Arnett's face was screwed into an amused smirk.

"What?" Jo asked.

"Love it when Wolverine Jo makes an appearance. It's been too long."

"If I have to be a mustelid, I prefer honey badger, thank you very much. Some people just need a little jolt to remind them why it's worth being a decent human being."

He made a chef's kiss gesture. "Couldn't agree more."

"Next up, Kiernan Wendiss. We need to know where he was yesterday."

When he answered the phone, Jo gave him the news about Madison as gently as she was able. He broke down, his tears quiet but insistent, with an undercurrent of hopelessness that ripped at Jo's heart. When they tapered off, she repeated her condolences, then forced herself to ask the question. "For the record, we need to know where you were yesterday."

He sniffled, and blew his nose. "I understand. I was studying at Dickenson Library at OakhurstU from about nine in the morning until about four-thirty for my midterm tomorrow. I took a break for food around, I think, twelve-thirty-ish? But I grabbed a sandwich and a Coke at the library's café, and I'm pretty sure they have cameras everywhere. Then I went home to watch some TV before my shift at Gino's. You showed up right before I headed out for work."

A possibility popped into Jo's head. "Are you a member of Lucifer Lost?"

"Lucifer Lost? What's that?"

"Never mind." If he was a member, he wasn't planning on admitting it. "Thank you for answering our questions. I know how hard this must be."

He made an odd sound, something between a grunt and a choke. "What's important is finding out who did this to Madison. Anything you need from me to get that done, I'm down. Phone records, access to my social media, whatever—just tell me where to sign."

Jo jumped on the opening. "Would you be willing to give us a DNA sample so we can exclude you as the baby's father?"

"Just tell me when and where."

Jo gave him the information, again expressed her condolences, then ended the call. "Well," she said to Arnett. "That alibi should be easy enough to check. And it's a good sign that he's willing to give a DNA sample."

"Let's see if he shows up before we order his medal," Arnett said. "He wouldn't be the first to pull out when push comes to shove."

Jo wagged her head in acknowledgment and clasped on to her necklace.

———

When the GPS announced they'd arrived at Brad Pratt's house, Arnett pulled up in front of a large rectangular cream-clapboard colonial subdivided into four apartments.

"How much are we gonna tell the kid?" he asked. "I say we go for full shock, see how he responds."

"What do we hold back, then? The figurine?" Jo asked.

Arnett nodded. "It's all we need to verify a confession."

They identified which of the apartments belonged to Pratt and rang the bell. The door opened, sending a nor'easter of marijuana smoke past them and revealing a skinny young white man, probably not more than a few days over twenty-one, with shaggy brown hair and a graphic tee with a pentagram on it.

He gave them a once-over. "Where's the burritos?"

Jo shifted her blazer to reveal her badge. "I'm Detective Josette Fournier of the Oakhurst County SPDU, and this is Detective Bob Arnett. We're—"

His eyes sprung wide open, or at least, wider open. "Marijuana's legal and I'm not a dealer and you can't come in without a warrant."

Jo held off on explaining to him that the tidal wave of olfactory evidence gave them more than enough probable cause to check whether he was over the legal possession limit. "We're investigating a murder and we need to ask you a few questions."

His eyes turned eager. "Murder? Who died?"

Jo hid her surprise at the unusual reaction as she pulled up Madison's picture on her phone. "Do you know a woman named Madison Coelho?"

He stared at it, fascinated. "Maybe. She kinda looks like a lot of people, if you know what I mean."

Jo reminded herself to be patient. "The circumstances of her murder suggest it was part of a Satanic ritual."

Brad's face instantly shifted to scorn. "This is such bullshit. You're just afraid of what you don't understand. Lucifer Lost would never murder anyone."

Given his odd reaction, Jo made a split-second decision that agreeing with him would be the best way to get him talking. "We believe someone is either trying to shift responsibility onto your organization or a disturbed individual adjusted your beliefs to their own warped goals."

Brad was thrown by her capitulation, but after a confused moment decided to run with it. "See, people are so jacked up. Anything different—people crap all over it. That's why Lucifer Lost is so important. We're about freethinking, allowing people to do and say and be what they want, as long as they don't hurt anybody else. Nothing to do with Satan."

Arnett gestured to Pratt's shirt. "So why the Satanic symbols and pentacles and animal skulls in the middle of the woods?"

Brad raised and waved his hands as though erasing an invisible whiteboard. "Unlearn what you think you know. Like, there were no animal skulls. If the report said that, some cop added it in. And you said pentacle, but you mean pentagram."

"Sure." Arnett was terse.

Brad hooked his thumbs through his belt loops, warming to the topic. "Pentagrams have been around for thousands of years. There are *Christian* churches that have pentagrams on them, even supposedly evil upside-down ones, like Amiens Cathedral. They symbolize life and the earth."

"Is that why you meet out in the woods, at night?" Arnett asked.

Brad smirked. "Many religions have rituals that are performed at night. Druids, Wiccans, Christian candlelight vigils. Shabbat starts at sundown. Ramadan has evening services. Unless you're saying *they're* all evil?"

Jo hurried to head off the debate, one Brad was clearly enjoying. "We don't want to make assumptions. Can you explain what the rituals were about? We need to know if we're looking at a copycat situation."

"What happened?" Brad asked.

"We can't release details. But if you give us a general sense of what you do, we can ask about any relevant specifics," Jo answered.

His eyes narrowed slightly as she spoke, most likely weighing whether she was setting a trap. "We gather, read our tenets aloud, go over any outstanding business, and reaffirm our commitment to our beliefs."

"And that involves building a fire and drawing pentacles on other people's property?" Arnett asked.

"Nature is everybody's property. And, yes, we incorporate all four elements into our rituals, since they're the basis of all things." He gestured down. "Earth, also symbolized by the pentagram. Water, sprinkled around us if we can't find a natural source. Campfires or candles for fire, and we burn sage to invoke the air we breathe."

Jo pulled up the Lucifer's Sigil included in Lacey Bernard's article. "What does this mean?"

"It refers to Lucifer. We use it as our group identifier, for obvious reasons." The color drained from Brad's face. "The killer used *this* symbol? How?"

"We can only say we found it at the scene," Jo said. "Can you tell us why that might be?"

His posture stiffened. "It has layers of meaning, and to us symbolizes nature's duality. If someone used that symbol, they chose it specifically to throw suspicion on us."

Jo allowed her brows to raise. "What makes you so sure of that?"

"Pentagrams, people know. Goat horns, people know. People don't know the Sigil of Lucifer."

Arnett mimicked his earlier shrug. "Anybody who read the article would have seen it."

"Precisely my point," Brad snapped.

"Could it be an off-shoot of your group?" Jo asked. "Or somebody who left on bad terms?"

"There are other chapters, but all of our original members are still in ours."

"We'll need a list of their names," Jo said.

"I can't give them to you."

"Why would your members need to hide?" Arnett asked.

Brad's previous insouciance returned, now with an angry edge. "Look at the tone of your question and your initial assumption our group practices Satanic worship. Is it unreasonable that our members might not want an ignorant public to draw dangerous conclusions about them?"

Jo pulled his attention back. "Many religions throughout time have incorporated animal sacrifice or human blood into their rituals. Is that an aspect of Lucifer Lost's practices?"

His stance widened, and his arms crossed over his chest—the fun of the debate had disappeared. "One hundred percent not. Our most basic tenet is no harm to others, including animals. We even encourage vegetarianism."

"Can you share with me what all the tenets are?" Jo asked. "That will help us rule out anyone not legitimately a member of your group."

Pride washed over his face. "We believe in personal autonomy and responsibility: all individuals may believe and act as they like, as long as their actions don't harm others. We believe in treating our fellow beings with empathy. And we believe in putting words into action, so we pledge time and money to support the autonomy of others."

"And what happens when members fall short of those tenets?" Arnett asked.

"Part of our pledge is that when we fail, as all humans do, we atone for that failure, including rectification of the harm caused by our actions."

"Who enforces that?" Jo watched his face carefully.

He shifted in place. "Nobody has authority over another member."

Jo held back her skeptical smile—where there were rules of any sort there was a need to enforce them, even if that only meant expulsion from the group. "Do you know of anyone who'd want to paint Lucifer Lost in a bad light?" Jo asked.

Brad's arms swept a wide circle. "You mean besides everyone?"

"Any specific threats?" Jo asked.

"Nothing specific," he admitted grudgingly.

Jo switched gears. "We have to ask where you've been this weekend, starting at ten yesterday morning."

His arms crossed over his chest again. "You're looking at it. Watching TV and kicking back."

"Alone?"

"For the most part. A friend came to chill last night for a couple of hours."

"What time?"

"From about ten last night to about one in the morning."

Which left plenty of time to abduct and kill Madison. Jo pulled a card from her pocket and handed it to him. "We'd appreciate it if you'd let the other members of your group know we'd like to speak to them. And if you think of anything that might be useful to us, we'd appreciate hearing it."

Brad glanced down at the card, then back up at her. "They won't be able to tell you anything else."

Once back inside the car, Arnett grunted in disgust. "Guy's the real-world equivalent of an internet troll. And 'personal autonomy as long as it doesn't harm other people'—who determines what constitutes harm?"

Jo stared down at the picture of Madison lying naked and dead in the woods. "And would demanding a man provide for a child he'd fathered be seen as infringing on his autonomy?"

CHAPTER SEVENTEEN

Arnett's head snapped up. "You think the father was a member of Lucifer Lost?"

"I don't know what to think." Jo's hand flew up to the diamond at her throat. "But quite a few things about all this bother me. One is the complete lack of struggle on her part, even assuming she was drugged. How did the killer get her out so deep in the woods with no fuss?"

Arnett nodded. "Fairly easy if they had her at gunpoint."

"Except for the dog. Dogs don't know to be quiet in the face of a gun."

Arnett's brows shot up. "Good point. And even an affable golden retriever wouldn't be okay with a stranger forcing Mom off the trail. So we're looking at someone she knew."

"Easy enough to claim you wanted to show her an interesting landmark or some such. But why would someone want to kill her? The only possible motive I can see involves that baby."

"Or maybe Brad just fed us a line of bullshit, and Lucifer Lost took her out there to participate in a ritual."

"Maybe she was even a member, and participated willingly,

thinking the ritual was something else." She rubbed the bridge of her nose. "Far-fetched, but possible."

"Why bring the dog, if so? More likely someone came out of the woods and claimed someone was hurt. The dog would have gone along if Madison seemed okay with it."

Jo exhaled deeply. "You're right. Everyone says she was kind. If someone was in distress, she'd have wanted to help, especially if it was someone she already knew." Jo's phone rang, and she connected the call. "Jo Fournier."

"This is Doctor Huang. You called about Madison Coelho? Is she all right?"

Tayla's fear of incarceration apparently hadn't compelled her to pass on any details. "No, I'm afraid she isn't. She was murdered."

Dr. Huang's voice caught. "What—how?"

Jo gave a brief explanation. "Did you work closely with her?"

"Yes and no." Her voice was thick. "It's a small office, so we worked in close proximity. But I spent most of my day with patients."

"So you all didn't eat lunch together, anything like that?"

Dr. Huang gave a choked laugh. "I'm lucky if I have time to eat in my office while I respond to patient emails. But it's not relevant anyway because her shifts weren't long enough for her to have a meal break."

Jo paused. "I thought she'd recently started working for you full-time?"

"Why would you think that?"

"Didn't she ask for more hours?"

"No." Dr. Huang was dismissive. "We have one full-time staff member, and the other two split the shift, four hours each. She knew we wouldn't be able to give her more time without taking time away from Dana, our other part-time employee."

Jo shot a confused look at Arnett. "How much did you know about her personal situation?"

"Not much. I believe in keeping a professional relationship structure in place for everyone's benefit. She was pregnant, she was a student, she was efficient, on time, and was a self-starter."

Jo's mind flew to her own micro-managing lieutenant and wondered if a boss like that would be heaven or hell. "Got it. We'll need to talk to everyone who worked with her."

Something rustled, like Dr. Huang was shifting the phone. She then rattled off a phone number for another chiropractor, a nurse, and the two other staffers.

"To be thorough, I also need to know where you were this weekend, starting at ten-thirty yesterday."

"My mother and father came down from Maine to visit. Since I'm on call we've stayed home, my mother and I playing cards while my husband and father watch football. You can verify with them if you like." She called her mother to the phone. After her mother confirmed, she took the phone back. "Is there anything else I can do to help? Either you or her family?"

"Her mother is her only family. I'm sure a call from you would be appreciated."

"I'll call her now."

When the call ended, Jo turned to Arnett. "If she wasn't going to school and she wasn't working extra hours, where the hell was she spending her time?"

CHAPTER EIGHTEEN

As Arnett continued back to HQ, Jo contacted the other employees of Blue Bay Chiropractic, trying to find any lead on Madison's mystery time-drain. Both the other doctor and the nurse shared Dr. Huang's good-fences-make-good-employees approach to relationships with their staff. Dana also had little to say about Madison, not surprising since they'd spent very little time together. But Jo's hopes deflated when Beth, the full-time assistant, also had very little to say about Madison.

"We got along fine," she said with a shrug in her voice after a chorus of *oh-my-Gods* and *how-horribles*. "But we weren't, like, close. She was really into her work, if you know the type. Like she was trying to prove something to somebody. I'd've thought she was trying to get a promotion, but there's nowhere to be promoted to. So it made no sense, and all it did was annoy Dana."

"Why did it annoy Dana?"

"Because it was like she was trying to show Dana up. I been there longer and I'm full-time, so *I'm* sure not going nowhere."

Jo suspected Dana wasn't the threatened one. "So you never hung out after hours, nothing like that?"

"Nah. I have my own friends outside of work."

Jo thanked her and hung up as they pulled into the HQ parking lot. "Lopez texted saying she brought the phone back here. Think she's found anything useful?"

"The way this is going?" Arnett said, striding toward the building. "I sure hope so."

They found Christine Lopez hunched over one of her desks, headphones on, her long black ponytail threatening to dip into her open can of Rockstar. One of Jo's favorite people, Lopez had partnered with Arnett during Jo's brief stint as lieutenant; when Jo asked to be made detective again and re-partnered with Arnett, Lopez helped clear out a backlog of tech analysis while waiting for a new partner. Her expertise quickly became invaluable, so she transferred in permanently and had helped Jo and Arnett solve more crimes than Jo could count.

"Good to see you," Jo said.

Lopez didn't respond. Jo stepped over and tapped her shoulder.

Lopez jumped into the air, sending her chair flying backward. "Holy crap," she said once she recognized Jo, hand clasped to her chest. "I told Janet headphones weren't a good idea. Anybody can sneak up on you." She ripped them off and tossed them on the desk like poisonous snakes.

"Thank goodness we weren't zombies," Arnett deadpanned.

Lopez narrowed her eyes at him. "Laugh now, Arnett. You won't have time to laugh when the zombies arrive."

Jo tilted her head. "I can never tell if you're serious or not about the pending zombie apocalypse."

"I'll take her seriously when she builds a bunker," Arnett said.

Lopez pointed to Jo. "The Covid pandemic? One mutation away from a zombie virus." She swung the finger to Arnett. "My cousin already has a bunker. I have knife skills and the ability to open cans without any equipment whatsoever."

Jo's brows popped up. "Well. Reserve me a spot, because I can outrun anybody when we need to replenish supplies."

"How many times do I have to tell you not to encourage her?" Arnett grumbled.

"Hey, you're the one who brought up the Z word. I'm just being pragmatic." Jo turned to Lopez. "I don't suppose the phone records have come back, or you've cracked into the phone?"

A smile spread over Lopez's face as she pulled her chair to the desk and plopped down. "Sure have. Whatcha want first, the bad news or the surreal news?"

Jo had learned to humor Lopez's flair for the dramatic, but still stopped short of appreciating it. "Whichever gets us to our killer fastest."

"Okay, well, I still have a few things I need to check, like for hidden apps, all that."

Jo placed her hands on her hips.

"The bad news is, I can't find any record of Kiernan Wendiss being in contact with Madison since the seven months ago he claimed. The last text was an uber-sweet heartbreaker where he said he was confused about why she broke up with him but said he respected her choice. He pledged his love, said he hoped she'd change her mind, and told her either way he'd always be there for her."

"Wouldn't be the first guy to switch tacks after the sweet route didn't go his way," Arnett said.

"True, but like I say, there's no record of any further contact. I put in the warrant for his phone records, because maybe he was harassing her at work or something. But no evidence so far," Lopez said.

"Got it," Jo said.

"And her lack of a personal life is real. No friends other than the ones you talked to—Naomie Alexander, Chelsea Whitens, and Julia Gagnon. Mostly the first two, but there's a group chat that involves all four of them. Nobody else but enforced study buddies."

"Enforced study buddies?" Arnett asked.

"You know, when your professor forces you to partner up with someone for a group project and you're stuck in living hell until you get your grades back," Lopez said.

"Gotcha," Arnett said.

"And, worst of all, there's no record I can find of any other guy, either since or before Kiernan. No flirting, no sexting, not even a dick pic. She tracks her appointments in Google calendar, and nothing suggests even coffee with a romantic prospect. By the way, you went to see her mother—do you have a laptop for me?"

Jo shook her head. "Madison couldn't afford one. She checked one out from the community college when she needed one for school." Jo dug into her jacket pocket. "But she had this thumb drive. I could only find term papers on it, but maybe you can find something we didn't."

"Or maybe she has a burner somewhere and her mother hasn't found it yet," Arnett said.

Lopez swung her chair back and forth, looking like the cat who'd eaten Tweety Bird. "I don't think that's likely."

Jo's radar perked up. "Why's that?"

"Because if she had one, I'm pretty sure she'd have used *that* rather than *this*"—she held up Madison's phone with a triumphant gleam in her eye—"when calling her secret night job at the strip club."

CHAPTER NINETEEN

Naomie sat at the white laminate desk in her solarium, furiously jotting notes and searching through her contacts. Generally the white-and-navy decor soothed her, made her feel like she was out sailing on her father's boat, but today she jumped like a bundle of raw nerves when the phone rang. Fully expecting it to be one of the vendors she'd contacted about Madison's celebration of life or Rhea Blondell, her co-founder at Triple-B, she hit the connect button without registering the caller's name.

"Naomie?" her administrative assistant Sandra's voice came over the line, hesitant and shaky.

Naomie's stomach tightened. "Sandra—are you okay?"

"I'm so sorry to bother you on a Sunday, but I just got your email about Madison."

"Oh, right." Naomie's eyes squeezed shut. Before she jumped into organizing the memorial, she'd sent an email to the staff of Triple-B letting them know that Madison had passed, but she hadn't expected anyone to get the message until they arrived at work Monday.

"What happened?" Sandra asked.

"The police aren't sure yet." She explained what little she knew, carefully holding back her tears.

"Oh." Sandra's pause was uncomfortable. "It's just that... well... I don't want to make a fuss and I know you said you were going to talk to Madison about it and I'm sure you already did but at the same time I can't help but wonder—"

Naomie held in an impatient sigh. Sandra was an organizational whiz with the mind of a computer, but the people skills of a rabid raccoon. Naomie cut Sandra off in her most reassuring voice. "Whatever's on your mind, you can tell me."

"It's—it's that grant issue I told you about. I hate to bring it up again because I know you said you'd look into it—"

The grant issue. Naomie's eyes flicked to the stack of papers she'd set aside once she'd received the call about Madison. It included an anomaly Sandra brought to her attention late the previous week regarding a thousand-dollar grant for Madison, a disbursement from a fund that helped mothers buy necessary supplies for their coming babies or newborns. Each grantee was only entitled to one endowment per calendar year, but somehow Madison had received a second pay out.

"I emailed Madison, but we didn't have a chance to talk about it. And, now, well... now it doesn't matter. I'm sure it must have been some sort of clerical error. We'll write up the discrepancy and report it to the board, but I don't think it'll be a problem. In our five years, this is our first issue." Naomie's gaze dropped to the list of potential caterers in front of her.

"But the thing is... I don't want to seem like I'm... But I just think it's strange. All those CSI-type shows say there's no such thing as a coincidence. It's strange that right after this discrepancy crops up Madison turns up dead."

"That's TV." Naomie struggled to keep her attention away from the memorial plans. "In the real-world coincidences happen every day." She pulled over the relevant forms. "The most likely explanation is Janelle misfiled the application, didn't realize it had been paid, and paid it again. It's easy to make mistakes when you're new."

"I asked Janelle about that, and she was adamant there's no way. She always prints out the approval and staples it to the application form."

"Everybody makes mistakes, Sandra." Naomie paged through the file. "And if this was really a second application, where's the first? There's no other application in here, no printout of the approval, nothing."

"But that's just it," Sandra said. "Janelle's predecessor taught her to make photocopies of the applications in case something gets lost or there's a problem with the review. And she pulled the backup and showed me the first application."

Naomie's full attention turned to Sandra now. "There are two different applications?"

"Yes. With two different dates, although the rest of the application is the same."

"The handwriting's the same?"

"Well, no. Madison filled the first one out by hand, but the second one was filled out online and then printed. Everything's typed except her signature."

"Do the signatures match?"

"Yes. And the log signature at time of receipt matched, too. So I pulled the checks. The first was deposited to Madison's bank account, but the second was signed over and cashed at a different bank, not deposited."

"Do those signatures also match?"

"They do."

"That suggests Madison cashed it." But her brain balked at the thought that Madison would have done that, to Triple-B, or to her. "Can you make me a copy of that original application? I'd like to take a look at it."

"I took pictures of it because Janelle didn't want to let it out of her office. I can email them to you as soon as we hang up."

"Have you told Rhea about this?" Rhea Blondell was the woman who'd co-founded Triple-B with her; she handled the administration, while Rhea functioned primarily as the financial officer.

"I thought I should talk to you first," Sandra said.

"Keep it under your hat for now. I'll take care of it." Naomie thanked her, then disconnected. True to her word, Sandra sent the attachments within a minute of hanging up the call, and Naomie printed them out.

Running her finger down both sets of documents, she compared the contents of each field. Sandra was right, the contents of the second application were identical to the first, word for word—that seemed unlikely unless someone was typing in the responses from the first application. And Madison wouldn't need to do that—only someone who wasn't sure of the details would.

But the signatures were definitely a match.

Tears filled her eyes, and she shoved the file away. None of it mattered anymore—Madison was gone, why run her reputation through the mud when she wasn't there to defend herself? Most likely it was an innocent mistake—pregnancy brain was real, Naomie was learning that herself. Maybe Madison filled it out by hand first but wanted it to be neat and submitted them both by accident. No matter what, the best thing to do was to just let it go. Naomie pulled her notebook back over and reoriented her energy to Madison's memorial.

But a nagging doubt pricked the back of her mind, whispering to her that something important was wrong.

CHAPTER TWENTY

Jo's mouth dropped open. "Madison worked at a strip club?"

"The Velvet Volcano over in Springfield. I found emails, calls, texts, digital paystubs, and schedules. But what put it over the top for me was the angry text from her boss when she didn't show up for her shift on Saturday night." Lopez held up the phone so Jo and Arnett could see the text.

After peering at it, Arnett dropped into an empty chair. "No wonder she kept her cards close to her chest."

Jo held up a hand as she paced the room, sorting through the implications. "Let me guess—this started about six or seven months ago?"

"That's a bingo." Lopez tapped her nose. "The end of March."

Arnett picked up her logic. "Right when her mother was placed in the emphysema category."

Jo's teeth raked her lower lip. "A lot of things happened right at that time. She also broke up with her boyfriend for no apparent reason."

"You think she was too embarrassed to tell him she was

taking the job at a strip club? Worried that he wouldn't accept it?"

"I think that's exactly what happened." Jo's mind continued to race. "And—based on what the ladies told me about her due date, she got pregnant shortly after that time. So, a girl who has zero trace of dating anyone starts working at a strip club and turns up pregnant shortly thereafter—"

"Hang on," Arnett said. "That's a good point. She's six months pregnant—she couldn't have been stripping. At least not recently."

Jo and Lopez exchanged a glance.

Arnett followed it. "What?"

Lopez gathered her ponytail. "It truly warms my heart that with everything you've seen on this job, you're genuinely unaware that pregnant strippers are a thing."

Arnett glanced between them, then narrowed his eyes. "Bullshit."

"I'm afraid not," Jo said. "Some men pay very well for it. To borrow an expression from my father, it takes all kinds to make a world."

Arnett's face dropped.

"But if it makes you feel better," Lopez hurried to add, "it's also possible that once she couldn't hide the baby bump, she switched to cocktail waitressing."

"Also on the positive side, Laura will be glad to know you're blissfully naive when it comes to gentlemen's clubs," Jo added. "But back to the point I was making—No boyfriend, starts at a strip club, becomes pregnant. Do we think that's a coincidence?"

"You think she was doing more than stripping?" Arnett asked.

Jo grimaced, and bounced her fist on her thigh. "I don't know. But that would explain why she hasn't told anybody who the father is."

"Damn. Sweet kid with everything going for her—good grades, good heart, just wants to help animals—and life comes along and punches her repeatedly in the face until she ends up dead." Lopez wrapped the ponytail around her hand. "And I can just hear the jerks who'll shrug and say 'she made her choices' like she had anything to do with the fact that her mother got sick and it's impossible to earn a living with only a high-school diploma these days."

Jo nodded for a long moment. It was one thing to know life wasn't fair, but some situations brought it into heartbreaking focus.

Then she stood. "Looks like we need to take a trip out to The Velvet Volcano."

———

The Velvet Volcano turned out to be located in a window-free gray-slab building that looked like an industrial sheet cake somebody left out too long. If the GPS hadn't directed her to the location, Jo would have missed it; there were no exterior markings other than a single, sad banner with the club's name bookended by girls in flame-covered bikinis.

"This is just depressing," Arnett said. "Not lurid, not seedy —just sad."

"They're definitely not targeting drive-by traffic. Maybe that's why Madison picked it." Jo ran her eyes over the half-filled parking lot. "But they're not hurting for business."

"Not bad at all for just after nine at night."

What the club lacked in curb appeal it made up with sheer sensory assault inside. Competing rows of pink, purple, and blue neon stripes outlined everything—the trio of stages, the bar at the back right, even the walking paths of the floor—and pulsed in time with blaring music. Three disco balls sent glittering neon reflections dancing over the chairs and tables that crowded the three jutting stages, and off the sequined curtains that periodically disgorged naked women. And an odd vanilla-jasmine scent with hints of talcum powder and baby oil saturated it all, causing Jo to rub her nose.

"This place should come with a seizure warning," Arnett said.

"It's like an electric unicorn exploded." Jo passed the cashier to the immediate right and pushed aside the visual clutter to peer at the far ends of the large room. "Two doors to the right, probably to the dressing room and management's office. The three doors on the left look like VIP rooms."

"Can I help the two of you?" The cashier, a forty-something woman with black back-combed hair a few shades too harsh to be natural, stood up, hand slipping under the counter as she did so.

Jo showed her badge. "We have some questions regarding the death of a woman who worked for you. I'd ask you to call out your manager if you hadn't just done that already."

The woman had the nerve to look indignant. She picked up the phone in front of her and spoke into it. "Two detectives are asking to talk to you." She listened, then hung up. "You said this is about one of our employees?"

Jo held up a picture. "Madison Coelho. You know her?"

The woman flinched. "Amber." She met Jo's eyes. "She's dead?"

A tall, lanky man with spiked brown hair and a tan suit appeared, pulling his office door quickly closed behind him. Over the carefully arranged smile on his face, his hard eyes lasered in on Jo and Arnett.

Despite his speed closing the door, he sauntered over to Jo and Arnett. "I'm Travis Hartley, the owner. How can I help you, Detectives?"

Jo ran through her introductions and showed the picture to Hartley. "Madison Coelho was found murdered today."

His smile faded. "Let's talk in my office."

Eyes followed them as they passed by the right-hand stage—several customers and the woman straddling the pole watched closely.

The throbbing music disappeared once the door closed behind them, and the refreshing lack of neon allowed Jo's eyes to relax. She took a seat in front of the large oak desk that dominated the surprisingly normal office. "When did Madison start work here?"

"Let's take a look." He opened a drawer to his right and rifled through the files there. When he found Madison's, he flipped it open on his desk and ran one finger down the front page. "Madison Coelho. She started March twenty-eighth of this year."

"As a stripper?" Jo asked.

"Yes," he said.

"What's your pay model?"

"Minimum tipped-employee wage per hour, currently six dollars fifteen cents, plus forty-five percent of their take in tips. Additional tips to the DJ and security are optional," he said. "While she was learning the ropes she danced three nights a week. Once she was up to speed she moved to five."

"And when it became obvious she was pregnant?" Jo asked.

His eyes narrowed so quickly she almost missed it. He flipped to a page in the file, rotated it, and pushed it toward Jo.

She leaned forward to scan the document. A liability waver signed on July twenty-fifth, releasing responsibility for anything that might happen to her unborn baby as she continued to dance for the club.

"How did that go down?" Arnett asked.

Hartley leaned back in his chair and crossed one ankle over his knee. "When we couldn't ignore it anymore, I told her she had three choices. Continue dancing specialty rooms, switch to waitressing, or go on hiatus. She kept dancing."

"With no pressure from you?" Jo asked, watching him carefully.

He smirked and raised both hands. "None at all. She was excited for the opportunity. It's a specialty, meaning people pay more to see it. And since it's a rare, limited-time situation, our girls jump at the chance."

"Did she perform any other *specialties* for extra pay?" Jo asked.

"You mean lap dances?" He shrugged. "Of course. All the girls do, with a strict no-touch policy."

"Private rooms?" Arnett asked.

"Not always." Travis steepled his fingers over his lap. "But some of our customers value privacy."

"Well, a *sort* of privacy," Jo said. "You have cameras in those rooms to monitor for abuse, right?"

"One hundred percent."

"But I'm sure you delete the files almost immediately after the fact," she said.

"Within the week."

The smug smirk on his face told her all she needed to know. An extra hundred flipped those cameras right off, and she'd bet her salary Travis had a pile of recordings at home for his own personal pleasure—or blackmail.

"Any chance you can check the recordings you haven't deleted yet?" Arnett asked.

"Not without a warrant. I'd never get another customer if it got around I let you see who comes in here."

And by the time they got the warrant, he'd have them deleted anyway. "Customers get out of hand from time to time. Any instances with Madison?"

He shook his head. "I'd've heard. But check with Chuck, he's our head of security. If there were any incidents, he'd know about it."

"Did Madison have any regulars?"

Travis shrugged again. "Nobody particular I know about."

"How did she get along with the other dancers?" Jo asked.

Hartley threw both hands up. "I don't track the pajama parties. But all my girls know if they don't treat the others with respect, they'll be out of a job."

Jo forced down the revulsion that pushed into her throat. "Then I'm sure you wouldn't mind if we talked to your employees about it?"

"As long as you don't keep them from their work," he said.

———

He left them alone in the dressing room, which told Jo the room had cameras or mics or the dancers knew better than to tell them anything. Sure enough, while they expressed shock and sadness and talked about how sweet Madison had been, when Jo asked about the working conditions, regulars, or problematic patrons, their answers became rote and practiced. Chuck the security guard was mostly monosyllabic, and claimed to remember no incidents with Madison whatsoever.

As they made their way toward the exit, Arnett jutted his head toward the men's room. "Gotta see a man about a horse."

As Jo waited, she scanned the crowd in the dim, pulsing light. A blonde cocktail waitress in a short, corseted blue-and-white lace concoction that had probably come from a Halloween store headed in her direction; Jo stepped forward to move out of her way. But the woman also maneuvered at the same moment and, teetering on her five-inch heels, crashed into Jo. The partially filled drinks on her tray spilled down the front of Jo's pants.

"Shit, I'm so sorry." The waitress grabbed a stack of napkins out of her teensy apron and swiped at Jo with them.

Jo gently pushed her hand away. "Please don't worry."

She met Jo's eyes with an odd intensity. "No, please, you

have to let me help clean you up. Take these and I'll grab some more."

Not surprised when her fingers hit something more solid than tissue, Jo made a few cursory swipes at her legs before slipping half the napkins, and the card hidden under them, into her pocket.

"You're never gonna believe this." Arnett appeared in front of her and jutted his chin to the door. "Outside."

Jo reassured the waitress again, then strode out behind Arnett. As she slipped into the passenger side of the Crown Vic, he tapped at his phone.

"This is one of those places that lets people cover the stalls in decals. Guess they figure it's better than graffiti." He held up the phone and pointed to a large sticker, a black rectangle slashed with a now-familiar white symbol.

The Sigil of Lucifer.

CHAPTER TWENTY-ONE

"So one or more of the members of Lucifer Lost frequents The Velvet Volcano," Jo said. "Or works there."

Arnett's expression was grim. "Maybe you're right, maybe this thing is playing a bigger role than we thought it was."

"No matter what, it leaps Lucifer Lost up the ladder of possibilities." Jo reached into the wad of napkins she'd shoved into her pocket. "And, we have another clue."

She flipped The Velvet Volcano business card over to the hastily penned message scribbled on the back: *Can't talk here. Meet me tomorrow at four at the Starbucks on Columbus.*

"What are we, stuck in some dime spy novel?" Arnett said. "She can't just call HQ?"

"Could be some sort of setup." Jo tugged her seat belt on over her shoulder. "But given how little we know, we have to take the risk. Honestly, I'm not at all surprised. Any place that hides itself from street traffic and has a panic button up for when the police show isn't what it seems to be. What's your take?"

Arnett's eyes scanned the building's entrance. "I keep going back and forth between a front for a prostitution ring or money laundering."

"Why not both?" Jo reached for her phone. "My first thought was organized crime, so I'm thinking we should check in with the Springfield Detective Bureau and see what they have to say."

"Don't want to screw up something they're trying to keep a quiet eye on," Arnett agreed.

Jo put through the call and left a message for whatever investigator might be keeping an eye on The Velvet Volcano.

Jo tapped the card on the corner of the phone. "Another possibility is if this is some sort of organized crime setup, Madison may well have gotten herself mixed up in something far more dangerous than she initially realized. She may have seen something she shouldn't have, or upset the wrong person. Academic achievement doesn't necessarily translate into street-smarts."

"So they took her out into the woods and killed her, and made it look like it had something to do with the Lucifer Lost group to put the attention elsewhere?" Arnett asked.

"I doubt anything happens in that club that Hartley isn't aware of, including the decals that show up on the bathroom stalls. A guest may even have struck up a conversation about it with him, especially if the rest of the members enjoy discussing the Lucifer Lost principles as much as Brad did. Easy enough to tuck the existence of Lucifer Lost into the corner of his mind for future use."

"Brad himself may have been here," Arnett said.

Jo glanced down at her phone. "I'm guessing we're not going to get a phone call back this late on a Sunday night. And we haven't heard back from Marzillo, which means they're still processing."

"So there's not much more we can do tonight." Arnett fired

up the engine. "I say we head home, get some sleep, and get a fresh start first thing in the morning."

———

As much as she needed sleep, Jo also needed to check on Sophie. She'd been so close to reconciling with David, and the situation with Chelsea had shaken that up. Sure enough, when Jo drove past, the living room light was still on.

Sophie answered the door with her hair pulled back into an uncharacteristically messy bun, remnants of make-up smudged over her face, and a nearly empty glass of red wine in one hand.

She stepped back to let Jo in. "This is a surprise."

Jo leaned in as she passed to kiss Sophie's cheek. "I was on my way home and thought I'd swing by. How are you doing?"

"I've been better, but I'm far better off than that poor murdered girl." She led Jo into her newly repainted sage living room and gestured to the wine sitting on the coffee table. "Can I get you a glass?"

"No, thanks. I'm already tired, and I have to drive. Pouring wine on top of that isn't wise." She sat on one end of the couch. "You said you've been better."

Sophie dropped on the other end and pulled a pillow into her abdomen with her empty hand. "I just—I don't know. I've spent the last few hours trying to convince myself I'm being paranoid."

"Paranoid how?" Jo asked.

"I know I overreacted earlier to Chelsea's call. And I'm sorry for taking it out on you. But I'm telling you, she's trying to get her claws into David."

"I don't think you overreacted. I was just as unhappy about her calling as you were." Jo picked her words carefully. "But as much as it sucks, Chelsea already has her claws into David, and will for the next eighteen years minimum."

"Believe me, I'm well aware. But that's not what I mean." Her face twitched, like she was smelling something bad. "I think she's trying to break up our marriage."

Jo didn't hide her confusion. "Wasn't she the one who broke things off with David? Didn't she say if he hadn't told her a bunch of lies about how bad your relationship was, she'd never have slept with him? Why go to all that trouble if she wanted him back?"

"That's why I keep telling myself that it doesn't make any logical sense." She took a gulp of her wine. "But something inside me keeps screaming this is a way to keep close contact with David. Maybe she changed her mind about wanting him, and this is a convenient excuse. She called him *twice* today."

"What about?"

"The first time because you wouldn't tell her what she wanted to know about her friend's murder. Which I admit I sympathize with because if one of my friends had been murdered, I'd want details, too. But then she called back panicking about being alone." She stared directly into Jo's eyes. "I've known girls like that, Jo. They're masters at manipulation, and they know how to get what they want while making you look crazy in the process."

Jo nodded. "How do you know about the calls?"

"One of the things I told David I needed if we were going to try again was complete transparency. We have each other's phone and computer passwords, and have a location tracking app so we always know where each other are. He also suggested that since he has to be in her life, he'd let me know exactly what was happening and why at all times."

Jo nodded, keeping her neutral face on—if she showed any emotion, Sophie would see it as judgment—but she didn't like that one bit. On the face it sounded like healthy communication, but it was rife for manipulation and abuse. What was Sophie supposed to say if he needed to talk to Chelsea or see her? *No, don't go take care of your child because the woman carrying it makes me jealous?* It put the onus of acceptance on Sophie, making her the villain if she expressed her true feelings.

But, then, what *should* David do? Keep what was happening from Sophie?

"If it helps," Jo said, "Chelsea was right to be worried about Madison. Whether she's milking it I can't say, but finding out her pregnant friend was just abducted and murdered probably hasn't been the best thing for her peace of mind."

Sophie took a sip of her wine as she weighed that. "No, that wouldn't be pleasant to go through. I've never felt as vulnerable as when I was pregnant. Except maybe now."

Jo reached over and squeezed her sister's arm. "Hang in there."

Sophie clutched the pillow harder into her stomach. "I think that's the problem, the 'hanging in there' isn't finite. Her difficult pregnancy will only be the beginning. There will be midnight calls when she can't stop the baby from crying, and scads of emergencies she doesn't know how to handle. I already feel like I'm waiting to catch my breath and I'm just not sure that day will ever come."

Jo sighed. Part of the life-long struggle of her relationship with Sophie was Sophie's self-centered tendencies—something Sophie surely felt about Jo, as well. Bringing that up, however gently, was a minefield—but if the situation were reversed, Jo would want Sophie to be upfront with her.

"I realize this has been thrust upon you in a particularly ugly way," she said. "But millions of people have to navigate exes and shared custody of kids from other relationships. It's not pleasant, but you're one of the strongest people I know."

A brief half-smile flashed over Sophie's face, which then quickly returned to a worried grimace. "I wonder what percentage of those involve the ex actively trying to destroy your relationship."

"We don't know that's what's happening, and there's good reason to believe she's just upset right now. You're in a difficult situation that you're already second-guessing, and this isn't helping. If you've made the decision to let David back in, you may just have to put your trust in that."

Sophie stared at the wall behind Jo's shoulder, and sipped her wine. After a long, tense moment she said, "Only time will tell."

CHAPTER TWENTY-TWO

Jo woke unsettled the next morning, anxious to dive back into the investigation. What she really wanted to do was track down the waitress from The Velvet Volcano, but she couldn't risk alienating her. Instead, she dumped an extra shot of espresso into her travel mug and headed out to HQ.

Arnett wasn't in yet when she arrived and her messages were frustratingly empty, so she clicked on her monitor. First things first—the most recent significant other. She dove into Kiernan Wendiss's alibi and background by requesting the video footage from the library. They also immediately checked his student ID swipes; the records verified his claims, as did records of material requests from just before ten and again at two in the afternoon. All well and good, but until she saw his face on the video footage, she couldn't be sure someone else hadn't used his card, or that he'd slipped in and out of an exit-only door. Jo'd seen one too many friends during her teen years sneak into movie theaters via one-way exits to ever fully trust them.

His background was clean; not so much as a parking ticket, and both the university and the pizza parlor where he worked confirmed his good standing and reliability. Of course, countless killers had glowing recommendations from unknowing friends, family members, and colleagues.

She switched gears to Brad Pratt, who worked as a teller at Citizens Bank. He had no criminal records, but Jo found another Lucifer Lost article where Brad credited the group with helping him 'clean up his act.' He'd been a troublemaker in high school, he told the interviewer, because he felt misunderstood. Once he discovered the freethinker approach of Lucifer Lost he realized what he was really rebelling against was the repression of traditional religions. Since Jo couldn't find any record of that troublemaking, it was either confined to school-based discipline, a sealed juvenile record, or he was making it up for a good story.

Her phone rang; the display identified the number as Springfield PD. "Jo Fournier."

"Detective Fournier, this is Senior Captain Ben Silva. I received your call about The Velvet Volcano. My understanding is you're inquiring about any active investigations we have relating to the establishment?"

"Yes."

"I did a double-check on this, and can't find anything active," Ben said. "It's a relatively new club, so that's not necessarily surprising. In terms of organized crime, we don't have anything ongoing. Suspiciously off the radar, in fact."

Arnett arrived at his desk and set a large Starbucks in front of her.

"My partner just walked in. I'm going to put you on speakerphone." Jo hit the button, then picked up where she left off. "We got the impression that's exactly what they were trying to do, fly under the radar."

"Ye-ah." Silva drew out the syllable. "Despite our best efforts, the battle with mafia in Springfield rages on. Sounds like it's time to add The Velvet Volcano to our watch list. I'd be interested to hear about anything else you learn."

"Since you're asking, one of their waitresses slipped me a note as we were leaving asking to meet today."

"Interesting. Keep me in the loop."

"Will do." Jo hung up and grabbed the new coffee. "Thank you for this."

"Up bright and early, I see," Arnett said. "I'm starting to think it's a ploy to make me buy the coffee."

She laughed, then caught him up on what she'd found. "Next up is Travis Hartley."

"I checked in with Rankin on the way over. Several people came forward claiming to have seen Madison. Several were one hundred percent certain they saw her Sunday morning, well after we know she was already dead."

Jo nodded. That was common—memories were notoriously faulty and easy to influence, and when people were trying to help, times and exact details shifted and shimmered. "I'm sure there were plenty of cute, brown-haired girls walking their dogs at Crone Ridge all weekend. Differentiating the right one in people's memories will be tough."

"At least now we know what she was wearing. That'll eliminate most false alarms."

Jo's phone pinged. "Marzillo wants to update us in the lab."

They grabbed their coffees and headed in. Marzillo looked predictably tired, with shadows under her dark eyes and curls peeping out of her bun.

"How late were you out there last night?" Jo asked.

"Close to midnight. Not a big deal, because Zelda's away and I hate being alone in the house anyway." She wiped her wrist against her forehead, careful to swipe above the nitrile glove on her hand. "Funny, isn't it? When you first start sharing a bed, it's hard to sleep with their movements and sounds. Then, after you've been together awhile, it's hard to sleep without the movements and sounds."

Jo smiled. "Humans are complicated, aren't we?"

"Preach," Lopez said, stepping through the doorway behind them. "Especially when it comes to relationships. Did I miss anything?"

"Just getting started," Marzillo said. "The ME confirmed what I assumed. Cause of death was the slash to the throat; the knife to the abdomen came after. As suspected, the substance used to write on her is blood, same type as Madison's. We've sent it out for DNA testing. No other wounds, defensive or otherwise, and no sexual assault. Tox screen is in the works, as is a DNA sample from the baby."

"Kiernan Wendiss gave us a sample this morning," Lopez injected.

"Oh, good, he showed up," Jo said.

Lopez leaned onto a desk. "Oh, yeah. Bright-eyed and bushy-tailed, waiting in the lobby when I got here. Couldn't give the sample fast enough."

Arnett's brows popped. "Either he's innocent or he's got some sort of God complex."

"Both equally likely," Lopez said. "He seemed like a good kid, but those are often the ones you gotta watch out for."

Marzillo continued. "Next up is the clothing. No blood or other obvious fluids on them. Dirt from the park, and dog hair that matches Ginger's. We're in the process of testing for touch DNA on the clothes, the phone, and the keys, but since our killer wore gloves, it's not likely anything transferred."

"Hope springs eternal," Jo said.

"On to the rest of the scene. The candles and the knife are both sold widely, same with the plastic baby she was holding. Both Party City and Amazon sell the exact model."

"I made a few quick calls," Lopez said. "Tracking the candles and the knife will be nearly pointless, but I have the managers of all Massachusetts Party City stores compiling purchases of plastic baby figurines within the last year. Apparently they fly off the shelves in February, but not this time of year, so maybe we'll get lucky. I'm in negotiations with Amazon to see if we can track down any recent purchases sent to this area."

"Either way, it's a long shot," Arnett said.

Lopez nodded. "I finished scouring Madison's accounts. Nothing other than the strip club turned up, although there was a decided shift in her social media usage about six months ago—next to nothing since she took the job at the strip club."

"Keeping a low profile," Jo said.

Lopez nodded. "When Wendiss stopped by to leave his DNA sample, he also gave us written permission to access his social media accounts, etc., so that's my next project."

"Thank you," Jo said. "Can I add a few more names to the list?"

"Hit me," Lopez said.

"Brad Pratt, part of Lucifer Lost. We'd really like to nail down who the other members of the group are. Also, Travis Hartley, who runs The Velvet Volcano." Jo filled her in on what had happened the day before.

"Sounds good. I'll see what I can dig up for you. In exchange I want to know every word that waitress says to you the minute you're done."

"Deal."

CHAPTER TWENTY-THREE

Naomie slipped into Beautiful Bouncing Babies at eight Monday morning, an hour and a half before the staff normally arrived. Usually she loved the peaceful calm of the early morning; it reminded her of going to church when nobody else was there, alone to allow her mind to focus and refresh. But today the silence lent a menacing quality to the surroundings, and a shiver ran along her neck as she locked the door behind her.

She'd barely slept the night before, and amid the tears and shock of Madison's passing the mysterious double grant application loomed as she tossed and turned.

Fraud. Embezzlement. She'd tried to tell herself that those words were too strong. But she couldn't talk herself out of them, or out of *betrayal*. Triple-B was *her* brainchild and *her* passion—Rhea had come on board only because Naomie didn't have all the needed skills herself—and she'd convinced herself that she'd created a family. A place where everyone cared deeply about each other and the shared mission. The realization that she'd been naive made her physically ill.

Only a handful of people had easy access to Madison's file and could have removed the original grant application: Sandra,

Rhea, or Janelle, Rhea's administrative assistant. Madison might have been left alone with the approved file while an admin helped someone with something else. Any of the four possibilities broke Naomie's heart, but only one was finite. If Madison was responsible, there would be no more theft. But if one of the others was, the situation could recur. She had to find out the truth.

After a quick walk-through to make sure she was alone, she beelined for the janitor's closet. Bracing against the sting of cleaning compounds, she pulled the mop and bucket away from the safe tucked in the back. After tapping in the code and extracting the suite's passkey, she hurried to Rhea's office.

What she was about to do was an enormous breach of trust. While she technically had the right to see any of Rhea's files, the respectful thing would have been to go to Rhea directly. But if Rhea was involved, telling her wasn't smart; she had the ability to cover any tracks before Naomie even figured out how to investigate. She wasn't sure what she was looking for; she figured the best approach was to work her way backward from what she knew. In addition to Madison, nine other young women received grants during the past fiscal quarter; if Madison's double application was part of a larger scam, their files seemed like the best place to start.

With a final glance over her shoulder, she unlocked the office. She left the door open so she could hear any noise outside, then hurried over to Rhea's gray filing cabinet. The metal shrieked as she pulled the top drawer open—she winced and checked the quiet again before proceeding. Then, with shaking fingers, she flipped through the drawer and extracted the ten files. She snapped a picture of the name tab on the first folder, then photographed every page inside as quickly as she could. Rhea often came in half an hour early, and Naomie couldn't risk getting caught.

As she closed the first file, she checked the time. Seven

minutes to photograph that file, and some of the others were thicker—she had to move faster. Her shaking hands blurred the next two photos, and she had to reshoot them—she took a deep breath and forced herself to focus, striving for a balance between speed and accuracy.

The second file took six minutes.

The third took five.

The fourth took ten.

As she reached for the fifth, something rumbled down the hall. She whipped around and bolted to the hall, then into the shared space a few doors down.

A printer was ejecting printed pages. Someone had sent a print job remotely. She laughed, hand on her chest, and returned to the office.

She finished the remaining files with ten minutes to spare. After returning them to the cabinet in their proper order, she hurried to Rhea's desk, where she tugged open the side drawer and extracted the funds-received log. Ten pages of signatures related to the current quarter; she aimed her phone and began to snap pics.

Something thudded softly outside the office door.

Adrenaline shot through her, and she flew into the hall again. She looked left, then right, but found nobody. She ran down the hall toward the reception area, straight to the door. She pushed it open and scanned the parking lot.

Nobody.

She was sure she hadn't imagined the noise. But maybe it had been a rodent in the walls? A raccoon on the roof?

She hurried to finish the pictures, then shoved the log back into the drawer. After locking the door and returning the passkey to the safe in the janitor's closet, she forced herself to walk at a normal pace to her own office. Once the door behind her was closed she sank into her chair, trying to steady her breathing and her pounding heart.

With Rhea and the others due any minute, she didn't want to be caught studying the pictures she'd just taken. So, when she regained her composure, she began her routine work for the day. First up, her filing. She hated filing, so when she finished with a given folder, she added it to the top of a pile that grew throughout the week. Then, each Monday morning she'd take the files she'd worked on over the weekend, add them to the pile, then put them all away so she could start the week fresh. She organized the stack alphabetically, then scooted her chair over and opened her filing cabinet.

She instantly froze. The row of files was uneven. Some sat slightly higher than others as if someone had carelessly pulled out and replaced a slew of folders. But that wasn't possible—she had several organizational quirks, and one was the need to have her files lined up exactly, with the tabs in line and at the same height. Opening a perfectly aligned drawer of files gave her the same feeling as a newly vacuumed rug, or a perfectly mowed lawn, and she always patted them into precise place every time she removed or replaced files—it was one of the reasons she saved her filing to do at the same time. And while it was possible she might have displaced *one* if she'd been in a particular hurry, to have *all* of them misaligned? Absolutely not.

Someone had been in her office.

CHAPTER TWENTY-FOUR

Chelsea paced the floor of her bedroom, hand bracing her lower back, frustrated and angry and scared.

David wasn't taking this seriously enough. This wasn't a game, this was *his son*.

Yes, he'd fixed the window. Yes, he'd spent the night—on the couch, he wouldn't even use her guest bedroom—so she could get a decent night's sleep. But then he'd bolted out of the door first thing in the morning, shoving a list of alarm companies at her. That was his idea of taking care of her?

She stopped the pacing and gazed around the room, eyes flicking over the perfectly filmy curtains she'd spent hours picking out, the perfectly pink sofa she loved to curl up on, the perfect parquet floors that had convinced her to buy this house over several others. Normally her little safe haven, her enclave of comfort. But it didn't help today. Nothing helped. Maybe she'd made the wrong choice to put off looking for jobs after she graduated in June until after the baby was born and she'd established a routine with a nanny—she had far too much time to think about it all.

She couldn't go for a run. She couldn't have any wine. She

couldn't vape. All she could do was read, that was all she'd been doing lately, and her eyes were about to fall out of her head. She'd called everyone she knew—sorority sisters, people she'd known in graduate school—they were all sympathetic and took time to listen, but they all had lives of their own and their concern for her only extended so far.

She started pacing again—waddling, really—and shook her head. Because, really, what did it *take*? He knew her friend, *another pregnant woman*, had been kidnapped and murdered. Why didn't that worry him? If he wasn't concerned for her safety, shouldn't he at least be concerned about her state of mind? He'd seen the doctor's letter that warned she shouldn't have any stress. And now with the strange flutterings in her abdomen, he should be seriously beside himself.

She lowered herself onto the couch, trying to find a comfortable position with the help of a stack of pillows. She flicked on a true-crime show—so appropriate—and watched the cops take the killer into custody. She forced herself to follow how they'd caught him, something about a chestnut, but it made no sense. But it was ending and another one was starting, so maybe she'd be able to lose herself in that. She paused it, then went to grab a cold soda.

She pulled a glass out of the cabinet, added some ice from the maker, then grimaced as she pulled out a can of Diet Sprite. Another restriction—no caffeine. She'd *absolutely kill* for a Diet Coke, but Julia had insisted she'd stunt the baby's growth if she had *even one milligram* of caffeine. She poured the Sprite over the ice, and took a long gulp.

Time was the real problem. She had a month at most before the baby was born. It was going too slowly and too fast at the same time.

With a sigh, she pushed herself away from the counter and headed back toward the couch. She'd be fine, everything would be fine, she just needed to stop obsessing about it. Maybe she should call Sienna to distract herself. Sienna wouldn't want to talk to her again so soon, but given Madison's murder she'd at least listen—

Chelsea's foot hit a fallen ice cube and slipped out from under her. She went down hard, landing on her tush and her empty hand as the soda in her glass splayed a wave across the room. Stunned, she sat still and took inventory, checking for pain, testing out each of her limbs. Nothing broken, and everything could hold her weight. Her son kicked inside her abdomen, and she closed her eyes in relief. A smile spread over her face.

Moving slowly and carefully, she got up and crossed into the living room to her phone. She picked it up and tapped David's contact.

CHAPTER TWENTY-FIVE

Naomie's normally cozy banana-yellow walls felt close and tight, and drew in further as she struggled with the discovery that someone had rifled through her office.

The first admin had arrived shortly after Naomie slammed the file cabinet closed. Seeing Naomie in her office, she instantly appeared with a problem to be solved, and although Naomie dealt with it as quickly as possible, two more landed on her desk before she'd finished the first. The day had continued like that, without time for a breath, the specter of her rifled filing cabinet refusing to let her mind completely focus on anything else.

The first respite came at four, when it was technically time for her to leave for the day. She closed her office door and blinds to give the impression she was gone, then tapped open the pictures on her camera. Her pulse sped, erasing the fatigue left by the nonstop day.

She studied the first file, then compared it with the rest. Nothing popped out in it or in the second, and she began to hope Madison's was the only application that had been tampered with. But then, in Ellie Fields's file, she found a grant application that had been filled out online and printed out. She scrolled to her pictures of the payment log. Ellie Fields had received a thousand-dollar grant two months before the date on her application—then a second grant just two weeks ago.

Cold dread spread down her arms and legs. She grabbed her bottle of water and chugged half of it down, hoping it would ease the queasy feeling in her stomach. When she returned to the client files she found a third woman with a typed application who'd also received a duplicate grant payment. She sent the relevant pictures to the printer and hurried to pick them up before someone could intercept them, then once safely back in her office fired a text off to Sandra. *I need to see you in my office ASAP.*

Sandra appeared within moments and closed the door behind her without being asked. Naomie handed her the print-outs and explained what they were. "Despite double payments noted in the log, the original applications are no longer in the files. I need you to check to see if Janelle has copies."

Sandra reappeared with a gentle knock five minutes later and silently handed Naomie the backup copies. As Naomie sorted them by name, she said a little prayer. If Madison's signatures matched but nobody else's did, that would strongly suggest Madison was responsible for all the fraudulent payments—of course she'd be able to match her own signature, but not anybody else's. But if all the signatures matched, they had a talented forger in their midst. And if so, Sandra might be right—Madison's death and the missing monies might be related. Naomie took a deep breath, then pulled the pairs of applications together one at a time.

All the signatures matched.

Sandra's expression showed she understood the significance, too. In a voice that sounded small and far away, Naomie asked her to keep what they'd discovered to herself, and told her to go home.

Alone again, she stared at the Renoir print on her wall, sorting out the implications and narrowing down the possibilities. Whoever had done this had gained access to her office, and Rhea's. Both offices were locked after hours, but during the day the atmosphere at Triple-B was relaxed and friendly enough that they both left their doors unlocked—often wide open— whenever they stepped out for coffee, printouts, or bathroom breaks. Anybody with enough nerve could slip in and go through whatever they wanted.

Whoever it was needed to know the procedures for grant applications, and for picking up the checks. But that also wasn't much help. The application instructions and form were online, and just about everybody knew the procedures for receiving payments from Triple-B funds. Even if they never received grant payments, most employees were reimbursed for expenses during the course of their responsibilities.

One thing was certain—she'd made bad choices. She and Rhea tried to put as much of their funding into helping expectant mothers as possible, and as a result had eschewed expensive business software or other systems that would have added security. That would have to change; they'd also need to put security cameras inside the building rather than only at the two entrances. She dropped her head into her hands—that would transform the environment she'd worked so hard to create, replacing one of trust and camaraderie with mistrust and micromanagement.

But the logistics were just a distraction from the more important question: had someone killed Madison to keep Naomie from discovering what was really happening with these forged applications? And if so, what on earth could she do about that?

After several minutes considering her options, she picked up the phone.

CHAPTER TWENTY-SIX

"She called again." Sophie sounded like she was talking through gritted teeth.

Jo reluctantly pulled her attention away from the monitor where she was doing her background check on Travis Hartley to Sophie's call. "Chelsea? Why?"

"She said she fell. She 'just wanted to let him know' she was driving herself to the ER to make sure the baby was fine. Of course David told her it was dangerous for her to drive herself and went over to drive her, just the way she knew he would."

Jo cleared her throat. "Just asking to consider all sides—is it possible the fall's legit?"

"Of course it's *possible*. Each and every thing she calls about is *possible*. It's the confluence of all of them together that's highly improbable." Sophie's pitch edged upwards.

Jo jotted information from the screen in front of her onto her notes. "I'm sorry, Soph. I know it's not easy. But if you let her drive you crazy, isn't she winning?"

"Oh, please. She doesn't give a red rat's tush about me or my mental state. It's David she wants."

Jo glanced resentfully at the monitor and struggled to remain patient. "But if you're at David's throat every five minutes about Chelsea, isn't she turning you into the sort of harpy-shrew wife that pushes her husband away?"

Sophie went silent.

Jo swore to herself—now Sophie was angry. She rubbed her hand over her brow, bracing for the pending explosion.

"You know what?" Sophie finally responded. "You're exactly right. I'm just playing into it, aren't I?"

Jo released the breath she'd been holding. "You're not *not* playing into it," she said tentatively.

"Thank you, Jo. That's just what I needed to hear. I'll let you know what happens." She hung up.

Jo stared down at the phone, now worried she'd released some sort of soccer-mom kraken onto Chelsea—no matter how she followed that scenario through, it didn't end well for anyone involved.

Arnett's voice broke into her thoughts. "Three-thirty. We need to get a move on if we're going to go meet that waitress." He registered the expression on her face. "Unless you're in the middle of something and want me to go alone?"

"No, I'm good." She pushed her chair away from the desk and stood up. "Just a weird phone call from my sister. She's worried Chelsea is trying to steal her husband."

"And you think she's not?" Arnett looked amused.

"I believe you can't steal a man who doesn't want to be stolen. But that's a helluva lot easier to believe when the husband in question isn't mine."

———

By the time they pulled up to Starbucks, the bright, crisp skies of the Pioneer Valley morning had turned to steely gray, portending the sort of soul-sucking icy rain that burrowed itself into your hair and clothes and stripped the trees of all remaining leaves. Jo pulled her jacket closer around her as she pushed through the door.

Once inside, the aroma of freshly ground coffee laced with seasonal pumpkin spice greeted her like an old friend, filling her with happy memories of falls past. She drew in a second greedy breath as she scanned the cafe.

A petite blonde in the back raised one hand. Jo nearly did a double take; the woman last night had been slashed with garish make-up, hair teased to high heaven, large breasts cinched so high they constantly threatened to fall out of her tiny corseted dress. This woman wore an elegant chignon, the barest hint of tasteful make-up on her face, and a cream-top-tan-pants ensemble so elegantly understated Sophie would envy them. If it weren't for the large, frightened brown eyes poking out of it all, she'd swear this was a different woman.

Jo chastised herself mentally. She knew better than to assume people only had one side. She made her way to the table with Arnett behind her.

"Thank you for meeting me here," the woman said, gesturing to the empty chairs. "Nobody from the club comes here."

"Not a problem." Jo slid onto one of the black metal chairs, and Arnett took another. "I'm Detective Josette Fournier, and this is Detective Bob Arnett. I'm afraid I didn't catch your name last night."

"No, sorry. I'm Hailey. Hailey Chartrain." She shifted her chair so she could continue to watch the door.

"I'm glad to meet you, Hailey." Jo slipped into a voice she hoped projected confidence and security. "What did you want to talk to us about?"

"The guys said Amber had been killed. Is that right?" Her eyes widened still further.

"The guys?" Arnett asked.

"Chuck the security guard and Dan the bartender."

"We know her as Madison, but, yes, that's right. Were you friends?" Jo asked.

"Not friends exactly, because she kept mostly to herself. But I liked her." Her long nails tore at the cardboard sleeve on her cup. "She didn't belong at the club."

"I'm not sure any woman *belongs* in a strip club," Jo said. "But sometimes life forces us to make hard decisions."

"You can say that again." Hailey took a deep breath. "But there are strip clubs and there are strip clubs, if you get my meaning. Amber—Madison—got more than she bargained for."

"What's different about this strip club?" Jo asked.

Hailey's nails tugged harder at the sleeve, and her voice dropped. "I don't ask questions because the less I know the better. But I know two things. Pairs of guys are in and out of Travis's office two, three times a night, always with some sort of duffel-bag-like satchel. And, the girls give more than lap dances in the private rooms."

Jo glanced at Arnett—exactly what they'd suspected. "Any idea what's in the satchels?" she asked.

Hailey raised both palms. "When they come in, I stay away. But I've glimpsed stacks and stacks of money. Not the kind you need for changing twenties to singles."

"And to be clear—the women have sex with customers in the private rooms?" Jo asked.

"No doubt. It's understood that if you want to strip at Volcano, you're expected to have sex with Travis's associates, the guys with the satchels."

"Just them, not other customers?"

Hailey shrugged. "You can if you want to as long as the house gets its cut. But if you aren't willing to go with the other guys, your life gets very difficult."

Jo held up a hand. "Just to be sure I understand. Is that why those men come in, to have sex with the women?"

"No, sorry." Hailey waved apologetically. "I'm not saying it right. They come in for some other reason, but sometimes they'll hook up with one of the girls. Like how sometimes when you go out to dinner you get dessert, and sometimes you don't. The dinner's the main event."

Jo's brows rose. "Got it. And in those cases, the women don't have the option of declining."

"Technically they do, but..." A rip appeared in Hailey's cup sleeve.

"Did any of them come for Madison specifically? Or any other customers?"

"Not really, which surprised me. I'd have expected she'd get a few guys looking for a girlfriend-experience situation because of the wholesome thing she had going on." Her face screwed up. "There was that one guy, but he wasn't there for Madison. He always showed up when we had any pregnant dancer."

Jo leaned in. "You know his name?"

"I don't. Strictly cash, and he was always in the specialty room. White guy, medium height. Wears a baseball cap and dark glasses, so I didn't get a good look."

"Dark glasses inside?" Arnett asked.

"Yup. Some people don't want to be recognized." She shrugged.

Jo scrolled up the pictures she'd pulled from Kiernan Wendiss's and Brad Pratt's driver's licenses. "Could it be one of these guys?"

Hailey's face scrunched up again. "Could be. It's hard to say."

"If he comes in again, can you take a closer look? Maybe even snap a picture?"

Fear flared in her eyes. "I can try. But I doubt he'll be back anytime soon since we don't have any other pregnant girls right now."

Jo nodded, and cleared her throat. "I'm sorry to have to ask, but I'm assuming you know what happens in the rooms because you've had to participate?"

Hailey's eyes latched on to her. "No, I never wanted to strip. Waitressing at clubs pays really good tips. And also I didn't want to—" She stopped abruptly.

Jo's radar went up. "Didn't want to what?"

She shifted in her chair. "Pay the *Travis Tax*."

Jo's stomach clenched.

Hailey continued. "He says it's an *audition*, that he has to know what he's selling. It's only supposed to happen once, but it's common knowledge that he'll ask again and if you say no your time's gonna be hard."

Jo's phone buzzed; she ignored it. "Hard how, exactly?"

"If you're on his good side you get the good time slots and the more vanilla guys. If you're having a bad day and need a rest, he'll give you a break. If you need more money, he'll send more work your way. Otherwise he'll go out of his way to give you whatever you *don't* want."

"So why not just go work at another strip club?" Arnett asked.

"The girls make triple what they can make other places, usually even more. He's got more girls wanting to work there than he can handle."

"Are the women ever harmed in the course of their work? Forced to take drugs?" Jo asked.

Hailey shook her head. "Nothing like that. Travis wouldn't put up with anything that took his girls out of circulation for the next customer. He likes to think he 'takes care of his girls.'"

There was a tone to her voice that contradicted what she was saying. "But you felt you had to speak to us in secret."

The sleeve ripped in two and dropped to the table. "He may

have delusions about how he treats women, but he's deadly serious about not talking to the police."

Jo's brows knit. "How serious?"

Hailey swallowed hard, and seemed to make a decision. "Check out what happened to Louisa Lyndak. Travis spotted her talking to a cop outside Volcano. She turned up dead before the week was out."

CHAPTER TWENTY-SEVEN

"I'll drive again, you call your contact at Springfield PD," Arnett said as they left the Starbucks.

"On it." Jo put through a call to Senior Captain Ben Silva.

"Detective Fournier," Silva said. "I didn't expect to hear from you again so soon."

Jo gave him a quick recap of what Hailey Chartrain had told them. "So possible evidence for either drug trafficking or money laundering, and definite evidence for prostitution."

Silva's pen scratched in the background. "This may be enough for us to get some sort of surveillance on them. After our last call I talked to the guys on the organized-crime task force, and their ears perked right up," he said. "This fits in with some current activity they've been following. If you can put us in touch with the waitress you mentioned, I'd appreciate that."

"I'll reach out. In the meantime, we'd appreciate any details you have on Louisa Lyndak."

"The name doesn't ring a bell. Hang on a second."

The clack of keys replaced the scratch of his pen. "Young woman, twenty-four, found dead in her apartment last April of a heroin overdose. Toxicology report detected xylazine as well."

Jo shot a look at Arnett, whose brows went up in response. Xylazine was an animal tranquilizer that had been making its way into street drugs; nobody knew for sure exactly where it came from or why, but the theory was it extended opioid highs. However, it also extended the possibility of an overdose.

"Any chance we can get a copy of the file?" she asked.

"I'll shoot it over to you. What's your email address?"

She dictated it, thanked him, and then hung up.

"Xylazine. That's tricky," Arnett said.

Jo opened her email. "Certainly is. I'm going to forward this to Marzillo and see if there's any way she can check the tox screen. If they assumed this was an overdose rather than a potential homicide, they might not have thought twice about it." Jo skimmed the rest of the file. "From everything I can see, I'm not sure I'd've thought it was anything other than an overdose. Tracks on her arm showed it wasn't the first time she'd used. Her door was open but the only prints found were hers."

"I have a couple of CIs that hang out in Springfield. When we get back to HQ I'll give them a call, see if they've heard anything about her or The Volcano."

"Sounds good." A notification on Jo's phone caught her eye. "That's right, a call came through while we were talking to Hailey. Naomie Alexander, and she left a message. I'll put it on speaker."

Naomie's voice filled the car, its normal confidence gone. "Detective Fournier? I'm calling because I've discovered something you may want to know about. It's probably not related, but I'm working on the assumption you'd rather hear about something that turns out to be nothing than *not* hear about something that turns out to be something."

The Naomie she'd met was far more self-possessed than this rambling indicated. "Something has her spooked," she said to Arnett.

"One of our admins found a discrepancy with some funds

we awarded to Madison. Long story short, she received two grants instead of one, and I think the second was forged because today I found two other clients with the same situation. I emailed Madison about the problem but didn't get a chance to talk to her before she died, and now I'm wondering if it's related to her death. If you're able to call me back, I'd appreciate it." After a series of clicks, the call ended.

Jo tapped to return the call. "Dammit—voice mail. Let me try again." She did, but Naomie didn't pick up; Jo left a message and told her to call again as soon as she was able.

"I don't like the coincidence that there's some pregnancy-obsessed creeper hanging out at The Volcano," Arnett said.

"Me neither, but there's not much we can do with that description. Nobody else mentioned the guy when we asked, and they must all know about it."

"We'll just have to hope he comes back," Arnett said. "I need food."

"I need caffeine," Jo said. "I meant to order coffee before we left Starbucks."

"Sal's has Diet Coke." He threw her a sideways glance. He was supposed to be cutting back on his meatball-grinder intake, and he knew Jo knew it.

"You can always get one of their grilled-chicken salads," she said.

"You can always get a tall ice water," he retorted.

"Hey, you don't have to get nasty about it." She laughed and threw up her hands in surrender. "I just have to be able to tell Laura I tried."

After a satisfying half hour with their sandwiches and sodas, they headed back to HQ, beelining for Marzillo's office in the lab.

"Any updates?" Jo said.

"By which you mean, have I had time to look at the Lyndak

file you sent me?" Marzillo said, eyes on her monitor as she entered something via the keyboard.

"We know you have a thousand things on your plate," Jo said. "No pressure."

Marzillo half-smiled, finished what she was doing, then pulled the file up on her monitor. "I noticed you were uncharacteristically vague regarding what you wanted me to look at, so I assume you want me blind to whatever hypothesis you have about Louisa's death."

"Can't get anything by you." Arnett eased himself down into one of Marzillo's empty chairs.

"Standard disclaimer. I'm not an ME—"

"But you worked with them closely enough for long enough to be helpful," Jo short-circuited.

Marzillo raised her brows. "I double-checked a couple of things with one of the MEs I used to work with back in the eighteen hundreds. For the most part, it looks like Louisa died of an overdose. Heroin laced with xylazine."

"For the most part?" Jo asked.

"There's this." She pointed to one of the numbers on the toxicology report. "The level of xylazine is much higher than I'd expect to see in this sort of an overdose, where street drugs are laced with tranq. Of course, the levels we see vary from month to month, so I verified with my contact. She agreed, even given the variation she's seen over the last year, this is much higher than what she'd expect."

"Which means what?" Jo said.

"That's where it gets even trickier. Could be she took several hits, and that drove the level up. Could be she was playing with xylazine on her own, and took too much. Either way, it's strange." Marzillo turned from the monitor. "So, what is it you think happened?"

"We had an informant insinuate she was murdered. Possibly related to Mob activity," Jo said. "If she's right, that would mean somebody purposefully administered a dose of xylazine that was meant to kill her."

Marzillo wagged her head. "The results here are consistent with that. The problem is they're consistent with several other possibilities, too.'

"Understood," Jo said. "Thanks for taking a look at it when you're already so busy."

Marzillo gave a quick nod. "Whatever it takes to catch this killer."

CHAPTER TWENTY-EIGHT

Julia stepped on the gas pedal as soon as the crosslight turned red. She absolutely could not show up late.

A notification buzzed the burner phone. She glanced quickly at it, keeping her eyes off the road for only a second. A text from Rick. Thank God—she needed a little positivity right now. What she really needed was to feel his arms around her and his heart beating under her cheek, but for now fleeting texts would have to do.

At the next red light, she grabbed the phone and read the text.

I have a plan so we can see each other.

Her heart sped, but she clamped down on the response—there wasn't any point getting worked up about something that couldn't happen. She tapped the screen to put through a call to him.

"Hello, my love." His voice brimmed with optimism. "I didn't expect you to call, but I'm glad you did."

"I'm on my way to grab dinner before class, so I only have a few minutes. And I don't mean to be a downer, but I just can't see how—"

"Hush and let me tell you what I did."

The glow in his voice stoked a teeny ember of hope in her heart. "Tell me."

"You meet clients at home, right? Pre-visits and all that for home births?"

"Ye-es." She drew out the word skeptically.

"So, what I'm thinking is, what if my sister was pregnant and was interested in a home birth with a certified nurse midwife?"

"Is she?"

"Of course not. But she lives in a big apartment building in Oakhurst with multiple entrances, and her friend in the building is going away to Hawaii for two weeks. My sister has the keys to her apartment. So, the plan is, you come for a supposed consultation with her. If anyone's watching you, they'll see you enter the building. She'll Venmo you a payment to make it legit if Pete's goons are monitoring you. But she'll be over her friend's place, and I'll be waiting in hers. If you want, she'll even be here to open the door for you, and then will go across the hall to her friend's."

The ember burst into a small flame. "That's a lot to ask. Are you sure she won't mind?"

"It was her idea."

Her mind kicked into overdrive, searching for flaws. "But she's not really pregnant, so if Pete's investigators look into her—"

"Her primary care physician is in a group building that includes an ob/gyn. And with HIPAA laws, nobody can ask which doctor she saw. And if she's using a midwife, maybe she decided not to even bother with an ob/gyn. They can't know her stance on that."

"But I'm assuming you don't want to do this just once, and

eventually it will become obvious she isn't pregnant to anybody watching."

"You said we only have to be careful for a few months, right? So, before it's time for her to show, the story will be that she had miscarriage, and then you'll stop coming here. By that time we won't need to worry."

She winced—the few months' estimate had been highly optimistic. But she'd learned the hard way as a midwife that the best way to deal with complications is one step at a time, with what's in front of you. This would work in the short term, and she could deal with the next phase when they came to it.

And after the last few excruciating days, she desperately needed a safe space with someone who loved her.

She squeezed her eyes shut and blurted her response before she could second-guess herself. "Let's do it. When?"

"Tonight."

Her anxiety spiked. "I'm not sure it's a good idea to do it so soon. It would be better to have her set up an appointment with me ahead of time. Make it all look above board."

"She'll call you as soon as we're done here, and you'll just happen to have time to come talk to her tonight."

She laughed, shaking her head. His child-like excitement was intoxicating and joyful, like bubbles in champagne. It made her feel valued and important that someone was willing to do all this for her—and she couldn't remember the last time she'd felt like that.

"When should I come over?"

"When is your class done?"

"Eight-thirty. I could be there about nine?"

"Perfect. I'll see you then." He hung up quickly—most likely to keep her from changing her mind.

She smiled to herself, but a tiny thread of anxiety pulsed in the back of her mind. She had so many balls in the air right now —was throwing up another one just courting disaster?

As if in answer, the burner buzzed again—with a text from The Mistake. She stared down at it, chest tight and her hands clammy.

I'll be in your new neighborhood later today. Can I swing by?

The words punched her in the gut—he'd made the effort to find out where her new place was. The uncomfortable sense of danger she'd felt toward the end of their relationship came rushing back, like a peach pit lodged under her sternum.

It's not a good idea. I'm sure Pete has someone watching my place.

So we'll meet somewhere.

Fuck. She wiped her clammy hands one at a time on her pants.

Her mother's voice ran through her head: *You play with fire, you're gonna get burned.* She shook her head to push it away—she'd been so sure she'd played it right, so sure she'd dodged the bullet. How could she have been so stupid?

But she knew why. Because Pete falling out of love with her had left her damaged and lost, questioning her life and her very identity, something she'd never once had to do before. And she hadn't handled it well.

Self-esteem had never been an issue with Julia. Not that she was conceited, she just knew her strengths and weaknesses. In a photograph, she'd probably be rated a seven out of ten, but in person she had a presence that pulled men to her like metal shavings to a magnet. They turned when she entered a room, even when more objectively attractive women were present. They listened when she spoke and laughed at her jokes. She'd never doubted her ability to entrance whoever she wanted—and she'd wanted Pete Gagnon.

Once they were married, she never felt the need to fan other flames. But Pete had called on her to do just that, strategically, to help build the Gagnon empire. She had a gift for getting important men to talk about things they wouldn't otherwise, 'better than a hundred-year-old bottle of Scotch,' Pete would joke. She came to suspect it was actually a turn-on for him that she was able to deliver contracts other family members couldn't secure. But as she got older, her charms waned. The powerful men were still happy to flirt with her, but they weren't hypnotized the way they'd once been. It hadn't bothered her because the only head she wanted to turn was Pete's—but it bothered Pete, and their intimacy disappeared. Not just physically, but mentally as well—even when they were in the same room they were in separate places.

So she found herself counting wrinkles, pinching sagging skin, hurrying to cover the gray creeping into her hairline. But no amount of facials or makeovers or gorgeous dresses rekindled his attention. The affair was her damaged ego's way of putting a bandage over that wound, of convincing herself she was still worth what she used to be worth. And while reveling in the reassurance of being desired again, she'd failed to see the lurking warning signs.

At the next red light, she responded.

Pete's reach is powerful. He won't just come after me, he'll come after you.

Fuck that, he responded with lightning speed. *Let him come for me.*

Her mouth went dry. He'd never discounted Pete before, and that wasn't a good sign. She wasn't sure what it meant or what exactly he was capable of, and she couldn't risk finding out.

He used me for all of these years, and I deserve my fair share. If you love me like you say you do, help me get it.

She held her breath as she waited for his reply.

There's no reason why we can't at least talk over the phone.

Except on the phone she wouldn't be able to choose her words with care and he'd be able to pin her down. She had to dodge.

I'm late for class, and I have a memorial I need to help with, AND I have clients every night this week. I need you to be patient.

One minute ticked away, then two.

Finally the response came: *I can be patient for now, as long as I know you want me.*

She stared down, unable to swallow. If she didn't say it, he'd freak, and she couldn't risk putting herself and the man she loved in danger. She had to keep his hope alive, and she had to do it fast, because he was counting the seconds and too long a delay would be just as damning as no response at all.

She forced her thumbs over the keyboard, silently asking Rick to forgive her as she typed.

I want you.

CHAPTER TWENTY-NINE

Jo's hand tapped frenetically at her leg as she and Arnett returned to their desks. "I'm not sure how happy Silva will be if we dig deeper into Louisa Lyndak's death since it's not our jurisdiction. I'm going to text him." She typed out a message as they slid back into their chairs.

Arnett pulled out his own phone. "A text just came in from one of my informants about Lyndak. Pretty straightforward: 'Bitch didn't know how to mind her business.'"

"That's in line with what Hailey told us, but not much more helpful," Jo said. "In terms of what we can do, Travis Hartley is my number-one suspect for Madison's murder at this point."

Arnett ran his thumbnail along his jawline. "Agreed. I'm thinking Madison either saw the wrong thing or said no to the wrong person."

Jo's pen rapped on her notepad. "And she didn't do drugs, so a faked overdose wouldn't get them what they needed. They'd've had to branch out. If he met a member of Lucifer Lost in the club or spotted the sticker in the bathroom and researched it, he might have decided it was a good way to get rid of the threat."

"Fits with what happened in the woods. If he 'ran into' her and hit her up for sex in the woods, she might not have felt she could say no."

"And it would have been easy for him to say he didn't want the dog watching. Matt won't let Cleopatra in the room when—"

Arnett's hand shot up. "TMI. But I agree. It would also explain why she took her clothes off without a struggle."

"If she thought it was sex, he could've pulled out a knife before she realized what was happening."

"There's also a strong possibility Travis or one of his 'associates' is the baby's father. If a broken condom was involved, she'd know who. Maybe she confronted him and he decided she'd be too much trouble."

"That would explain why she wouldn't tell anyone who the father was." Jo dropped her pen and sat forward. "So the question is, how do we get any evidence? We need DNA samples from the 'associates' but we don't even know who they are yet."

"We'll have to see what Springfield PD comes up with about The Volcano. Meantime we can try for a warrant for Travis's DNA. But we'd need at least a sworn statement from the waitress, and even then I'm not sure it'll walk. And if we get it and serve it, that could step on Springfield PD, because it'll let The Volcano know we're watching," Arnett said.

"I'll text Silva, see what he thinks. We might as well get started on the warrant just in case. And we can show Travis's picture to the people who claim to have seen Madison at Crone Ridge, see if any of them recognize him. We'll do the same with any photos Springfield PD gets of the people going into The Volcano. If we get a hit, that might help with probable cause for the warrant."

"We might as well take a stab at getting a DNA sample from Brad Pratt, too." Arnett swung back to face his desk. "You work up the paperwork for Hartley, and I'll take Pratt. With a

little help from the warrant gods, we could have samples by the
end of the day tomorrow."

———

After finishing up the warrant paperwork, Jo and Arnett headed
home. Matt wasn't there when she arrived; he'd been called in
for an emergency surgery and texted he'd hopefully be home by
eight-thirty. The threatening rain had started to fall, beating a
steady rhythm on her windshield as she carefully navigated the
newly wet roads.

The house felt strangely empty without him in it. As she
made her way into the kitchen for a snifter of calvados, she
marveled at how quickly that shift had taken place. Only a
couple of weeks before she'd been resentful and grumpy as a
result of having to share her space, but now she was bothered by
the quiet. She still needed time alone to de-stress and think now
and then, but he no longer felt like an invasive presence in *her*
home—he now felt like a part of what made it a home.

Cleopatra, the Sphynx cat she'd accidentally adopted,
rubbed up against her leg as she pulled open the cabinet. Jo
squatted down to give her a cuddle. "I should probably eat
something before I throw any booze on my stomach," she told
the cat. "And Matt'll be hungry, too. What do you think? Breakfast for dinner, since Matt loves that? If I start now, I can have
bacon and hash browns ready by the time he gets home, and
then I can just throw on some eggs."

"Browwr." Cleopatra bumped her head against Jo's chin.

"I'll take that as a yes." Jo set Cleopatra on one of the
kitchen chairs. "Although probably what it really means is
you're hoping for some of the bacon. I'm no fool."

As she laid out rashers of bacon in a skillet and grated pota-
toes for hash browns, Jo told the cat about her day, including the

twists and turns of what they'd learned and the theories in her head.

"It's all very frustrating," she summed up. "This poor girl—life took everything from her, none of it due to any fault of her own. The least I can give her is the justice of finding her killer, but unless her killer is the baby's father, we may never be able to find any evidence of anything. So if you have any Sphinx-kitty magic lingering behind those huge blue eyes, feel free to send it my way."

Jo's phone, perched on the table next to Cleopatra's chair, shrilled.

Jo popped her brows at the cat. "Impressive. If I'd known it was that easy, I'd've asked ages ago." She wiped her hands on the towel hanging from her oven, then crossed to pick up the phone.

She frowned down at the number—Chelsea was calling.

Jo's jaw clenched—maybe she'd written off Sophie's concerns about Chelsea too quickly. No matter what, obviously she hadn't been clear enough about proper boundaries.

She stabbed at the phone. "Chelsea? I thought I was pretty pointed about the fact that—"

"Please, Jo, I'm not calling for myself. This is about Naomie. She's missing."

CHAPTER THIRTY

"Dammit, I should have gone to see her in person," Jo said to Arnett, who she'd picked up en route to Naomie Alexander's house.

"You returned the call," Arnett replied. "There's no reason to believe this has anything to do with a paperwork error."

Jo's eyes flashed to his. "Other than the fact she's now missing?"

He raised a hand. "You're jumping to conclusions, and that isn't like you. She may be fine."

Jo tried to convince herself he was right. She tried to remember the exact wording of the message as she scanned the traffic, fighting back her frustration at the drivers staying below the speed limit, held back by the steadily falling rain.

Four cars were already parked in the wide driveway of the Alexanders' sprawling red-clapboard farmhouse. Although newly built, the covered front porch and narrow eaves mimicked classic New England architectural elements. Modernity with a nod to the past, but the pre-fab feel came up short.

A medium-height, blond white man burst through the front door as they stepped from the car. His classic blue button-down matched his eyes and the creases on his black chinos were still crisp, despite whiskering across his lap. Chelsea and Julia slipped out of the doorway behind him; Chelsea, hands firmly clutched at her abdomen and eyes wide, hurried to pace him while Julia, face pale and tight, hung back.

"Detectives?" the man called while they were still a good hundred feet away. "I'm Chris Alexander, Naomie's husband. I hope I'm not overreacting, but with what just happened to her friend..."

Jo hurried through the now-sheeting rain to the porch, then shook his hand. "It's always better to be safe than sorry. What exactly happened?"

He rubbed the hair on the top of his head as though trying to scrub it off. "Naomie went out for a walk around five o'clock, and she hasn't been back. That isn't like her."

"She went out for a walk after what happened to Madison?" Jo asked. "Why?"

He pulled his phone out, tapped at it, and thrust it at her. "This is what she sent to me."

Jo read the text showing on the screen, sent at five twenty that evening: *Had a stressful day, can't seem to shake it. Gonna go for a walk to re-center. Shepherd's pie needs an hour in the oven, pull it out if I'm not back.*

"So about half an hour before sunset. She didn't say where she was going," Jo said, and scanned the cars in the driveway. "Is one of these hers?"

Chris pointed to a champagne Lexus 500h. "That one. When she goes for walks, it's usually at Haptin Pond. There's a trail just down the road that leads right to it, about a quarter mile away." He gestured north, where Jo could see a narrow, paved path marked by two wooden posts disappear into a copse of trees.

"Does she go for walks often? How long do they usually last?"

"She used to go all the time, but lately she's been doing a prenatal exercise class instead. When she does, it's about half an hour."

Jo considered the time. Nine-fifteen, which meant she'd been gone for over four hours, far longer than any walk would warrant. "And you tried calling her?"

He tapped the phone and held it up again. The display showed five calls to Naomie beginning at six-fifteen, interspersed in the last hour with several calls to other numbers. "She didn't answer. I left several messages asking her to call me back as soon as possible."

"With the pregnancy, is there any chance she stopped to rest and fell asleep, something like that?" Arnett asked.

"When Chelsea got here, she waited while I checked along the main path. I didn't see her anywhere," he said.

"That's when I told him I thought we should call you," Chelsea said. "I don't understand why she would do this. Why would she go out for a walk alone after what happened to Madison?"

Julia wrapped her arms across her chest, gripping her upper arms. "Crone Ridge is in a much more— She wouldn't have considered this area unsafe. I know I wouldn't have."

Chelsea shook her head incredulously. "Because you're not pregnant. I've barely been able to sleep with the nightmares I've been having about getting abducted."

Julia's fingers dug into her arms. "Naomie's always thought she can do anything. And mostly she can."

"But there's something else," Chelsea said. "I forgot to tell you this until I mentioned it to David the other night. There was a man watching us in the parking lot of the smoothie bar the other night."

Jo's jaw mentally dropped, and she struggled to keep her annoyance from showing. "A man watching you?"

"Yeah. Well, I don't know for sure he was watching *us*," she hedged, "but he was sitting in his car, like looking down in his lap. It gave me the creeps."

"Why didn't you mention it before?" Arnett asked.

"I—um—I didn't think too much of it. He didn't follow us out of the parking lot, but maybe he did from a distance and I just didn't notice." Her eyes looked everywhere but their faces.

"What did he look like?" Jo asked.

"I couldn't really tell. He had a cap on, and dark glasses, and he was looking down."

"Dark glasses at night?" Jo asked, her mind flying back to Hailey's description of the man at The Volcano.

Chelsea shifted her weight from foot to foot. "It was hard to tell. It was dark, so they might just have been regular glasses. But I couldn't see his eyes."

"And you didn't happen to see the license plate?" Jo asked.

Chelsea shook her head.

Jo turned to Chris. "Could Naomie have had an errand to run, something like that?"

Chris pointed back to the house. "Like her text said, she had a shepherd's pie in the oven, and intended to come back for dinner."

"And she doesn't forget things like that," Chelsea said.

"I might believe she forgot if she was half an hour late, but four hours?" Chris said. "And now it's pouring rain?"

Jo held up a hand to short circuit the growing panic in their tones. "Given the circumstances, I agree with you. There's strong reason to believe something may have happened, and time is of the essence. We need to start searching, now."

———

The wind shifted as they waited at the entrance to the park, blowing icy rain in a slicing diagonal, now with a barrage of leaves and twigs from the surrounding trees. Jo drew the hood of her jacket tighter in a futile effort to stay as warm and dry as possible, and said a prayer of thanks when the search and rescue team deployed by the State Police Special Operations Section arrived, again overseen by Incident Commander Roscoe.

"Same procedure this time," he told Jo and Arnett when the initial team arrived. "We'll send the K-9 unit and the helicopter out immediately, and organize the grid search as they do the initial hasty search. With luck we'll get a resolution quickly enough to bring her back alive."

As with Crone Ridge, the woods around Haptin Pond extended for several hundred acres to the north. Using the IMAT's topographical maps, Chris showed them which of the two trails Naomie favored, and how far she normally went.

Ivan Geary nodded, and pointed down the road. "Rocket and I will start at the trail head entrance by the house, since we know she was most likely there. You have a shirt of hers?"

Chris handed over a sweater. "I grabbed this from her hamper. She wore it yesterday. Hopefully the scent will be strong enough even from then?"

"Don't you worry. Rocket can pick up her trail from something she hasn't worn in years." He turned to Jo and Arnett. "You two coming with me?"

Jo glanced over to Roscoe. When he nodded, she and Arnett moved into place a few feet behind the dog.

Ivan held the sweater up for Rocket to sniff. "Find her," he said.

Rocket took off; Jo tried not to think about what they might find as she and Arnett hurried behind. Still tugging the hood of her jacket closer, she alternated focus between Rocket's slightly slanted gait and the trail in front of them. After about a quarter of a mile, Rocket veered off the trail into the forest, and Jo's concentration intensified as her feet slipped and slid in the newly formed mud of the shifting forest floor.

As the trees drew closer together, the rain came in fits and starts: slowing to fat intermittent drops when the trees created mini canopies, then blasting them with downpours of water and leaves and twigs in between. She eyed the shrubs and moss and dirt ruefully—whatever footprints or other evidence might have been present was long since destroyed.

Rocket's pace seemed to quicken, and he curved sharply to the right. Jo projected Rocket's trajectory forward to a large boulder in the distance—a sickening déjà vu slammed through her.

Rocket rounded the boulder, with Geary right behind. Jo's chest tightened.

"Good girl, Rocket. Good girl."

Jo forced herself forward around the boulder.

Naomie Alexander lay naked, hair spread out behind and arms crossed over her chest like a woodland angel—but with her neck slashed, and a knife protruding from her blood-anointed abdomen.

CHAPTER THIRTY-ONE

As Marzillo and her team began the systematic steps of processing the scene, Jo pushed down the nausea roiling through her. The similarities flew at her, shifting her off balance like a swarm of bees: two of the rocks behind Naomie's head had been used as a makeshift altar, complete with candles arranged in the same configuration they'd seen by Madison; the same symbol was drawn on her, and an identical hunting knife protruded from her abdomen; the hands clasped across her chest in the same position, and the expression on her face just as peaceful.

"The same killer, without a doubt," Arnett said.

Jo nodded, then shook her head against her disorientation, afraid the memory of Madison's scene would encroach on her ability to properly evaluate this one. But the harder she tried, the more crushing the sensation became, like a car alarm she couldn't cover her ears to stop. She squeezed her eyes closed, took a deep breath, and opened them again, forcing her mind to hunt for any differences that might exist.

"Four boulders, not three, and smaller," she said aloud. "The biggest one doesn't look so much like a gravestone."

"Beggars can't be choosers," Arnett said.

"And these were the first large free-standing boulders we came across." Jo circled the scene, noting how the vantage point changed the details. "The body is facing a different cardinal direction, so what's important about the positioning is the relationship to the stones."

Arnett gestured a circle. "And the killer cleared a section for her. Just dirt here, but everything else has a layer of scrub. Different from the first scene."

"Her baby bump isn't nearly as big." Jo tried to remember how far along Naomie was. "I think she was just coming up on six months, and Madison was past seven. Janet, can you see if she's holding a plastic baby figurine?"

Marzillo shifted position to reach the hands without disturbing anything else. "Rigor has set in to the smaller muscles of the fingers." She pried the fingers apart, then lifted the arm. "But it's not yet complete in the upper arms. Normally I'd say that means she's been dead for two to four hours at most, but the cold would delay rigor somewhat. So, I'll adjust to three to five hours."

Jo glanced at her watch. "It's ten now, so between five and seven o'clock. That fits with when she left the house."

Marzillo lifted the second hand, revealing a figurine. "And here it is, the twin to our first plastic baby."

The wind shifted, sending a shower of drops into Jo's face. She gestured to the makeshift altar. "No way those candles were burning once this rain started. But the wax has spilled over, so they were burning for a fair time before the rain started."

"When exactly did it start?" Arnett asked, pulling out his phone.

"About eight," Jo answered. "And based on how long it took us, I'd say it would take at least twenty-five minutes to walk at a moderate pace from the Alexanders' house to where we are now."

"The candles had to have been burning for what, an hour at least?" Arnett asked.

"We can buy some and test that out," Marzillo said. "But I'd say closer to two. The surfaces are relatively flat, so it would take a while for enough to pool to overflow."

"So, if that's right, they'd have been lit no later than six or six-thirty," Arnett said. "That narrows things down."

Jo's hand flew up to the diamond at her neck. "There's something—"

"What?" Arnett asked.

"I don't know. It feels like stage dressing again, but I'm getting something else as well." She pulled out her phone and scrolled to the photos from Madison's crime scene. She picked one, then shifted to the equivalent vantage point—and gasped. "Bob, Janet. Come around and look at this."

They shifted behind her, then compared what was on the screen to what was in front of them. "Holy shit," Arnett said. "The positioning is *identical*."

Peterson came over to see. "That's creepy AF. And given how creepy this already is, that's saying something."

Jo nodded. "It's like he used the first scene to guide the second."

"Detectives." Alicia Sweeney's voice came from behind them. "We found her clothes."

———

Jo and Arnett followed Alicia the few hundred feet to where the neatly folded stack of clothes, along with a phone and a ring of keys, sat waiting on a table-like boulder. A canopy of tree branches had kept them relatively dry, but not unscathed. Jo pulled up a photo of Madison's clothes for comparison purposes, now welcoming the déjà vu.

"Same exact configuration," she said. "Either the killer placed them himself, or he directed them very exactly where to put everything."

Sweeney went through the procedure of examining and bagging the belongings. Beige bra and underwear. Red tunic, plain except for a small bow placed to rest at the top of Naomie's pregnant belly. Black maternity leggings. Black hooded cargo-style rain jacket. Trainers with socks stuffed in at the bottom of the boulder. Phone powered on.

When she'd finished, Jo and Arnett trudged silently through the mud back to the temporary command center. They ducked in under the tarps to get out of the rain and poured themselves cups of black coffee from the portable urn.

"I'm feeling like I've been thrown out of a car down the side of a steep hill," Arnett said. "So much for our mobbed-up strip-club theory."

Jo took a deep breath. "I'm not so sure we can toss it out just yet. From what we heard from the group of friends, Naomie was close to Madison, like a big sister. If Madison told her something she saw or something that happened, Naomie may have intervened on her behalf."

"You think she was that stupid?" Arnett's grimace was skeptical. "Why wouldn't she just come to us?"

"It may have happened some time ago, long enough for her to think it wasn't relevant. You're right that Naomie seemed like a smart enough woman to know better than to keep something like that from us, but we've seen people hold back on worse for less. And Julia said something about Naomie thinking she could do anything, and mentioned before that Naomie was very big on keeping people's secrets. I think we need to talk to Julia, find out more about that."

Arnett's face nodded, still skeptical. "Maybe, but it seems

extremely unlikely. I think in light of all this we need to dust off our other theories."

Jo nodded. "I agree it's not the most likely possibility at this point. If I take a step back from this, like I was just discovering both scenes at once, I'd strongly lean toward a random serial killer snatching pregnant women. But if that's right, it's a pretty big coincidence that the two victims were close friends."

Arnett scratched his chin. "How many pregnant women are out walking this time of year? Pretty shallow pool to dive into."

"Good point," she conceded. "But could he even have known she was pregnant just by sight? I don't think her bump would have shown under her jacket."

"He'd've had to know she was pregnant beforehand."

"But the whole reason Naomie and Madison were friends was *because* they were pregnant, so less of a coincidence." Jo tapped her thigh. "They became friends through the prenatal class. And there's that guy Chelsea says might have been watching them outside the juice bar Friday night, whose lack of description sounds very much like the man at The Volcano."

"So maybe our killer was watching one of them, and stumbled on the rest?" Arnett said. "Maybe he followed Madison to the juice bar, or even the class itself at Triple-B. One-stop shopping destination if you're looking for pregnant women."

"So we need to expand our canvassing immediately to include Beautiful Bouncing Babies and the juice bar where the women went after class. See if anybody noticed anyone strange hanging around." She tapped at her phone, sending out the information to the rest of the team.

"Theory three, this has something to do with Lucifer Lost." Arnett gestured toward the crime scene. "The precision of the crime-scene layout? Sure seems like the killer was following some sort of diagram or procedure that outlined exactly what to do."

Jo nodded. "Could be both theories two and three together.

We know someone from Lucifer Lost was at The Volcano. Maybe they stumbled on Madison there, followed her, and discovered the other women."

"So we add in a picture of Brad for our canvassers and see if anybody recognizes him," Arnett said. "And Kiernan's for good measure, until we get that security footage back. Maybe he's unstable, and his anger toward Madison leaving him crept out to her friends. Especially if he thought they were covering up something for her."

Jo tapped at her phone. "And we still have to figure out the discrepancy with the money at Beautiful Bouncing Babies."

Arnett grimaced. "Seems like a non-issue to me. Madison needed money, that wasn't a secret. She was already being pushed to do things she didn't want to do, would she have stopped at grabbing some extra from an organization that's there to help? And a thousand dollars—is that really worth killing two people over?"

"If the issue is staying out of jail, then yes. And Naomie didn't think it was Madison, and Naomie didn't strike me as the sort of person who caved to flights of fancy," Jo said. "If the information about the missing money had come from Chelsea I'd brush it off, but Naomie was level-headed. And for her to turn up dead within hours of discovering the discrepancy? I think we have to at least consider the possibility that something deeper is going on, and someone killed both Madison and Naomie to cover their malfeasance. Making it look like a Satanic ritual would be an effective cover-up."

Arnett gestured back to where Naomie's belongings had been found. "We have the phone again, so hopefully Lopez can find us something. Stupid of the killer not to dump it somewhere, or at least remove the battery."

Something about that tugged at Jo, but she couldn't land on what. She tapped out a message to Lopez. "If anything's there, she'll find it. But I think at this point we also need to talk to the people who work at Triple-B."

"We need to canvas there, anyway."

"So, we have a solid plan." Jo took in a deep, slow breath. "Which means there's no more putting it off. We need to go tell Chris his wife's dead."

CHAPTER THIRTY-TWO

Jo's passion for her job had always been absolute. The long hours, the office politics, the budget limitations—none of it mattered as long as she could spend her days hunting down the men and women who destroyed other people's lives. It was her way of bringing light to the darkness, of adding more to the world than she took from it, and any downsides along the way seemed relatively negligible.

Except telling people their loved ones were dead.

It never got easier, no matter how many times she'd done it. There were no words to make it easier to hear, no words to ease the pain once the news was delivered. There were dozens of different reactions, but one thing remained the same—the disbelieving pain in their eyes as their world shattered.

It shredded her heart, every single time.

Chris Alexander's knees buckled out from under him when she delivered the news. Thankfully, he was standing next to the dining room table and caught himself into a chair. He sat for a moment staring straight ahead, saying nothing as Chelsea and Julia peppered Jo and Arnett with tearful questions. Chelsea's were loud and effusive, punctuated with sniffs and hiccups; Julia's were silent, tears streaming down her cheeks, the tendons in her neck strained and tight as she struggled to maintain control. Then, Chris gasped, sank his head down into his hands, and sobbed.

Chelsea pulled a chair to his side and put her arms around him as best she could. Julia left the room, returned with a blanket that she placed over his shoulders, and poured him a glass of water. Then she retreated to the spot where she'd been standing by the kitchen counter, her eyes sliding continually around the room, searching.

After walking them through the grief-counseling resources available to them, Jo gently told Chris that when he was ready, she'd need to ask him a few questions.

He sat up straight and rubbed a hand over his face. "Ask me now. You need to catch this guy."

Jo nodded. "I noticed a camera by the front door. Do you have any others?"

Chris shook his head. "We just have that one so we could make sure nobody stole any packages that were delivered. There isn't much other crime in this area."

"We'll need to check the footage," Arnett said.

"That's not a problem," Chris said. "But it won't tell you much. When we go for walks we go out the back, since the path is closer to the backyard than the front."

"It's possible that whoever is doing this may be someone known to Madison and Naomie, or it may be someone who has been following them." Jo checked each of their expressions. "Has anything strange happened to her recently that you know of?"

"No, nothing," Chris said, then looked to Chelsea and Julia.

"Just that guy at the juice bar," Chelsea said, cheeks pink.

"Can you tell us anything about the vehicle?" Jo asked.

She nodded. "It was a dark color, like black or maybe charcoal. Mid-size. I'm sorry I didn't notice the type."

"You said you couldn't tell what he looked like because of the cap and glasses," Jo said. "But you're sure it was a man?"

Chelsea blinked. "I assumed it was, but maybe it wasn't. All I really saw was the cap and sunglasses. But you can't think a *woman* did this?"

"No facial hair, nothing like that?" Arnett asked.

"No, not that I remember."

Jo glanced around at each of them. "Anything else? Even if it seemed insignificant at the time? Did Naomie have any enemies? Anyone with a grudge?"

They all shook their heads. "Naomie spent her life helping people," Chris said. "There wasn't any reason for anybody to be upset with her."

Jo had yet to meet the person who had no enemies, whether known to them or not. "No employees she had to fire, or business competitors?"

Chris turned to Julia, who shook her head. "Not that I'm aware of."

"Any recent stresses at work or elsewhere?" she asked.

Chris's eyes scoured the table. "Work was always stressful, but nothing in particular. In fact, yesterday she put her work mostly aside to arrange the memorial for Madison."

"A memorial service? When?" Jo shot a quick look at Bob, distracted from the bomb she was about to drop. A memorial service would be an excellent opportunity for them to do some surveying; killers sometimes came to such gatherings and might well do so here.

"Tomorrow evening, isn't it?" He glanced at Chelsea and Julia for confirmation.

"Yes. She decided to hold it in the classroom at Triple-B," Chelsea said.

"I know this is a strange request, but is there any way you can still hold it?" Jo asked. "We'll want to attend so we can watch who comes and what they do, and we'll send a tech in beforehand to install some hidden security cameras."

Julia answered, voice thick. "From what she told me, all the arrangements have been made. We can use it to honor both of them."

Chelsea wiped away two new tears. "If you have a spare key to the classroom, I can be there to oversee the setup."

"I don't," Julia said. "But I can make sure someone lets you in."

As Arnett jotted the details, Jo returned to the main subject. "Naomie left me a message earlier about a problem at work. Some money that had been fraudulently paid out."

Julia stiffened, and shifted forward. "What money?"

Jo carefully considered her wording. "She claimed Madison applied twice for a grant she was only entitled to receive once. There was some missing paperwork that led her to believe the disbursement wasn't accidental."

Julia's face clouded over. "I can't believe Madison would do something like that. How much?"

"Two grants of a thousand dollars each."

"There's *no way* she'd do that," Chelsea cried out.

"Madison needed money badly," Jo said.

"That doesn't mean she'd steal." Chelsea's face screwed up indignantly. "And two thousand dollars? How could that possibly be related to their deaths? Who would kill over two thousand dollars?"

Julia shot Chelsea a scathing glance. "For a lot of people, two thousand dollars is the difference between life and death."

Chris looked alarmed at the news. "And if someone killed them because of it, it's not because of the money, it's because they don't want to be caught and sent to jail."

Jo continued to watch their faces carefully as she continued. "Were you aware Madison was working several nights a week at a strip club called The Velvet Volcano?"

Chelsea appeared genuinely stunned by this news. Chris looked confused. Julia's face went blank.

Jo zeroed in on Julia's reaction. "Did you know?"

She shook her head stiffly. "I didn't. But it makes sense, given her mother's medical needs."

"But she was pregnant," Chelsea said, expression stunned.

"Turns out, that's not a problem," Arnett muttered.

Chelsea stared at him, horrified.

Jo's gaze returned to Julia—something about her reaction wasn't sitting well. But she sensed Julia wasn't the type who'd respond well to pressure while in front of others, so she momentarily switched gears, turning back to Chelsea. "Did she mention anything to you?"

"No." Chelsea rubbed one of her upper arms. "But I don't understand. What does the money have to do with anything if this is about some creeper watching us?"

"Hold on." Julia frowned. "Naomie did say something about someone going through her files. I just figured she was being paranoid, because why would someone do that? Everyone at Triple-B has clearance to look at whatever client files they need to without sneaking around behind her back."

Chelsea's head whipped around. "But the *clients* don't, right?"

"No, absolutely not. Only staff," Julia said.

Jo followed Chelsea's train of thought. "Are the files locked away?"

"Yes," Julia answered. "Either in Naomie's office or Rhea Blondell's office. Rhea's the CFO."

"But they leave the offices open all the time," Chelsea objected. "I went to have lunch with Naomie last week and I sat in her office alone for ten minutes while she finished up talking with someone else in another area."

Julia's nod was reluctant. "No, that's true. Once you're past the reception desk, there are no cameras or anything. We never had reason to worry."

Jo turned back to Chris. "Did she ever bring work home with her? Does she have a home office where she keeps records?"

"The only records she keeps here are whatever files she's currently working on. She has a home office of sorts, a desk in the solarium. She likes to work in the natural light, with the view. Liked." He choked on the last word, then stood and left the room.

———

They followed him silently through the house. The solarium, enclosed by three walls of floor-to-ceiling windows, would have created a beautiful space during the day. But now, with the wind howling and the rain chattering across the glass, Jo felt oddly exposed, like the darkness had stripped away all protection and was waiting to swallow them whole.

"There, on the desk," Chris said, pointing.

Jo pulled her eyes away from the glass and crossed to the minimalist white table in the far corner. A squat vase of fresh white daisies, a cup of pens and pencils, and a computer monitor were the only accoutrements, all placed pristinely as though readied for a magazine photo shoot. A brown satchel hanging from the top of the office chair added to the effect, like a purposeful addition meant to make the room look casually lived in.

She mentally shook herself. "Do you mind if we take the bag with us?" Jo asked.

"Take whatever you need," Chris whispered.

After a quick trip to the kit in the trunk of her car, Jo bagged the satchel and gave Chris a receipt. "We'll get it back to you as soon as possible."

"Take your time." Chris's eyes filled with tears again. "She doesn't need it now."

Jo cleared her throat. "In the interest of checking all the boxes, we need to know where you all were between five-twenty and nine."

"At five-twenty I was on the way back to the office from an on-site assessment," Chris said. In response to Jo's confused expression, he paused to explain. "I have to go out to damaged properties for insurance claims. I got back to the office around five-thirty, closed everything out, and left about six. I got home a short time after, I'm not sure when. I grabbed a beer and started watching the Bruins game I'd recorded. When the kitchen alarm went off, I pulled out the shepherd's pie thinking Naomie would be home soon. When she didn't show up, I called Chelsea and Julia, and you know what happened after that."

"Would your front-door camera show when you got home? And was there anybody at your job who saw you return?" Jo asked.

"Yes, the camera should show the exact time. And yes, not only do we have key cards to get into the building, my job is open concept. Several people were there when I got back, and we all left around the same time." He gave names, which Arnett jotted down.

She turned to Julia, who answered before she asked. "I had two one-on-one appointments for midwife clients up to about four-thirty, then I went to pick up an early dinner before my Lamaze class at seven. I was just about to start class when Chris called."

Chelsea volunteered her answer when Julia finished. "I'm not working right now. I was at home, trying to set up the crib I just bought. Then I was going to head out for the Lamaze class, because that's one of the ones I attend. But then..." She lifted a limp hand, then plopped it back down again.

"Thank you," Jo said. "There's one last issue. Chelsea, Julia.

I don't want to alarm you unnecessarily, but there's a possibility, especially if the person you thought was watching you at the juice bar is the one who did this, that they might come after one of you next."

Chelsea's head bobbed in furious agreement—this wasn't news to her.

"So we need to be sure you're protected," Jo continued. "The ideal situation would be for you to leave the area, go stay with a friend or relative. We can put a patrol on each of you until you figure that out. Do you both have someone like that?"

Chelsea's face screwed up, and her brow furrowed. Julia stiffened, and something strange flitted across her face before she covered it.

"I—I can't leave," Chelsea said. "I could go into labor any day. My doctor says you never know with first-time mothers, and my sister and David are here. I'd rather just have the patrol officer stay with me."

"We wouldn't be able to continue a patrol for long," Jo said. "Ideally just until we can get you somewhere secure."

Chelsea's gaze jumped between Jo and Arnett. "But who's to say I'd even be safer somewhere else? Why wouldn't he just follow me?"

"That's not likely," Jo said, "unless there's some reason why the killer wants you specifically dead. Do you know of some reason that would be?"

Chelsea shook her head as she studied the table in front of her. "The only person I know who has any reason to be upset with me is Sophie, and I don't see why she'd have anything against Madison or Naomie. I can't even think of anybody who knows all of us. We only know each other through Triple-B."

At the mention of her sister's name, flames rose up Jo's chest, and she struggled to contain her reaction. "Then it's far more likely this is a killer who's seeking whatever pregnant women are convenient. They'd have no reason to follow you."

Red spots appeared on Chelsea's cheeks. "I just can't go out of town. I'll take the patrol officer, please."

Jo pushed down her frustration and moved on to Julia. "Do you have someone you can stay with?"

"That won't work. I have clients who depend on me," Julia said.

"We'll get a patrol on you as well, then," Jo said. "We can't maintain it for long, but hopefully we'll find the perpetrator quickly."

Julia gave a single sharp head shake. "That won't work, either. Some of the people I work with don't come from the best circumstances, and having a police officer following me into those neighborhoods would compromise the trust I've built with them and their families."

"But you need to stay safe," Chelsea said, preempting Jo's objection. "Surely that's more important than—"

"Than their safety?" Julia asked. "My life is more important than theirs, for some reason?"

"But you're in *immediate* danger, and they aren't," Chelsea said.

"I disagree. If this psycho is looking for pregnant women to kill, he's not going to come after me." Her hand fell to her flat stomach. "But if my clients—or their families—refuse to let me come help with their home births, they could die in childbirth."

"At least let them put the officer at your house, then," Chelsea said.

"What's the point? I'm hardly ever home, and it would just keep an officer off the street protecting someone else." She turned to Jo. "No, I'm sorry. I'll just have to take my chances."

Jo's mind raced, trying to track what was happening. Julia wasn't the first person to turn down personal protection, and her reasons for it made sense. The fact was, under-served communities sometimes had tenuous, if not downright distrustful, relationships with the police. And yet, Jo was certain something else was going on.

"We won't force you. But if you change your mind, let us know." Jo turned to Chris. "We're so sorry to ask you to deal with this right now. Please know we're deeply sorry for your loss."

Chris met her eyes, and his voice came out as a hoarse whisper. "Please. Just find whoever did this to her—before anybody else gets hurt."

CHAPTER THIRTY-THREE

After Jo assured Chris they'd do everything possible to catch Naomie's killer, she turned to Julia. "Can we speak to you for a moment outside on our way out?"

Julia look startled, and stepped forward with a jerk. "Of course. Actually, I need to leave anyway. Cecile and Fred need to be told. Naomie's parents," she clarified, then looked at Chris. "I don't think this is information they should get over the phone."

Chris's face fell and his stare bounced between Julia and Jo. "Oh, God, you're right. In the shock of it all, I didn't even think —" He stood up. "I'll come with you."

Julia started to respond, but Chelsea jumped in. "Chris, you're in shock. Let Julia handle it. In fact, I'm not sure you should be alone tonight. Do you have a friend who can come over? If not, I can stay."

"Chelsea's right." Julia's nurse voice kicked in. "You need to take care of yourself right now. And I'm already persona non grata with them. If they're going to get bad news, it might as well come from me."

Jo watched a series of emotions battle across Chris's face;

finally, he gave in and sat back down. "You're not persona non grata. And you must be in shock, too."

Julia nodded, her eyes blank. "Part of my job is getting people through crises. I'll be fine."

Jo considered her reaction, again struck by the sense that something wasn't quite right. She added it to the list of things she needed to ask Julia.

Chris still looked uncomfortable, and like he wanted to object. He put on an awkward smile. "Thank you, Julia, I appreciate that. And no, Chelsea, I'll be fine on my own."

"You're sure?" Chelsea's hand lightly touched his forearm.

"I am." He looked down at her abdomen. "You need to take care of *yourself*, too."

Chelsea nodded, and Jo caught the quick flash of relief that flit across her face. "Okay, if you're really sure. But call me the second you need anything."

He promised he would, and saw them all to the door. After Julia helped Chelsea into her car, she returned to Jo and Arnett, who'd pulled out a pair of umbrellas from Jo's Volt.

Even amid the pelting rain, Jo kept her voice low. "What did that mean, when you said you were persona non grata with Naomie's parents?"

Julia took a deep breath and waved away the question. "Chris is right, it's probably an overstatement. Divorce is never easy, and they're a close family. Of course they'll side with him."

"Was Naomie siding with him?" Jo asked.

Julia suddenly looked exhausted, and her voice came out as a husky whisper. "No. She was always a good friend to me." She looked up into Jo's eyes. "But you said you wanted to talk to me *before* I said that, so there must be something else."

Jo nodded. "When I mentioned that Madison worked at The Velvet Volcano, you had a strange reaction, like there was something you wanted to say, but not in front of the others."

Guilt washed over Julia's face, along with a quick flash of relief. Julia glanced back over her shoulder at the front door. "It's hard to explain. No, not hard at all, just embarrassing. One day I pulled Madison aside after class because she looked like she wasn't well, and with the pregnancy, I was concerned. She said she was just stressed because her mother needed some test and their credit cards were already maxed out. She burst into tears, and believe me, she wasn't the sort to burst into tears."

Jo nodded—from everything she'd heard, she didn't find that hard to believe.

"She told me about the fellowship to UC Davis and the dreams she'd given up. It hit me hard because I know exactly what that's like. So I told her how much I admired how hard she was working to make a better life, because I had a similar story and had gone another way. I told her how my mother gave up everything to give me a chance to become a doctor, and then my little brother got sick. How trying to save his life meant I was on my own to pay for school. But the way I chose to pay for it had been stupid and irresponsible, and I'd put myself at risk because I wanted a shortcut. I was trying to build her up, let her know what she was doing would be worth it some day. So I told her I'd been a stripper."

Arnett responded. "You think you gave her the idea? She was already stripping by the time she met you."

She put a hand on her hip. "No, I don't think I gave her the idea, but I think she was at a crossroads and I think my story made her feel okay with being a stripper. As in, 'If Julia made herself so successful starting out this way, I'll be fine.' She said something about how she never would have thought someone as 'classy' as me did that. When she said that, I got on my defensive high horse and said yes, it was stupid and risky, but there's nothing wrong with using the assets you're given, and told her that being in control of your sexuality and making your own choices is empowering, and it's not about being 'classy' or 'not classy.' I saw this odd look of resignation cross her face that I didn't understand, and just thought it had to do with whatever situation ended her up pregnant. But looking back on it now, I think she was at a point where she might have gotten out of it if I hadn't legitimized it for her."

Understanding crushed Jo. "You can't blame yourself. You didn't know. You were trying to encourage her in what you thought she was really doing."

"But maybe if I hadn't called it stupid and risky she would have opened up to me about what she was doing, and I could have talked her out of it."

"Do you think Madison told Naomie she was working at The Velvet Volcano?"

"Maybe, I don't know. Naomie wouldn't have shared something like that with me without Madison's permission."

"How do you think Naomie would have reacted to that? Do you think she might have gone down to the club, said something to the wrong person?" Jo asked.

Julia's face clouded, and she rubbed her eyes. "I wouldn't doubt it. Naomie had a heart the size of the universe and zero self-preservation instinct. She was sheltered, and she thought she could save everybody." She shook her head. "And I gotta give it to her, the self-delusion allowed her to blow past warning flags and make things happen. Didn't matter what arena of her life—work, school, friends, marriage—she refused to acknowledge problems and obstacles. That's the whole reason Triple-B exists, because she didn't listen when she heard no. And every win made her more likely to try the next impossible thing. So, yes, if she got it into her head that Madison was working in the wrong situation, she'd have no problem taking it up with whoever was in charge."

"So she'd just walk in without protection?" Arnett said.

Julia held up a palm. "Naomie's the daughter of Ferdinand

Gagnon. Everywhere she went she had the protection of the Gagnon family's money and power and connections."

Jo nodded. The Gagnons were the sort of upper-echelon family that gave back copiously to the community, and so were highly esteemed not just for their money. "Just one more thing. I also sensed there was more to your refusal of police protection than you were saying."

Julia's hand dropped to her side, and her posture stiffened. "I'm not sure what gave you that impression."

Jo purposefully relaxed her own posture, trying to put Julia subconsciously at ease. "I just want to reassure you that our goals are to find out who killed Madison and Naomie, and to keep you and Chelsea safe, not to embarrass anybody. But we need all the facts to do that, even the ones that aren't related, so we know what *not* to pay attention to."

For a few seconds, Julia seemed to consider that. Then her eyes and expression hardened again. "I understand it may be hard for *you* to understand why some communities aren't comfortable with the police. But I work with women in all sorts of circumstances, and their safety has to be my primary concern. Appearing with an officer by my side will make other vulnerable women unwilling to use me for their births."

Jo held her eyes for a moment longer than necessary, trying to make clear what was really at stake, for everyone involved. "It's not clear at this point whether someone is targeting your friend group in particular, or Beautiful Bouncing Babies as a whole, but they're certainly aware of your and Chelsea's movements. That means it's not just you and Chelsea who are in danger, but all of Triple-B's clients, and your personal clients, too. You may be leading the killer directly to them."

Julia's face turned ashen. Jo said a prayer the dose of reality had worked.

But without another word, Julia marched to her car, climbed in, and drove away.

CHAPTER THIRTY-FOUR

"I've seen clams that couldn't slam shut that tight," Arnett said once they'd returned to Jo's car. "If she was really concerned about keeping her clients safe, she'd do whatever she had to in order to find the killer."

"She's hiding something. The question is what, and does it relate to our investigation?" Jo stared out the window. "How likely do you think it is Lieutenant Hayes would okay surveillance on her?"

"About the same as me giving up meatball grinders," Arnett said.

Jo pursed her lips and nodded. Lieutenant Lindsay Hayes, a new hire who'd been brought in from upstate New York, had taken an instant dislike to Jo. Surveillance teams were expensive, and while protecting a potential victim might be a priority, watching over one in the hope of finding out something that might not be related to the case would be an impossible sell. "Especially since smart money would be on our perpetrator going after Chelsea, since she's pregnant. What about a warrant to see Julia's phone records?"

Arnett grimaced skeptically. "Based on your instinct? Not likely. But we can always try."

Jo's phone rang. "Lacey Bernard," she said as she tapped to answer the call. "Lacey, how are you?"

"Not too bad. I'm calling about the murdered pregnant women."

Jo groaned inwardly at the use of the plural, but wasn't surprised that Lacey'd heard of the development—a group of press had started to form at the trail entrance when they left the park. "Right. We're still trying to get a handle on what exactly's happening."

"Can you confirm a second pregnant woman was found murdered?"

"Here's what I can tell you off the record." Jo caught her up on the situation. "So we have to proceed with caution. We need to make the public aware that there may be a killer targeting pregnant women, but while causing as little panic as possible."

"The horse is out of the barn on that one. I heard the pieces some of the local TV reporters are putting together. There's going to be a public outcry as soon as this hits the airwaves. You missed the evening news, but everyone will wake up to notifications on their phone and pieces on the morning news."

"Then we need to use it to our advantage. Be sure to make it clear all women should take precautions, but if possible, I'd like you to stress that the two victims were friends. That way, if the killer is picking his victims at random, he'll get a false sense of security, and if it is someone known to Madison and Naomie, it'll put him off his game."

"I can do that. Do we want to mention Beautiful Bouncing Babies specifically?" Lacey asked.

Jo shook her head slightly at Arnett with a question on her face, and he shook his back in response. "No," she said. "We'll hold that back, that may be our way to catch him. And, no point in giving them negative press if we can avoid it. We'll get a warning out to all Triple-B's clients directly."

"Anything else?"

Jo looked over at Arnett.

"What do you think about the Lucifer Lost angle?" he asked.

Jo considered. "If we're trying to smoke out the members, that'll make them dive deeper into the shadows. But since they've already dug in, I can't see how *not* mentioning them will help. So, yes, let's also put that anyone who has information about Lucifer Lost should contact us."

"I'll make it happen. And of course you'll make sure I know what's what before anybody else?" Lacey asked.

"Of course." Jo smiled and shook her head. "Thank you."

"Not a problem. Good luck with your lieutenant." Lacey hung up.

Jo winced. "She's not wrong. Hayes is going to call us pretty much any minute."

Arnett glanced at the time on the dash. "Most likely she's in bed by now, but who knows what emergency alerts she has set when it comes to you."

Jo gave a shudder that was only half fake. "The good news is we've got all our irons in the fire. Marzillo's team is all over the crime scene, the search team is looking for additional evidence, we've got canvassers leaving no stone unturned, and now we have Lacey laying some psychological mines for our killer. Going back to Julia, I'll have Lopez do a deep dive on whatever we can legally find." Jo tapped at her phone, then fired up the car. "So, given it's three in the morning, I think the smartest thing you and I can do is go grab a few hours of sleep so we can jump into this sharp and focused first thing."

————

Given the adrenaline and cortisol coursing through her veins, Jo slept better than she expected to, and actually woke refreshed after a mere three hours of sleep. The payment would come later—sometime around midday she'd crash, at least if she didn't keep the caffeine flowing. She showered quickly, threw on clothes, and gave Matt a quick kiss before running out the door with a pain au chocolat tucked in a paper towel.

The steady rain prolonged the fading darkness, making the morning feel like time had stood still since they'd left the crime scene the night before. She tried to shake off the illusion as she downed large gulps of mocha in between bites of the pastry, and by the time she pulled into the parking lot, a powerful blend of caffeine, sugar and fat elicited the punch of dopamine and serotonin she needed to refresh her optimism about solving the case.

She started with the security footage from Chris and Naomie's camera. As Chris predicted, it showed Naomie arriving shortly after four, but then showed nothing—not even a neighborhood cat walking across the porch—until Chris arrived home at six-fifteen. Naomie must have left the house across the back of the property.

Protective gloves in place, Jo removed the satchel's contents. A laptop—that would make Lopez's day—and a small stack of files and papers. By the time Arnett made it in half an hour later, she'd sorted through the stack carefully, preserving any potential fingerprints or touch DNA that might be present.

"What'd you find?" Arnett asked as he handed her another mocha.

She pulled off her gloves and took a large sip. "Several files for applicants to Beautiful Bouncing Babies, containing financial and other information. As best I can tell, she was evaluating them to see what they qualified for. But these"—she pointed in turn to three sheets of paper—"seem to be the fraudulent grant applications. That one's Madison's."

Arnett hunched over for a closer look. "Can't really tell much from them."

"No. I'm hoping Lopez will be able to find something on her laptop or phone that'll help."

"Speak of the devil, and she will appear," Lopez's voice said from behind them. "Did I hear you say you have a laptop for me?"

"We do." Jo gestured to the computer.

Lopez wiggled her fingers. "Give it to meeeee. Sounds like you have something specific you want me to look for?"

Jo filled her in on Naomie's phone call to her the day before, and the grant money issue she'd called about.

"Ah, well, that explains the pictures I found on her phone before I went home for my cat nap."

Jo perked up. "Do tell."

Lopez motioned for them to follow her out to her multi-desk setup, pulled a Rockstar out of her mini fridge and cracked it open, then pulled up a file on her main monitor. A grid of thumbnails appeared; after a double-click, the first picture opened. "These look like client files. There are ten of them, including Madison's. It looks like Naomie went through and took pictures of every page." Lopez scrolled through. "Then some pages of what look like a disbursement log."

"You said Madison's file is in there. Do you mind if I take a look through?" Jo asked.

"Be my guest." Lopez rolled her chair out of the way, and gestured to the empty chair sitting next to the desk.

Jo pulled it over, then began to click through the files. "The other two women whose disbursement sheets I found in Naomie's satchel are here as well, and in each case, there's a second, handwritten application for the same grant, with different dates. And"— she continued clicking through—"there are double disbursements for each in the log."

"That would be much harder for Madison to pull off,

accessing the other clients' applications," Arnett said. "Even if the offices were routinely left unattended, she'd have to know what she was looking for."

"I think Naomie realized that, too, and that's why she called us. So the next thing I want to know is whose fingerprints are on these grant applications."

"Most everybody has legitimate reasons for touching the files," Arnett said.

"True, but I also want to see whose prints *aren't* on the applications. If Madison's prints aren't on hers, that tells us something important."

"Smart." Arnett leaned forward for a better look. "Standard, non-coated paper. Unless someone wiped them off right away, the prints would have absorbed and be nearly impossible to wipe away."

"That's what I'm hoping. I was going to lift the prints myself, but it's been awhile, and we want to be sure we keep everything preserved. Since we need to head down to Triple-B to interview everyone anyway, I'll leave it to the pros."

"I'll make sure we have prints on record for both Madison and Naomie," Lopez said.

"Thank you," Jo said. "If someone is bilking thousands out of Triple-B, it's very possible they killed both Naomie and Madison to keep from being found out."

CHAPTER THIRTY-FIVE

Chelsea pushed the front-window curtain of her brownstone aside with a finger, just an inch, to stare out at the undercover officer across the street. She'd tried to bring coffee out to him half an hour before, but he'd chastised her, going on about how he couldn't be undercover if she drew attention to him. She'd shot off an angry text to Julia, expecting her commiseration since she hadn't wanted any surveillance at all. But Julia took his side, saying it wasn't just about protecting Chelsea, it was about catching the killer and she needed to be patient, blah blah blah.

Sighing, she let the curtain drop, then lowered herself onto the couch and snatched up her copy of *Persuasion*. But her mind wouldn't be distracted, and she found herself staring off into the distance, her leg bouncing so furiously it threatened to fly right off.

She hadn't thought through the police protection well enough. On the surface she'd thought it would get her what she wanted—for David to take the situation seriously. She'd talked him into spending the night again the night before—he couldn't turn her down in light of a second friend's death, and he couldn't now deny that pregnant women in the area were in danger. He'd seemed genuinely concerned about her—he'd watched a movie with her, talked to her, all very cozy and sweet. She told him he didn't have to sleep in the guest room if he didn't want to, that she'd actually prefer it if he slept in her room, because she didn't like being alone after everything that had happened. But he'd just smiled and acted like she was being funny, and went into the other room. Then when the under-cover officer showed up at the crack of dawn, he'd seemed relieved to hand her off to the protective detail, and hurried off to work, commenting how she wouldn't have to worry now that she'd have someone watching her twenty-four seven.

The words had hit like a punch to the stomach. She'd given away her leverage. She should have turned the detail down and told David she needed him—how would he have been able to say no? Except, if she'd turned down the detail, Jo would have been sure to tell David. Damned if she did, damned if she didn't.

Time was running out. Once the baby was born, it would be so much harder to pull David in. He knew she could afford a nanny, so claims of being overwhelmed would be easy for him to push aside. Even if he didn't, he could always just take the baby off her hands claiming she needed her 'alone time' rather than just staying with her. Because, originally, she'd been sure there was no way that wife of his was going to spend hours taking care of an infant that wasn't hers, and so David's visita-tion with the baby would necessarily be time spent with Chelsea. But now she wasn't so sure—she'd gotten to know Sophie well enough to know that if it meant removing an excuse for David to be with Chelsea, she'd change every diaper and warm every bottle in existence.

The mental image of Sophie cooing over the baby sent phys-ical pains shooting through her chest. No way was she going to let Sophie get her claws into *her* baby.

She pushed herself up and waddled into the nursery, feeling like a duck who'd swallowed half a loaf of bread whole. She was lucky, pregnancy hadn't changed her figure much at all, and from the back you couldn't even tell she was pregnant. But still, galumping around like a mini-elephant just wasn't cute. No wonder David didn't want to share a bed with her right now. She'd have to double-up and triple-up on the exercise to get herself back into shape as quickly as possible.

Which reminded her—she needed to order one of those post-birth corsets. And as much as Julia was going to yell at her for it, there was no way she was going to breastfeed. Formula all the way, and hopefully her milk would dry up quickly. Because pregnancy alone was going to do a huge number on her breasts, let alone if she spent months and months breastfeeding. Julia had tried to convince her that breastfeeding didn't change your breasts beyond pregnancy itself, but that was just ridiculous. No thank you—not worth the risk.

The point was, things weren't going the way she'd planned. Even Madison's and Naomie's deaths didn't seem to be making a difference, and she was worse off than at the start.

She had to adjust her plan.

———

Julia held herself up using her Formica counter, staring sightlessly out the duplex's kitchen window as her new single-serving Keurig spat coffee into her mug. When it finished, she grabbed it out of the machine and gulped without even adding milk. Once she'd drained the mug she pushed it back into the maker with a shaking hand, inserted a second pod, and started another cup brewing. Then she sagged into a chair at her kitchen table and dropped her head into her hands.

She needed to pull herself together.

The excuse to leave with the detectives before had been a

godsend, but talking to Cecile and Fred had been the worst experience of her life. Naomie, their only daughter, had been their alpha and their omega, and their pain was absolute. The normally unflappable Cecile had collapsed into a pile, screaming and literally scratching at the floor, so upset Julia was worried Cecile would have some sort of cardiac event. She'd had to give Cecile a pethidine injection in the hopes of calming her down. By the time Julia got home, it'd been almost five in the morning, and she had nothing left. But despite her emotional and physical exhaustion, she hadn't been able to sleep, and just slipped into a strange gray zone where Naomie's face loomed in front of her, begging for help, leaving Julia tossing in a pile of sweat-soaked blankets.

Now, after carefully monitoring her responses the night before, she finally had a moment to sit and allow her emotions to be what they were. But her brain wouldn't kick in and she sat numb, like she was the one who'd been given a sedative and it wouldn't wear off.

Everything was spiraling out of control. She couldn't let it.

Her burner phone, still in her purse where she'd dumped it, buzzed. A tiny hint of emotion cracked through her fatigued haze as she scrabbled for it, desperately needing the salve of Rick's text. He hadn't been happy when she'd had to cancel their plan the night before, but had understood why. She couldn't tell him everything, of course, because he'd never understand and she couldn't risk losing him. She needed him to be there for her more than she'd needed anything in this life.

She closed her eyes and paused for a moment. These racing thoughts weren't like her. She couldn't afford to fall apart.

She groped in the bag and her fingers hit smooth, cold metal. She pulled out the phone with a gush of relief.

I need to see you.

It wasn't from Rick.

Son of a fucking bitch. Adrenaline rushed through her, and she resisted the urge to hurl the phone across the room, clenching it so hard she was surprised it didn't crack under her fingers. *Take a fucking hint, you delusional piece of shit*, she typed in, relishing every letter. *Fuck all the way off.*

She forced herself to delete it. The upside was the adrenaline spurt had done what the coffee couldn't, and now she just needed a moment to think.

Nothing had changed with respect to this—pissing him off wasn't going to help. Her previous decision on how to handle him was the right one, and she needed to just stay the course.

Too much going on right now. I'll call when I can.

A minute later, the phone rang.
She refused the call, and quickly sent another text.

Can't answer now. With a client.

She waited a minute, then two, sipping her remaining coffee, eyes pinned to the screen.

After five minutes, he still hadn't responded. She took a deep, slow breath, and slipped the phone back into her purse. Thank goodness he'd let it go, at least for now. She had other fires she had to put out.

CHAPTER THIRTY-SIX

Beautiful Bouncing Babies was located just off downtown Oakhurst, far enough away from the main streets to be circumspect without being difficult to find. The half red-brick, half peach-stucco building was bright and appealing, with high, welcoming arches and a warm, joyful strip of mural of babies playing together. The inside was just as cheery, with banana-yellow walls accented with dashes of mint and splashes of mother-and-baby artwork. Jo could see how, especially to women with fewer resources, Triple-B would make them feel pampered, cared for, and in good hands.

At least, on days when the staff members weren't wiping away tears and struggling to speak.

Sandra, Naomie's administrative assistant, turned out to be a white woman in her mid-fifties with ditchwater-brown hair. She continually tugged at her generic work pants and top; Jo couldn't decide if it was a sign of poor fit or emotional distress. Sandra's pale-blue eyes were red and swollen, and her expression was grim and frightened.

She walked them through a hall, past cubicles and a multipurpose room containing office equipment, then unlocked a door. "This was Naomie's office. I thought you'd want to see it."

"Thank you. Has anyone been in here since she last was?" Jo asked.

"The janitorial staff comes in after hours. Other than that, I left when Naomie did, so I don't know if anybody besides that went in."

"Is that common for people to go into each other's offices?" Arnett asked.

"That depends what you mean. During the day, yes, all the time. We're a small organization and the officers often have to go into one another's files for one reason or another. But once people have left for the day, you need a key."

"Who are the officers? Do they all have keys to everything?" Jo asked.

"Naomie, of course, and Rhea Blondell. And Julia Gagnon, although she isn't technically an officer. Naomie and Rhea started the non-profit together, and Julia came on as an educator and medical professional. There's a janitorial passkey kept in a safe, and they all have access to that. The rest of us, it depends. I have a key to Naomie's office, and Janelle has one to Rhea's. I think that's it."

Jo asked her about the fraudulent grant applications. "Do you know who Naomie suspected?" Jo asked.

Sandra shook her head. "She didn't say."

Jo nodded. "Who do *you* think is responsible?"

"I've been worrying myself sick about it," she said, looking nauseated. "If I had to pick someone, and I don't like doing that, I'd say Janelle, Rhea's admin. Only because she's relatively new. She's only been here for three months, and she and I are the two who work closely with the financial records."

"Does she have money problems, anything like that?"

"Not problems exactly. But she—just like me—lives the kind of life where a thousand dollars would make a difference."

Jo could see the pain in Sandra's face as she answered. "Most people do, I think. I know it's hard to point the finger at a co-worker, but we appreciate your honesty. We'll need to talk to everyone who works here in turn, and we'll need to take everyone's fingerprints. Can you help us arrange that?"

"Sure thing, I'll set up appointments with everyone. The fingerprints should be easy. Everyone who works here has to get a background check done, including IdentoGo live scan fingerprinting. We require that they also submit fingerprint cards to us while they're employed here."

"That'll save time, thank you. Is there a room where we can talk to people privately?" Jo asked.

"We have a conference room. Will that work?"

"That sounds perfect." Jo glanced around. "I don't suppose you have any coffee here?"

Sandra gave a watery smile. "This place runs on coffee. Let me show you where it is."

They followed her into a small break room that looked more like a cozy kitchen. Sandra grabbed two paper cups from the top of an upside-down stack, and filled them with coffee from the large pot. "How do you take it?"

"Black, thank you," Arnett said.

"Just cream for me, if you have it," Jo said.

Sandra handed one of the cups to Arnett, then reached into a container by the side of the coffee pot but pulled her hand out empty. "Ugh. I hate it when people take the last of something and don't refill. Hang on." She pulled open the cabinet above the coffee maker, and grabbed an industrial-sized box of the creamers.

Jo gasped.

Behind the creamer box was a large bag of king-cake baby figurines.

CHAPTER THIRTY-SEVEN

Sandra jerked back at the sound of Jo's gasp. "What's wrong?"

"Do you know how those got there?" Jo pointed toward the bag.

Sandra followed the gesture, and her face relaxed. "Oh, those. Kinda creepy when you see them like that, aren't they? But they're just party favors we use for decorations when we have showers for the clients."

"How long have they been there?" Jo asked.

"Oh, over a year, at least. We try to save money where we can, so I picked up a gross of them. Why? Do you want to see them?" She reached for the bag.

Jo's hand shot out. "Please don't touch them. We'll need to take them into evidence."

Sandra's arm and face dropped abruptly. "Of course. Whatever you need."

Jo retrieved gloves and an evidence bag from the Crown Vic and collected the figurines while Sandra returned to work. "We may as well have them checked for prints, although I'm not sure how much use it will be. Anybody could have touched them at any time."

"But if we get a clear print, it may at least point us in the right direction," Arnett said.

After securing the evidence bag back in the trunk of the car, and asking Sandra to get a hold of the other two women who'd received double grant payments, Jo and Arnett turned toward interviewing the admin and support staff. Knowing too well how quickly office gossip spread, they started with Janelle Robinson, Rhea Blondell's administrative assistant. Janelle's alarm and confusion when asked about the fraudulent grant applications felt genuine to both Jo and Arnett, sending them into their interview with Rhea Blondell more confused than ever. They went directly from the conference room to Rhea's office to talk with her before anyone else, especially Janelle, had a chance.

Rhea rose from her desk when they entered and greeted them. Tall and thin, her brown eyes were puffed and her brown skin looked sickly—but her grief was layered with anger. Once they sat, she didn't wait for them to start.

"Two women, both associated with Beautiful Bouncing Babies, have been murdered. How is that possible?" Rhea crossed her arms and leaned back in her chair.

Jo kept her face passive as she weighed Rhea's response. Anger was a common response to death, especially unexpected, violent death. Pointing that reaction at law enforcement was just as common. But that sort of attack was also an effective strategy for putting someone off balance and maintaining control of an interaction—and Jo wasn't about to concede it.

"That's what we need to find out, as soon as possible," Jo said. "Have you noticed anything strange lately, any suspicious people or cars lurking in your parking lot, anything like that?"

She gave a single, sharp shake of her head. "Nothing."

So Rhea was a woman of few words. "Was anyone having an issue with Naomie?" Jo asked.

"Your question makes no sense." Rhea's eyes pierced hers.

"Madison was the first to die. Either she's the one who someone had a problem with, or a very sick individual is hunting pregnant women."

"We can't know what's important and what isn't until we have all relevant context," Jo said, carefully holding on to her neutral expression. "Were you aware that Naomie's administrative assistant stumbled on a fraudulent grant application submitted in Madison's name, and that Naomie was investigating who was responsible for it? And that she found two other clients with similar double disbursements?"

The question had the effect Jo wanted. Rhea's face paled, and red blotches appeared on her neck as she processed the implications. "Fraudulent grant applications?"

"Yes." Jo silently handed her a printout of the relevant documents.

Rhea's eyes flicked expertly. "Two disbursements, when they were only entitled to one." She glared up at Jo. "How did this happen?"

"You tell us. It's your job to monitor grant dispersals," Jo said.

Rhea's eyes bounced between the documents and their faces. "Why didn't Naomie come to me about this?"

Jo tilted her head. "That's a very insightful question, I think."

The blotches on Rhea's neck widened into a solid sea of crimson. "What are you implying?"

"I'm trying to find out why your business partner was murdered, and from what you said when we arrived, I assume you want that, too. If so, I need you to answer our questions instead of just turning them back to us. Did you know anything about this, and if so, what? If not, explain to us how it got past you."

For a moment Rhea looked like a pressure cooker about to explode. But then she flipped through the papers again.

"Grant requests come in to Janelle. She takes them, enters them into the system, then evaluates them. If they qualify, she brings them to me for signature. I admit, I only spot-check her work. I have to rely on her to do her job so I can do mine." She stood, opened her office door and stuck her head out. "Janelle, can you come in here?"

Janelle came in, her expression worried and her posture stooped. "How can I help?"

"Can you explain how two grant applications for the same period were approved for Madison Coelho?"

Janelle straightened slightly. "I didn't think to check through the disbursements from before I hired on. It didn't occur to me that someone would try to slip a second application past me. I apologize. It's completely my fault. I'll replace the funds from my own money."

Jo watched Rhea's expression as Janelle responded. Frustration and anger dominated, but something else mixed in—regret?

"That won't be necessary. The larger damage here is that we could be called to account for failing to have proper protections in place when dealing with disbursal of government funds. We'll need to write up an account of what happened and why for the grant report. I'll also need you to see if you can track what happened to the funds."

"We're already tracing that," Jo said. "In Madison's case, the check was taken to a Citizens Bank branch and cashed out. My guess is when we pull a copy of the canceled check, the signature on the back will match Madison's. We're also looking to see if they still have security footage for the transaction."

"Janelle should be able to get copies of the canceled checks for you before you leave today." The red began to recede from Rhea's neck. "Is there anything else you need from her?"

"No," Jo said. "But we do have a few more questions for you."

Rhea nodded at Janelle, effectively dismissing her. Once the door was closed behind her, Jo continued. "How well known are your procedures here? Meaning, who would have known about how these grant disbursements in particular would work?"

Rhea's hands gestured an arc around her. "Generally speaking, everyone. Even our janitor has submitted reimbursement requests for cleaning supplies, and all our disbursements are processed the same way."

"And," Jo said, "everyone knows Janelle is new to the job?"

Rhea nodded. "You see how small we are. It's impossible for everyone to *not* know when we have a change in staff."

Jo gestured toward the paperwork. "If you had to guess, who do you think is responsible for this?"

Rhea stiffened. "I don't like to speculate about things like that. Reputations are hard to repair once they're damaged."

Jo leaned forward. "I sympathize with that position. But we need to know who's responsible for this, and so do you."

Rhea shook her head at the ceiling. "I honestly can't see any of our employees doing this. But by process of elimination... Janelle seemed genuinely horrified about the error, and if Naomie were responsible, she wouldn't have ended up dead. To my mind, that leaves Sandra. But I've only ever known her to be a kind, honorable person."

"Sandra's the one who brought the problem to Naomie," Jo said.

"You insisted I pick someone. Maybe Sandra realized she was going to get caught and brought the issue to Naomie to make herself look innocent. I wouldn't have believed that yesterday, but I also wouldn't have believed someone was embezzling under my nose."

Jo braced herself for the response to her next question. "We need to know where everyone was after five-twenty last night."

Rhea looked affronted, but kept the reaction under control. "I had a doctor's appointment yesterday at three-thirty. I came back here after to finish the work that still needed to be done. I believe I got back around five-forty-five, and worked until about seven. There should be security footage of me coming and going."

"Was anyone else here in the building with you?"

"Sandra left shortly after I arrived. She should be able to confirm."

Jo stood up, Arnett right behind, and handed Rhea her card. "Thank you very much for your help. If you think of anything else, please let us know."

Once closed back into the conference room, Jo turned to Arnett. "At an operation this small, any admin responsible for reimbursements would be able to remember what monies they'd paid out without checking—at the very least, it would be a huge risk to assume they *wouldn't* remember. My guess is someone took advantage of Janelle's new-hire status to perpetrate whatever this scheme is."

"My money's on Rhea. She'd have trained Janelle, and it's easy enough to 'forget' to tell her to double-check the log," Arnett said.

"That would explain the preemptive show of anger," Jo agreed. "But we'll need to hope for some physical evidence."

They continued on with the rest of the interviews. Everybody had alibis for the time after five-thirty, and nobody could remember seeing anything suspicious.

Arnett checked his watch with a sigh. "If we hurry, we can go grab something to eat before the memorial service."

"I'm starving. And a quick trip to Sal's will give us a chance to be gone and off everyone's mind as they head into the memorial. Then we can slip back in and see what we see."

On their way to Sal's, a call from Lieutenant Hayes rang through on Jo's phone.

"Two pregnant women," Hayes stated without preamble. "Why is the first I'm hearing about this an ass-chewing from DA Barbieri?"

"We weren't certain until late last night," Jo said.

"You should have woken me."

Jo shot a look at Arnett, who rolled his eyes. If a detective woke her every time an ugly homicide came in after dark, Hayes would never sleep. But this wasn't about consistency or proper procedure, it was about any opportunity to slam Jo.

"I'll make sure to do that next time," Jo responded.

"Both the DA and the press are all over me. I need something I can give them that makes us look at least partially competent. Do you have a name for me?"

Jo gave her an abbreviated version of what they knew and how they were addressing it all. "We're hoping the memorial service will give us some insight."

"Update me when it's over." Hayes hung up.

Jo shook her head as Arnett parked and they made their way into the restaurant. Once they'd put in the order for their medium Sal's special, they compared notes on the day's interviews and checked in with the other officers and detectives helping with canvassing and the tip line.

"The officer who went over to Joy's Juice Bar and Café said one of the employees noticed some 'weird guy' hanging out in a car a couple of times when they took out the garbage," Arnett said through a mouthful of pizza. "It was hard to see much through the windows, and they didn't notice the make or the model, but said it was a dark midsize car."

Jo swallowed her own mouthful. "That fits what Chelsea said. And it fits the stalking serial-killer theory rather than an issue with fraudulent disbursements."

Arnett wagged his head. "Could be either. Whoever it was could have been stalking the group because of the disbursement situation, trying to figure out how to fix the problem."

Jo stabbed the air with a slice of pizza. "Two thousand dollars. If someone stalked these two women and killed them over two thousand dollars..."

Arnett shot her a skeptical glare. "We've seen people murdered over a dirty look. And you and Lopez razzed *me* for not knowing about pregnant strippers."

"No, I don't mean that, it's never that simple. It's about whatever fueled the desperation that lead them to steal in the first place. Or, like Chris said, about staying out of jail. I just meant it's heartbreaking."

"Fair enough," Arnett said, taking another piece of pizza. "But I've got a gut feeling about our buddy Travis."

As Jo took a large draw from her Diet Coke, her phone rang. "It's Lopez," she said, and answered the phone. "Christine. What's going on?"

"Hey." Lopez's voice had a quiet edge to it. "I stumbled on something possibly weird. When you summarized the embezzling situation for me, you said last night nobody admitted to knowing anything about it. Did that include Julia?"

"It did. She said Naomie told her something about someone going through her filing cabinet, but said she hadn't told her anything about fraudulent grant applications."

"Yeah, I'm calling BS on that," Lopez said. "Because right after Naomie left you the message about the grant applications? She immediately called Julia."

CHAPTER THIRTY-EIGHT

"Naomie called Julia immediately after she spoke with us? How immediately?" Jo asked.

"Like, the exact same minute. Her call to you ended at four-ten, and her call to Julia started at four-ten," Lopez said.

"How long did the call with Julia last?" Jo asked.

"Ten minutes."

"So they actually spoke." Jo's mind raced, working through the possible explanations. "Devil's advocate. It could be she'd planned to call Julia for something else, and was just working her way through her phone calls."

Arnett threw her a come-on-now look. "Julia was her close friend *and* aunt *and* business partner, and she didn't mention the fraud to Julia?"

Jo raked her teeth over her lip. "I'm not sure that's much better for Julia, actually. Because the only reason Naomie would have *not* mentioned it was if she was worried Julia was involved. So, Julia's either lying to us, or Naomie suspected her."

"But isn't Julia married to the other Gagnon brother? Don't they have gazillions of dollars?" Lopez asked.

"She's in the process of a divorce. Money's always compli-cated in divorces," Arnett said.

"Facts," Lopez said. "I'll look into it."

"Well," Jo said, "this memorial service is getting more and more complicated."

Jo and Arnett finished their dinner and slipped into the memorial service half an hour after the official start time, hoping to blend in as much as possible. Decorations were minimal, comprised mostly of photographs dotting the whiteboard, with Madison's on one end and Naomie's on the other. Just below, a long table with a linen cloth contained two journals with matching pens next to an elegant card asking guests to write a final message to Madison and Naomie.

"I think we need to see what ends up in those," Arnett said.

"Agreed. I'll talk to Chelsea about it," Jo answered.

They helped themselves to cups of coffee from the refresh-ments table, then retreated to the far corner of the room. A strange blend of emotions mixed throughout the room; several children, too young to understand the nature of the occasion, dove noisily into a box of toys, while several smaller ones in the arms of their mothers elicited coos and smiles from red, puffy faces. Jo caught enough snippets of conversation to deduce these were babies born under the guidance of Beautiful Bouncing Babies, whether assisted by classes, grants, or other programs.

Jo surreptitiously studied the dynamics across the room. About fifty adults were in attendance, most of them women. Madison's mother and Chris Alexander stood at one end of the journal table with an older couple who, based on the woman's striking resemblance to Naomie, must be her parents. Madison's mother looked like she was caught in a nightmare, unsure what to do with the strangers touching her shoulder, grabbing her hand, pulling her into hugs. Chris held himself with a stiff stoicism, trying his best to shield Cecile from the most egregious of these well-meant assaults as diplomatically as possible. Ferdinand Gagnon's arm circled his wife's shoulder, pulling her periodically into his chest when she could no longer fight back her tears.

Chelsea stood in the center of the room, holding court to a group of women peppering her with questions. Julia, hanging back from everyone on the far end of the room, clutched a cup of coffee and solemnly greeted the mothers who came up to her, glimpses of somber pride peeping out as she engaged with the babies. How many of them had she delivered?

Jo studied each individual in turn, looking for anything, or anyone, out of place. Nothing set off any bells: no telltale emotions, no furtive glances, no odd interactions.

About ten minutes after they'd settled in, Kiernan Wendiss appeared at the entryway, tear-filled eyes bouncing around like a lost child looking for his mother. When he saw Jo his posture tightened, and he beelined for them.

"Madison's mom told me there's been another murder. Is that true?" he asked.

"A friend of Madison's." Jo gestured to the pictures on the wall. "Naomie Alexander."

Desperation and anger battled on his face. "The article in the paper about Madison said something about a Satanic cult? Lucifer something?"

"We're pursuing several possibilities," Jo said.

"I looked them up, their group and their tenets and their sigil," he continued. "I don't understand. Why would they hurt Madison?"

As he spoke, Jo winced. Because over his shoulder Jo spotted Brad Pratt stepping into the room accompanied by another man—both wearing graphic tees with large silver Sigils of Lucifer.

———

Kiernan noticed Jo's reaction and turned to follow her gaze.

"You have to be kidding me—" He swerved on his heels and bolted toward Brad. "Hey man, what the actual fuck?"

The entire room jerked around to see what was going on. Brad turned to face Kiernan, a smug grin spreading over his face. Brad's friend lifted his cell phone to catch the interaction.

Jo and Arnett jumped to intercept, but Kiernan was faster than both of them. The second he was within reach, he pulled back a fist and swung.

Brad didn't even try to dodge the blow. Kiernan's fist landed solidly on his jaw with a stomach-churning crunch.

As Brad hit the ground, Jo grabbed Kiernan's arm and threw him back toward Arnett. Arnett grabbed him, snapping a handcuff on one arm, then the other.

Brad's hand flew to his chin, but he made no move to get up. "I want that guy arrested, right now. That's assault, and you all witnessed it."

"And I have it on camera," the friend said.

Chris appeared at Jo's side, face twisted with anger. "Assault? When you show up dressed like *that* to my wife's memorial?" He pointed down at Brad. "Arrest *him*."

Brad laughed incredulously. "On what charge?"

Chris's eyes narrowed dangerously. "Disturbing the peace."

"This is a public event, broadcast all over their website. I have every right to be here," Brad said.

"Wearing that is intentional infliction of distress. You came with the intention of provoking a reaction." His arm swung to the side, pointing to Naomie's parents. "What kind of a sick asshole would want to do something like that to grieving people?"

"I have a constitutional right to wear something that represents my beliefs, particularly when my organization is being accused—"

Jo had had enough. She stepped between the two men. "Chris, step back and allow us to handle this. Brad, do you need medical attention?"

"No, but that's not—"

"Then I need you to accompany me outside."

"I'm not—"

She pulled out the handcuffs she'd stashed in her blazer pocket and closed them around his wrists. "Now."

Brad stood, looking up at his friend. "You catching all of this?"

Jo crooked an index finger at the friend. "You, too."

"What did I do?" the friend said.

She jutted her head toward the door. "Feel free to keep recording, especially if you intend to continue refusing to cooperate with law enforcement."

He tapped at the phone and slid it in his pocket, then strode through the door. Jo herded them down the hall and through the main office of the building, then out to the sidewalk. Arnett followed her, Kiernan in tow. Thankfully, he was smart enough to remain quiet.

"I want him arrested," Brad repeated.

"To confirm, you want to press charges?" Jo asked.

Brad drew himself up taller. "Of course I want to press charges. He assaulted me."

Jo motioned to the undercover officer who'd been assigned to protect Chelsea, currently watching the building. "Then we'll send for backup to come take the three of you into custody."

Brad's brows rose in faux indignation. "The three of us?"

"Chris Alexander made it clear he'd like you charged with disturbing the peace at his wife's memorial service," Jo said.

"This shirt is protected by the constitution," Brad barked. "And we have the whole thing on tape. That jerk flew across an *entire room* to attack me."

"We *also* have the entire incident on tape," Jo said. "Several angles of it, in fact. All of which will show clearly that your friend had his phone out in anticipation of a reaction. They'll also show the expression on your face as you entered the room, and when you saw Kiernan coming at you."

Both the smugness and indignation dropped from his face, replaced with genuine shock. "You—you can't—"

"Let me explain it to you clear and easy," Arnett said. "No publicity is bad publicity, right? You want to be heard, and this'll get you attention. But judges and juries don't look kindly on people who cause emotional distress to grieving families to further their political ends."

Jo made direct, extended eye contact. "And, if you're willing to go to this extreme to bring attention to Lucifer Lost, I have to ask myself what other extremes you'd be willing to go to."

Brad's mouth snapped open and shut. "I have an alibi for Madison Coelho's murder."

"I hope you have an alibi for Naomie Alexander's too. Because you've also refused to put us in touch with other members of your group, which shows an unwillingness to help with a police investigation. Add to that this extreme demonstration of your contempt for the victims and their families and I don't think we'll have a problem getting a warrant to search you and your organization."

Brad's face turned white. "Look, I'm not really hurt. I don't need to press charges."

"That's very gracious of you," Jo said.

Arnett pulled out the key to his cuffs and released Kiernan. Brad lifted his hands toward Jo so she could remove his.

She didn't move.

"Officers are en route," Arnett said.

Brad's gaze bounced back and forth between them. "Wait— What? You're still going to arrest us even though I'm dropping the charges?"

"Sorry you misunderstood—this isn't a negotiation," Jo said. "You'll still need to explain to the judge why you showed up here today dressed like that. And we're more interested than ever to know who the other members of Lucifer Lost are and where they were at the time of these murders."

CHAPTER THIRTY-NINE

Once Brad and friend were bundled into squad cars, Jo and Arnett headed back into the memorial service. All eyes were on them as they attempted to slip back in.

"Whatever veil of discretion we might have had before has been obliterated," Jo said.

"But that little drama may have been exactly what we came here to see," Arnett answered.

Chris broke away from Naomie's parents and stormed over to them, demanding to know what happened. They calmed him as best they could, and advised him to continue the memorial like nothing had happened.

Once the crowd's interest in the altercation shifted, Chelsea took to the microphone to say a few words about both Madison and Naomie, then invited up anyone else who wanted to do the same. Both Madison's mother and Naomie's father gave short, emotional eulogies, followed by several people associated with Triple-B. Jo listened carefully to the speakers' words while scanning the crowd for reactions.

When the tributes finished, Jo and Arnett refreshed their

coffee, then sidled over to Julia. She hadn't moved from the far
edge of the crowd, her face and neck tight with strain.

"How are you holding up?" Jo asked her.

Julia drew in a deep breath. "As well as can be expected."

Jo glanced back at Chris, standing again with Naomie's
parents. "This has to be all that much harder when you're going
through a divorce from the family."

Julia gave a curt nod. "My soon-to-be-ex didn't show, which
helps. I'm sure he'll be at the family services, so he probably
figured he'd give me this space. Cecile and Fred have always
been good to me, but Pete is Fred's brother, and those types of
ties bind tight."

"So many life stresses all at once," Jo said. "I'm so sorry."

Julia's eyes narrowed and flicked over Jo's face. "It hasn't
been my favorite few months, no."

Jo made a quick calculation—Julia wasn't stupid, and she
wasn't the sort of woman who played games. Any attempts to
dance around the subject would just offend her and lose Jo the
element of surprise.

"You remember last night, we mentioned there had been
some fraudulent grant applications submitted to Triple-B, one
by Madison?" Jo asked.

"I do. Were you able to talk to Sandra about it?"

"We were. But something else came to our attention. I
mentioned Naomie called us the afternoon before she
died, upset and concerned about the fraud. We've had a
chance to look at her phone records now, and were
surprised to see that the minute she hung up, she called
you."

Julia's lips drew into a tight line. "She calls me almost every
day. Usually more than once."

"But she didn't mention the money situation to you at all?"
Jo asked.

Julia's arms crossed over her chest. "I told you she didn't."

Jo allowed her brow to crease. "That strikes me as strange. What *did* you talk about?"

Julia gestured an arc in front of them, one arm still tight across her chest. "The memorial. It was a short conversation."

"Huh," Jo said, brow still creased. "If you were talking about Madison, I'd think she'd be even more likely to tell you someone had committed fraud in Madison's name."

"She had a lot on her mind, and obviously Madison's death was our focus. She was probably just trying her best to get through what was a very bad day," Julia said.

"You two were close, right?"

Tears filled Julia's eyes. "She was the best friend a person could have."

"So it's hard for me to understand why she wouldn't tell you about a disturbing issue that cropped up at the business you both loved. You're exactly the person she'd turn to."

Julia's crossed arms tightened. "I don't know what to tell you. She didn't say anything to me. There's nothing I can do if you think I'm lying."

Jo popped her brows. "Oh, I think it's very possible she didn't tell you. But in that case, I have to ask myself *why* she didn't tell you."

Julia didn't flinch and she didn't color, but as the implication of the question landed, her pupils constricted to near pinpoints—a sign of anger or fear. Either way it meant there was something she wasn't saying.

"Naomie was a strong, considerate person. She probably didn't want to disturb me with another fire to put out, at least not until she had more information," she said, voice deceptively smooth and controlled.

Jo hadn't expected Julia to admit to anything, but the reaction told Jo she was on the right track. "You're probably right. She must have intended to tell you after she talked to Rhea."

"That must be it." Julia's face didn't move.

"I do wonder, though—why didn't you tell us she'd called you yesterday?"

Julia's eyes narrowed so quickly it looked like a twitch. "Why would I? Like I said, we spoke almost every day, sometimes more often. You asked me if she'd told me about the money, not whether or not we spoke."

Before Jo could respond, a scream rent the air behind them.

CHAPTER FORTY

Jo and Arnett whirled toward the source of the scream.

Several women Jo didn't know had dropped to their knees, while several other women, too pregnant to drop easily, turned and called for Julia. "Chelsea fainted!"

Jo crossed the distance in a few short strides, Julia at her heels. While Julia dropped to her knees and grabbed Chelsea's wrist, Arnett and Jo cleared a small circle around Chelsea.

"Someone call 911," Julia said. "What exactly happened?"

An unidentified blonde pulled out her phone. "We were just talking, and she collapsed."

"Did she show any signs of distress?" Julia asked, glancing at her watch.

"She said she was feeling a little weird, and she kept clutching the sides of her belly," a brunette said. "Like you do when you're uncomfortable from standing for too long."

Jo squatted to examine the small cup that had fallen from Chelsea's hands; no liquid was left in it. She pulled a nitrile glove from the pocket of her blazer, picked the cup up into the palm of her hand, then peeled the glove back off her hand and up over the cup. "Anyone know what she was drinking?"

"I do," the brunette said. "I got it for her. She asked for Pellegrino. She said even though it gives her gas since she got pregnant, she loves the bubbles."

"Her pulse is fine, and she's breathing." Julia looked up at the women. "Can someone grab a few of the pillows we use in class?"

Clearly relieved to be able to help in some way, several of the women hovering around the edge hurried to bring Chelsea an array of pillows.

As Julia lodged one underneath Chelsea's legs, Chelsea's eyes fluttered open. "What— What happened?"

"Don't move," Julia said, and shoved a second pillow under Chelsea's feet. "You passed out. Have you been having pain or discomfort?"

"Off and on for a couple of weeks," Chelsea said. "But the doctor says everything's fine."

"What did you have to eat today?" Julia asked.

Chelsea rubbed her forehead. "I had Cheerios for breakfast."

"What else?"

"A couple of the apple slices from the buffet."

"That's it?" Julia said. "I told you, you can't skip meals while you're pregnant."

"I haven't been very hungry this week, what with every-thing..." Chelsea's other hand flew to her belly.

Julia leaned back onto her heels and grabbed Chelsea's wrist again. "That's probably all this is then, emotional stress and low blood sugar. But we're calling an ambulance anyway."

Chelsea tried to push herself up. "No, please don't do that. I'll be fine."

Julia motioned to the blonde girl on the phone, who was in the process of telling the dispatcher that Chelsea was now awake and responsive. "If you don't want an ambulance, that's fine, but we need to take you to the ER. We need to be sure everything's okay."

"No, honestly, that's not necessary—"

Visions of both Sophie's and David's faces sprang up in front of Jo's eyes, David's filled with concern about his child, Sophie's filled with suspicion about Chelsea's motives. Whatever was happening here, she couldn't risk something happening to the baby, for everyone's sake. "I'll call David," Jo said. "He can take you."

Chelsea reached for Jo. "No, please don't do that. I've bothered him enough and I know he's with his girls tonight. Really, this is just because I didn't eat anything. I'll force something down."

Jo hadn't expected her to object. "Chelsea, don't be difficult about this. I won't call David if you don't want me to, but you're going to the hospital. We'll have the officer assigned to protect you take you in. He's supposed to be with you all evening anyway."

Chelsea looked from Jo to Julia and back again. "Okay. I guess that's the safest thing to do."

While Arnett went out to tell the officer what was happening, Jo and Julia helped Chelsea to her feet and slowly walked her to the door. They helped her into the officer's car, then watched as it took off down the street.

As soon as it was out of sight, Jo pulled out her phone.

"Who are you calling?" Arnett asked.

"Sophie, then David," she said.

"Chelsea didn't want you to do that," Arnett said in a sing-song voice.

"And I didn't want my brother-in-law to cheat on my sister. Life doesn't always go our way. But with someone out to kill these women, I don't like the timing of this one bit."

CHAPTER FORTY-ONE

After Chelsea was safely on her way to the emergency room, paper cup carefully preserved for the ER toxicologist to test, Jo and Arnett went back inside. A jittery tension had seeped into the room; the previously focused conversations were now stilted, and punctuated by nervous glances. As word made its way around the room that Chelsea was safe and being tended to, people made their excuses and left. When the room was nearly empty, Arnett glanced at his watch and signaled to Jo.

Once out in the car, Arnett's brows rose. "A fight and a fainting spell. Not what we anticipated, but interesting."

"Very. The question is, was any of it integral to our murders?"

"We'll find out soon enough, especially since Pratt's little stunt will almost certainly guarantee us a warrant to look into him and Lucifer Lost." He pulled out into the street.

Jo raked her lower lip with her teeth. "I'm just as interested in Chelsea's fainting spell."

He threw her a confused look. "You bagged the cup and sent it on. You think someone drugged her?"

"Actually, no. My first instinct was she'd faked it."

"Either way, what would that have to do with the murders?"

Jo drew in a deep breath before answering, then told him about Sophie's concerns. "She's convinced Chelsea is up to something, and up until now I've taken that with a large grain of salt. Huge, actually."

"She likes attention, that's for sure," Arnett said.

"No doubt. But..."

"But what?"

"Let's say Sophie's right. Let's say Chelsea is consumed with getting David back, and she's inventing or magnifying the problems with the pregnancy to get and keep his attention."

"Okay."

"And that didn't get her what she wanted, so she stepped it up."

"Playing up the pregnancy component of her friends' murders for the sympathy it gets her from David?" Arnett asked.

"Something like that." Jo tugged at her necklace.

Arnett slowed for a jay-walking pedestrian. "Spit it out, Fournier."

"There's nothing to spit out because I'm not sure what I'm thinking myself," Jo said.

"But then why didn't she want you to call David?"

"No, absolutely right. I'm looking for something that isn't there." Jo switched gears. "How do you feel about Julia's explanation of the phone call with Naomie?"

"If Naomie didn't tell her, it's because she suspected Julia of stealing the money."

"The more I think about it, the more I think if she did suspect Julia, she'd have been even more likely to tell her. As close as they were, I think she'd want to give her a chance to explain herself before she passed judgment." Her hands flew to her necklace. "Julia's lying to us."

"Seems strange Julia would kill someone she's so close to,

even if it meant going to jail," Arnett said. "But then, we haven't looked too closely at Julia. Maybe she has priors for embezzlement and she's not just looking at a short stretch. Wouldn't be the first person to turn on a good friend when push came to shove."

"It's possible," Jo said. "Because something here isn't sitting right. My internal radar was already up based on both her refusal to take us up on police protection, and on her demeanor, and now it's blaring and flashing red lights."

"You mean the stand-offishness at the memorial service?"

"I'm torn on that, actually. When I put myself in her place, I'm not sure I'd behave any differently. She's got a complicated relationship with the family, and as a health professional, she's also experienced in handling crises in a calm, collected way. She has to compartmentalize those emotions just like we do when we work a crime scene."

"Then what is it?"

"That's just it, I'm not sure." She shook her head and rubbed the bridge of her nose. "It's possible I'm overthinking everything."

Arnett glanced at the clock on the dash. "The team'll pull out the cameras and the footage as soon as the caterers have cleaned up from the event, hopefully something there will clear things up one way or the other. I say sleep on it, and see what your subconscious says in the morning."

Jo stared out the window at the slowing rain. "With Hayes and the press on us, I'm not sure how well I'll sleep until we have our killer. But you're probably right—we should at least try."

———

But after she climbed back into her own car at HQ and watched Arnett drive off, she still hadn't been able to get Julia's lie off her mind.

Which lie? The thought struck like a hidden snake, then echoed through her mind. Was it the slipperiness surrounding Naomie's phone call that was bothering her most? Or the deceit she'd detected when Julia blamed her refusal of police protection on her obligations to her clients? Or was it the very odd vibe she'd picked up whenever Julia dealt with her in-laws?

She'd verified that divorce papers had been filed, and Lopez had discovered several of Julia's credit cards were recently shut down. The divorce—and the rancor surrounding it—were real. And yet, she was still sensing deception around that situation that she couldn't put her finger on.

She shook her head—it made no sense.

Tapping a single nail on her steering wheel, she pulled out of the HQ lot. She needed to get over herself—she wasn't a human lie detector, and she'd been wrong before. But generally when she was wrong, it was because she failed to pick up on someone's deception, or that she was wrong about what exactly they were lying about, and whether that lie was relevant to her case. She'd never thought someone was being deceptive and had it turn out they were being truthful.

Instead of slowing down as she approached the turn to home, she sped up and passed it, instead heading back to Triple-B. She and Arnett had only been gone from the memorial for about fifteen minutes, so the clean-up should still be underway. Julia wouldn't necessarily stay until it was finished, but it wasn't likely she'd bow out without at least helping. Jo drove as quickly as she could without endangering anyone, easing up across the street from the Triple-B lot ten minutes later. She scanned the area— Julia's Mercedes was still there. She pulled into a side street kitty-corner to the building and parked herself in the shadows.

Twenty minutes later Julia emerged, speed walking toward her car as though late for an appointment. Why—and with whom?

Jo waited for Julia's tail lights to disappear around the corner before pulling out to follow. She sped up to cut down the distance between them, but turned at a casual pace onto the street Julia'd taken, staying as far back as she was able without losing sight of the car.

After a short stint on the pike, Julia pulled into the parking lot of a Staples office supply store. Jo selected a spot that allowed her to keep watch on both the store entrance and Julia's car and settled in to wait.

She had several calls to make anyway—perfect time to knock them out.

First, she called Lacey to update her on the investigation. Then, unable to face a call, she texted Hayes, who responded with a mini-rant about how the public was calling DA Barbieri continually with concerns about the safety of pregnant women. Finally, Jo brought up Sophie's contact and put through a call to her.

"Any news?" she asked when Sophie picked up.

"None whatsoever. David said he was going to call you directly," she said, with irritated hesitation.

"You sound strange. Everything okay?" Jo asked.

She blew out a prolonged puff of air. "I'm... confused. It doesn't make sense that Chelsea didn't want you to call David when she collapsed today."

"Yeah, Bob and I were just discussing that," Jo said. "But it's good news, right?"

"It should be," Sophie said. "Except I don't like it when things don't make sense. When people suddenly act out of character, it usually means something else is going on."

Jo smiled to herself—she and her sister had more in common than either liked to admit. "Or it could be that you, for very understandable reasons, are just hypersensitive to her motives right now. She had plenty of people around caring for her, so maybe she figured it didn't make sense to bother him. Or, maybe she realized her plan wasn't working, and gave up on it. Having your two best friends killed can reevaluate your priorities."

"No, that's true," Sophie said with another sigh. "You're probably right."

Julia appeared out of the store's sliding front doors carrying something large and bulky in a plastic bag, still striding like she was late for something. Jo sat up and turned the car back on. "Sorry, Soph, gotta go."

But this time Julia went directly home, to a little duplex with low-maintenance landscaping, flaking paint, and a detached garage she didn't park inside. The vehicle had barely come to a stop before she was out, door slammed behind her, hurrying up the front porch.

As Julia disappeared inside, Jo slid under the shadow of a large maple tree a block down from Julia's driveway. When Julia didn't come out again after several minutes, Jo considered leaving. She was probably wasting her time when she should be sleeping—Julia had probably crawled under her covers and was crying herself to sleep as she tried to process her dearest friend's premature death. But she'd definitely been in a hurry, and had stopped off to make some sort of a purchase, both things that suggested something else was going on. Maybe someone was coming to her house to meet her? She couldn't risk missing whatever it was, so it was worth hanging around a little longer to find out. She fired off a text to Matt updating him on where she was and what she was doing.

She'd barely finished the text when Julia's front door opened again. She emerged, carrying a plastic grocery bag tied in a knot at the top.

Jo hurried to tap open her camera app, then pointed her phone toward Julia trotting quickly across the porch and down her driveway—toward the trash can waiting at the curb for the next morning's pick up.

Jo's heart pounded in her chest. "Put the bag in the trash can—please put the bag in the trash can," she chanted. Because while she'd need a warrant to search inside Julia's house or her property, once the trash was on a public street in a city receptacle, it was legally outside Julia's curtilage. That took away any expectation of privacy, and the bag was fair game for Jo to snatch up. And if Julia urgently needed to be rid of this garbage, Jo urgently needed to see what was inside it.

Julia reached the can, lifted the lid and stuffed the bag inside. Then she returned to the house, glancing back once over each shoulder.

Repressing a yelp of joy, Jo quickly identified herself on the recording and stated the date, time, and place. Then, with the phone still recording, she waited, watching the seconds tick up on the recording counter.

When she'd waited five minutes, she made her move.

As quietly as possible, she got out of the car and closed the door behind her. Sticking to the shadows as much as possible, she strode silently toward Julia's house, camera pointed in front of her. When she reached the garbage can, she cautiously lifted the lid, then angled the camera as she peered inside.

Most of the bags in the can were black garbage bags. Only one, directly on top, matched the bag Julia had been carrying. Jo filmed herself grabbing it—so surprisingly light her hand jerked up when she lifted it—and lowering the lid back down.

Then, with a surge of triumphant adrenaline, she practically pranced back to the car.

CHAPTER FORTY-TWO

Jo flew as quickly as she could back to HQ, feeling like a child on Christmas Eve desperate to find out what Santa'd left in her sack of presents. To distract herself as she drove, she called the Staples Julia had visited and requested a copy of all video footage from the previous hour.

When she burst through the door to the lab, Lopez swerved wildly in her chair, dropping her highlighter as her hands reflexively clenched into fists.

"What the hell?" Jo jumped back from her.

Lopez dropped her fists. "I could ask you the same thing flying in here after hours like the Tasmanian Devil's second coming."

"I didn't expect anybody to be here. And who did you think was coming for you in the middle of a highly fortified law enforcement facility?" Jo said.

Lopez threw her hands onto her hips. "The ones to worry about don't check for badges."

Jo rubbed her brow with her free hand. "Much as I hate to admit it, Arnett and Marzillo might be right. Maybe it's time to cut back on the zombie-shooter games."

Lopez rolled her eyes before dropping her gaze to the bag in Jo's hand. "Whatcha got?"

Jo explained quickly. "So I need a space where I can carefully dump it out and see what's inside."

"Ah, garbage. That's always a good time." Lopez rose and led her to an empty workstation. "We can use this one once I throw some plastic liner over it."

"I don't think it'll be too bad, actually. It's surprisingly light." Jo bounced the bag to illustrate.

Lopez pulled on gloves, then spread the liner over the work table. "Have at it."

Jo set the bag down, pulled on her own gloves, and untied the knot. Then she carefully tilted the bag and pulled out the contents.

Thousands of crumpled white and yellow strips of paper. Which, as she started to pull them apart, seemed to multiply exponentially.

Lopez's eyes widened. "Looks like somebody had herself a shredding party. I guess we know what she needed to pick up at Staples."

Jo stared down at the infinite drifts. "The good news is, people don't shred things just for the fun of it, especially after racing home from a memorial service."

"True story," Lopez said, also staring apprehensively down at the piles. "Have you ever pieced together shredded documents before?"

"I have." Jo nodded slowly. "It's not fun."

"Your talent for understatement remains unrivaled," Lopez said. "It's not fun in the exact same way shoving flaming matches directly into your eyeballs is not fun."

"And, we're going to have to find some way to flatten them first." Jo sucked air in through her teeth. "We should probably just be grateful she bought a strip shredder and not a cross-cut shredder."

"That's what I love about you, Jo," Lopez said, still staring at the piles. "When life hands you a wildfire, you always remember to stop and enjoy the pretty glow."

————

While Jo sent a text telling Arnett what she'd found, Lopez hunted down an iron. "If we set this on a medium heat, it should flatten the paper without discoloring it."

"Won't that degrade any DNA or fingerprints?" Jo asked.

Lopez screwed up her face as she considered. "Fingerprints, definitely. DNA, depends on how hot we get it. My guess is we need to assume it will."

Jo grimaced. "Thank goodness I have a clear recording of her putting the bag into the can, and of me recovering it. How long do you think this will take? Our killer may be planning to strike again as we speak."

"Could be days. We're gonna need to start now, and hustle."

Two hours later, they'd only managed to iron about half the strips. "And we haven't even started matching them up yet," Lopez said, wiping the sweat from her brow with her wrist.

Jo glanced at the clock. "We both need sleep or we'll go cross-eyed. I say we come back and start in on this tomorrow."

"I should be able to get us some extra hands on it tomorrow," Lopez said.

They carefully secured the area, then headed out for the night. When Jo reached home, Matt was just finishing up a glass of wine, about to head for bed. She dropped down next to him on the couch, and reached over for a kiss. "How was your day, my love?"

"Productive. Mostly check-ins with patients, all of whom are progressing well. It's always a good day when that happens." His smile was tired, but proud.

"I'm so glad to hear it, but not at all surprised. You're a miracle worker." She leaned in for another, longer kiss.

"Oh, I almost forgot," Matt said as the kiss finished. "Did David reach you? He's been frantic."

"He's been trying to reach me? I didn't get—" Jo frowned, and pulled out her phone; sure enough, a voice mail was waiting for her. "I stand corrected. He must have called when I was wading through the piles of paper. My phone was on Lopez's desk."

"He said to call back as soon as you can, no matter how late it is."

Jo glanced at the time—almost midnight. "Well, he asked for it."

He picked up before the first ring finished. "Jo. Is Chelsea alright?"

She pushed down her irritation at his demanding tone. "I was going to ask you the same thing."

"Why would you ask me? You're the one who was with her."

"I wasn't with her, I was just there when she collapsed. And she was conscious before she left."

"I assumed you followed her in the ambulance." His words were clipped. "She's not answering her phone."

She paused and took a breath to keep control of her temper —it wasn't her job to watch over his mistress. "No ambulance, the officer assigned to her took her in. And you know how emergency rooms are, David. If you're not bleeding out of your eyes, it's quite a wait. And you're not supposed to have your phone on once they take you back."

He laughed a short, bitter laugh. "You've met Chelsea, right?"

He made a valid point—Chelsea was the sort of person who assumed those types of rules weren't for her.

"Did she say why she didn't want you to call me?" he asked when she didn't respond.

She paused. "She said she'd been bothering you too much."

"That doesn't sound much like her, either," he said. "Can you try calling her? Maybe they'll let her answer a call from the police."

"It's late, David. She's either still in the hospital and shouldn't be answering, or she's in bed and shouldn't be disturbed. I'll check on her in the morning."

"Can't you please just try now? If she's not picking up my call, something's wrong. And with this crazy guy out killing pregnant women, I just—I can't—"

He stopped abruptly, and the emotion in his words punched Jo in the gut. She pictured him, pacing in the living room he rented from Matt, ruffling the hair on the top of his head the way he did when he was agitated. He wasn't just *worried* about Chelsea and the baby—he was terrified. The realization brought up two warring reactions in her: empathetic heartbreak on his behalf and enraged jealousy on her sister's. If he was really done with this girl, why couldn't he wait until morning to hear from her?

Jo pushed away the inappropriate anger; she'd have to deal with it another time. No matter what the motivation, David wasn't wrong to be concerned. "Okay. I'll call you right back."

She hung up the call, then tapped Chelsea's contact. The phone rang twice, then she answered. "Jo?"

"Chelsea. I just got a call from David. He's trying to make sure you're okay. He says he called you?"

"Oh, yeah, right. He called when I was with the doctor and I just now got back." She sounded distracted.

"Is everything okay?" Jo asked.

"He thinks so. The baby's heart is still beating, and he said if it was going to trigger labor, it would've by now. So they sent me home and told me to follow up with my regular ob/gyn tomorrow."

"Do they know why you collapsed?"

"They said the same thing Julia said. Low blood sugar and stress. Oh, and exhaustion."

Jo waited for her to say more, but she remained silent. "Did they do any blood work, anything like that?"

"They always take a sample. I'm not sure what they looked for, though."

Jo's teeth clenched. For someone who normally loved the sound of her own voice, Chelsea was being ridiculously closed-lipped. But Jo was tired, and this wasn't her responsibility—she had a killer to catch. "I'm glad you're feeling better. Can you let David know?"

"I will. I'm sorry he bothered you," she said. "And thank you again for getting me the police protection."

"Let us know if you need anything," Jo said, still off-balance. When Chelsea confirmed she would, Jo hung up.

Matt's brows lifted. "All sorts of family drama."

She rubbed her eyes. "You don't know the half of it. I'm starting to think I'm in *The Twilight Zone*. First Chelsea is calling David every five minutes like a love-sick puppy and it's annoying him and driving Sophie crazy, so Sophie's calling *me* and driving *me* crazy. Now Chelsea *isn't* calling David, and *he's* suddenly the one freaking out that he needs to talk to Chelsea, and now *he's* calling me and driving me crazy. And it's *still* driving Sophie crazy, because she thinks it's just another tactic and she's going all Vizzini trying to figure out what Chelsea's strategy is. And now I'm fully caught up in it, completely obsessing because Sophie's got me questioning it all—why would Chelsea go from calling him constantly to telling me *not* to call him? People don't just one-eighty their behavior like that without a reason."

Matt's brows knit. "She's been through a lot, losing two

friends in as many days, and realizing the killer might be coming after her. Add that on top of the normal stresses of pregnancy and I'm surprised she's still standing."

Jo sighed. "Bob said the same thing, essentially. I'm just losing perspective on all of this. Now that she has the protective detail, she has somebody other than David to rely on, and I'm sure it's just that simple."

"There you go." Matt stood up and held her hand. "So, I say we head up to bed. I'm beat, and I know you are, too."

She took his hand and stood. "You're right. Let's hit the hay."

But as he followed her upstairs, a nagging doubt whispered to her that there was more to Chelsea's about-face than met the eye—and it left her deeply unsettled.

CHAPTER FORTY-THREE

Jo woke early the next morning after a block of dreamless sleep. Wanting to let Matt sleep as long as he could, she showered as quietly as she was able, made a travel mug filled with coffee for herself, and left another on Matt's nightstand with a note telling him to have a good day.

When she got to HQ, Lopez was already there. "How early does a girl have to get up to beat you in?" Jo said with a laugh.

"I only beat you by about ten minutes." She shook the yellow scraps in her hands. "I had a nasty nightmare where these little strips of misery were chasing me through an endless decaying mansion, threading their way around my arms and legs and into my ears and mouth. One even burrowed into my belly button."

Jo threw up a hand and squeezed her eyes shut. "I haven't had nearly enough caffeine to be able to process that."

"Tell me about it." Lopez turned back to the strips of paper. "But tell me while you're helping, because time's a-wastin'. I'm separating out the strips that have nothing on them, and the rest I've been lining up so the writing is in the canonical direction. Then we can try to match up strips with writing in the same locations. The white strips seem to be printed documents, while the yellow contain some sort of handwriting."

Jo pulled on gloves and dove in. Following Lopez's method, they made reasonably fast progress, and by the time Arnett arrived and tracked Jo down, they had most of the strips turned the right way.

"Holy shit." He surveyed the stacks of strips in front of him. "You weren't kidding in your text."

"No, I wasn't." Jo stood up, stretching the kinks out of her neck as she pulled off her gloves. "And I never thought sorting through footage of people standing around at a memorial service would seem like the brighter option for my day."

"Don't forget all the hotline slush we get to wade through," Arnett said.

Jo shook her head. "Still far preferable to this. But I *am* sorry to have to leave you on your own, Christine."

"Not a problem." She shrugged. "As the team trickles in I'll pull in some of the techs to take turns. That'll keep any one of us from going completely insane."

Jo grabbed the mocha Arnett had brought for her and chugged half as they walked to their desks. "And to think when I was a little girl I loved doing jigsaw puzzles."

They spent the next several hours going through the security footage, identifying all the attendees and tracking any suspicious movements. They watched every angle with eagle eyes once Brad showed up; with everyone's attention diverted, the altercation would have been a perfect time for someone to try something unseen. But as far as they could tell, nothing untoward happened.

Once Jo and Arnett escorted the three men outside, Cecile and Fred Gagnon came over to console Chris, then led him back over to where they'd been stationed at the remembrance table. Based on his flailing gestures, it took a fair amount of time before they were able to calm him. Julia shifted to Chelsea's side as soon as the drama began, and didn't leave it until Jo and Arnett were back in the room.

"That's an interesting choice," Arnett said, pointing to Julia. "Was she protecting Chelsea or waiting for some sort of opportunity?"

"Hard to say." Jo squinted at the screen.

After the dynamic returned mostly to normal, Jo tracked the blonde who had claimed to bring the Pellegrino to Chelsea before she collapsed; sure enough, she went to the drinks table, poured herself some coffee from the urn, then opened a new bottle of Pellegrino and poured some into a cup for Chelsea.

"Unless she's related to Penn or Teller, she didn't tamper with the drink," Arnett said.

"No." Jo watched the cup closely as Chelsea stood talking with the girls, checking to be sure nobody dropped something inside it when she wasn't looking. Nobody did.

But Chelsea did begin to shift her weight more frequently, and looked around nervously. One of the women reached out and touched her shoulder, then pointed toward a group of chairs in a corner of the room. Chelsea shook her head and smiled weakly—the woman must have been asking if she needed to sit down.

Then, Chelsea sank to the ground. Smoothly, like her legs were folding under. Her head fell sideways onto her arm.

"Is it just me or was that the most elegant faint you've ever seen in your life?" Jo asked.

"I haven't seen many faints," Arnett said. "But don't prep schools teach you how to do everything swanky? Or, maybe she's got automatic muscle memory from sports. When I played hockey, the first thing they taught us was how not to split open our heads when we slipped on the ice."

Jo winced at the visual. "You're probably right. I can't see the point of her faking it when she didn't want me to call David."

Arnett pointed his pen at her. "Unless she's one of those Munchausen people, the ones who pretend they're sick to get sympathy. Maybe she knew she was pushing the line too far with David, but couldn't resist getting all that attention from all the people at the memorial."

Jo's brows bounced up. "That's possible. Really likely, actually."

"Don't sound so surprised," Arnett laughed. "I manage to say smart things every now and then."

"Sorry." Jo squeezed her eyes shut. "I didn't mean it like that. I just meant I've been driving myself crazy trying to come up with an explanation of what's going on with her, but nothing makes sense. That does. But it has a new name, now, right? Factitious disorder, something like that?"

He shrugged. "Search me."

"And the streak ends," Jo joked.

Nothing else happened for the remainder of the service. As the guests left, Julia made her way over to her brother- and sister-in-law; they turned to her as she approached, not in a hostile fashion, but not warm, either. They had a small exchange that, based on gazes and gestures, seemed to involve offers to help clean up. Julia shook her head repeatedly, at which point Cecile, Fred and Chris left. Julia remained and, with the help of Sandra and Janelle, restored the room to its previous state. Then, Julia, now in her overcoat and with her satchel over her shoulder, exited out to the office area of Triple-B.

Jo checked the time stamp. "That's fifteen minutes before she left the building and I followed her home. What was she doing for fifteen minutes?"

"Could be taking care of some final errands before she left for the day. Like picking up some documents she needed to shred," Arnett said.

Jo jabbed her pen in the air toward him. "Why not just

shred them at the office? They must have a shredder there, and that would have saved her the expense of buying one."

"She probably figured we'd be snatching up the contents of all the shredders, which our guys did. And maybe some of the documents she needed to shred were back at her house anyway." Arnett glanced at his watch. "How is it already three? No wonder I'm hungry. I can't face those hotline tips until I get some food."

"Perfect. We can pick up the security footage from Staples on the way."

An hour later they hunkered down into their desks with meatball grinders. After verifying Julia had in fact bought a shredder from Staples, they settled into a rhythm of writing down the new hotline messages and triaging them in order of priority. Then, as the sun went down, they worked their way down the list in turn, following up where possible. Several people claimed to have seen either Naomie or Madison out walking, but when questioned, the timing or other details didn't match up. Several more claimed to have found evidence of Satanic cults around the areas in question, but when contacted, that evidence turned out to be unrelated.

When they were two-thirds of the way down the list, Jo's phone rang.

"It's Philby PD." She shot Arnett a confused look, then picked up. "Jo Fournier."

A young male voice came over the line. "Detective Fournier, I'm Officer Stanton of the Oakhurst PD. We have a murdered pregnant woman next to a culvert we think you need to see."

———

The culvert in question was tucked behind a strip mall on the outskirts of Oakhurst, next to a claustrophobic road cloaked in darkness. Jo and Arnett screeched to a stop, adding their head-lights to the illumination of the squad car waiting there; Janet Marzillo and her team followed closely behind. Two officers stood by the side of the road with a medium-height, thirty-some-thing black man huddled against the cold in a thin silver blan-ket, while the perimeter of crime-scene tape was monitored by a burly, dark-haired white man Jo quickly identified as Officer Stanton.

"What do we know so far?" Jo asked.

Stanton jutted his chin toward the man with the other offi-cers. "Wesley Williams came looking for his girlfriend, Helen Jackson. Every Wednesday after her prenatal exercise class she picks up food from Panda Express on her way home."

Jo exchanged a look with Arnett at the mention of a prenatal class.

"After class she texted to say she was on the way to get the food," Stanton continued, "but never made it home. After an hour and a half, when she didn't pick up his call or answer his texts, he came looking for her, worried that she'd gone into premature labor or had some sort of emergency. He found her car in the lot, but she wasn't in the restaurant or any of the other stores, so he searched the area. He found these clothes, along with her purse and phone, and immediately called us." Stanton pointed to a pile of objects. "He continued to search while he was on the phone with us, and discovered her at the bottom of the dip, near the culvert."

"Damn." Jo's throat tightened. The only thing possibly worse than losing the woman you loved and your unborn child was finding their bodies yourself. "We'd better go have a look."

Stanton pointed down. "That way, just out of sight. You'll see my partner as soon as you start down."

Joined by Marzillo and Peterson, Jo and Arnett hurried into protective gear, then headed down the bank of the small man-made ravine. Where it ended at a large drainage pipe, another officer guarded a large swath of cement adjoining the slowly flowing water.

Behind him, a petite, light-skinned black woman lay naked, her tight, black curls swept upward, away from her head, her arms crossed over her chest. Her throat had been savagely slashed, and a familiar knife protruded from her belly. As before, the Sigil of Lucifer was painted on her body in what looked like her own blood.

Rage and frustration erupted in Jo's chest, threatening to derail her. She took a series of deep breaths, struggling to keep herself calm and cool enough to evaluate the scene effectively.

"This location is mere feet away from a shopping area," she said when she'd pushed the emotion down. "Out of sight, yes, but very different from the kills set deep into the woods. Why?"

Arnett instantly met her train of thought. "Maybe he had to. We've warned pregnant women there's a killer on the loose, particularly in wooded parks."

Jo squinted toward the top of the culvert. "Why not just wait? I don't think I've ever heard of a serial killer who appears suddenly and kills three victims in one week."

Arnett rubbed his chin with his wrist. "Maybe they were killing somewhere else and relocated."

"We'd know if other pregnant women were being killed like this, wouldn't we?" Peterson asked. "Someone would have contacted us."

"He might have changed his MO to help cover his tracks, but I tend to agree—we'd have found any pregnant women showing up dead with any methodology as soon as we started checking," Jo said.

"Ted Bundy went on a killing rampage after escaping prison for the second time," Marzillo said. "Maybe it's someone who escalated while being locked up."

"It's possible," Jo said. "But if you know the police are actively searching for you, wouldn't you be more careful, not less? Go deeper into the woods rather than risk being seen by anyone who walks up to the edge? And what about the clothes?" She pointed up to the edge. "Why leave them up there where someone's almost guaranteed to stumble on them? Why not put them down near the body?"

"This late at night, back behind the buildings, I'm not sure how many people would stumble on them," Arnett said. "But your point is well taken. There must be a reason why our killer chose to do it that way. What are you thinking?"

Jo raked her lower lip with her teeth. "I'm not sure. But I also think what we're not seeing here is just as important as what we are. No impromptu altars. No candles—"

"And there's been a blow to the head." Marzillo pointed to an area of Helen's hairline, just above her ear. "See the swelling? And if you look closely, here, there's a scrape that mimics the shape of the swelling."

"So she was hit with some sort of object?" Jo asked.

"That would be my guess. It's possible she could have sustained an injury in that location from falling, but it would have been an extremely awkward fall," Marzillo answered.

"Our theory before was the women were subdued some-how, either with some sort of drug or at gunpoint," Jo said. "So maybe Helen had heard about the murdered pregnant women and decided to fight back?"

"Why not fight back right away, then?" Arnett pointed up. "In front of the restaurant where people might be able to help?"

"Could be she didn't realize what was happening. If what you've heard is women are getting murdered in the woods and someone pulls a gun on you in a parking lot, you'd think you're just getting robbed," Peterson said.

"But then he pulls her down here, and she realizes it's going to be more than that, so she fights," Jo said. "Could that contu-sion be from the butt of a gun?"

Marzillo peered back down at Helen's head. "It's consistent with that possibility."

"What about the baby figurine? Is she holding one?" Jo asked.

Marzillo pulled the clasped hands up and apart, revealing a king cake baby identical to the other two they'd found. "No rigor whatsoever, which fits with the time frame Stanton gave us."

"Okay, so," Jo said, forcing herself not to pace. "Our killer picked a different location, most likely because they didn't have a better option. They left off the ceremonial trappings, likely for the same reason. Helen wasn't one of the women who hung out with Madison and Naomie, which means they most likely had to branch out since we've got Chelsea under police protection and Julia isn't pregnant. They also weren't able to get Helen to go quietly, the way they did with the others, but still went through with it all despite the risk. What does that tell us?"

"They were obsessed," Peterson said.

"Or they had some reason why the murder had to take place tonight," Arnett said, hand in the air signaling he was trying to think. "From the start we assumed our killer latched on to Lucifer Lost to shift blame. But what if we're exactly wrong? What if this is some sort of three-part ritual that needs to be completed within a certain period of time? Either by actual Lucifer Lost or some psycho obsessed with Lucifer Lost?"

Jo nodded. "Okay, let's follow it through. We've been working with several theories. One is a fully random serial killer just looking to kill pregnant women—but most likely they'd go elsewhere or wait until it was safe to kill again. Our second theory is Travis or one of his associates from The Velvet Volcano is using the Lucifer Lost trappings to get rid of women who are problematic. That could create time pressure, too, if Helen was about to go to the police or some such," Jo said.

"So we need to find out if Helen has any connection to The Velvet Volcano," Arnett said.

"What about the embezzled money?" Marzillo asked. "Was Helen one of the other women who had a second grant taken out in her name?"

"Not according to the documents Naomie had on her, but that doesn't mean she didn't know something about it." Jo stared down at Helen's slack, frightened face. "So in addition to finding out if she's connected to The Volcano, we need to find out if she's associated with Triple-B, and if so, whether she got a grant from them." She started walking back toward the hill. "And we need to talk to the boyfriend asap."

CHAPTER FORTY-FOUR

But Wesley Jackson couldn't tell them where exactly Helen had attended prenatal class. She went to several different places for several different services; he'd lost his job as a restaurant manager during the pandemic and was struggling to find another, so money was tight and her medical insurance was limited. Helen hadn't had any issues with anyone following or harassing her, or any enemies that he knew of. He didn't recognize any of the other women's names, but that didn't mean Helen hadn't known them. She worked an unpaid internship, and spent her evenings with him—he'd have known if she was working at a strip club.

As Jo and Arnett strode back toward the buildings of the strip mall, she pulled out her phone and placed a call to Sandra at Triple-B.

"Helen Jackson?" Sandra answered Jo's question. "Yes, she's a client here. Why?"

"Did you hold classes today, or were you closed due to Naomie's passing?"

"We considered closing, but decided Naomie would want us to stay open for the sake of the clients. We scaled back our services, though, while we work out how to manage now that Naomie is..."

Jo saved her from struggling to find the right words, and zoned in on the implication. "I don't know much about non-profits. How will that work? Can they hire someone else to fill in, or does whoever takes over need to be vetted by the board?"

"That's part of what they're trying to work out. But for now, Julia and Rhea are covering as much as they can."

Jo made a mental bookmark for that and returned to her original topic. "Was Helen one of the people who attended your prenatal class today?"

"I'm not sure. We have two, one at five and one at seven. I do remember seeing her today, though."

"Did she know Naomie or Madison? Or Chelsea and Julia?"

"I'm sure she's met Naomie, all of our clients did, and since Julia teaches most of our classes, I'd assume she knows her, too. I can't say regarding Madison or Chelsea." Her tone rose. "You're using past tense. Is Helen okay?"

Jo stopped walking, and explained as quickly and diplomatically as she was able. "I have two important favors to ask you. First, is there some way you can send out another email blast to all your employees and clients asking if anyone knows or saw anything out of the ordinary today, especially regarding Helen?" She dictated the number of the tip line.

"Of course. I'll send it now."

"Thank you. The second is, can you look into Helen's accounts and make sure there's nothing strange going on with her grant applications or anything else?"

"I can double-check first thing in the morning." She sounded doubtful. "But I've already been going over everything since we found the other discrepancies. There's not really any other way Helen or any other client could have accessed money they weren't entitled to."

"I understand. Thank you so much." Jo disconnected the call and stared up at Arnett. "So that's three people associated with Triple-B. No way is that a coincidence."

Arnett nodded. "But are we looking at a killer inside the ranks of Triple-B, or outside of it?"

Jo shook her head and tapped on Chelsea's contact. When Chelsea picked up, Jo dove straight in.

"Helen Jackson," Chelsea said. "No, that doesn't sound familiar to me. Maybe we were in class together or something but we never hung out."

Jo thanked her and hung up the phone. "Dammit, dammit, dammit."

"What? This narrows things down considerably," Arnett said as he swung into a turn. "Helen didn't have a personal connection to the other women, and she wasn't involved in the money issue. Her boyfriend is sure she wasn't a stripper. That leaves us with an obsessed psycho stalking Triple-B, looking for pregnant women to kill. Now that we know what kind of monster we're working with and where to look, we'll catch him in no time."

"Something's not right. It doesn't fit—something doesn't fit. This murder just doesn't mesh with the other two. Unless—" Jo cropped one of the pictures she'd taken at the crime scene so it only included Helen's face. "We need to verify she didn't work at The Volcano. I'm sending this to Hailey. She'll know if Helen worked there."

The text came back within a minute—Hailey hadn't ever met Helen at The Volcano or elsewhere.

"Dammit," Jo said again. "I don't understand."

"I don't understand what you don't understand," Arnett said. "That clinches it, and now we know where to point our resources. Lopez will have the phone shortly and will find any other connection that exists." He pointed to the shops in the strip mall. "Meantime we canvas these stores and check out their security footage. If he intercepted her coming or going into the restaurant, somebody saw something or caught something on film. Worse comes to worst, we at least have options now. We can even send someone in to Triple-B undercover to pretend to be a pregnant client and try to trap him that way."

"Right. Let's get on it," she said gruffly.

"No, hold up." Arnett grabbed her arm as she passed. "Talk to me."

"I don't know." Jo rubbed her eyes again. "The logical part of my brain says that there's clearly only one answer here—a serial killer who's stalking women in Beautiful Bouncing Babies. But the rest of my brain is screaming *that makes no sense*. Multiple murders in just a few days is generally a spree killer with a personal motive, not a serial killer unknown to the victims. And the trappings at the scene—why go to all the trouble to build the altars and paint strange symbols, then suddenly abandon most of that? And the choices he's making— leaving the phones on, leaving the clothes on the bank where anyone can see them—it's almost like he's trying to get caught. Nothing is lying right, and I feel like a child that's being taught to repeat a poem without understanding what the words mean."

"I hear you," Arnett said. "But we've done solid work to bring us to this point, and we're narrowing in on him. We need to trust this is getting us where we need to go."

"Right," she said, and started toward the buildings again. "But it better get us where we need to go fast, because this guy is killing at a furious pace and doesn't show any sign of stopping."

CHAPTER FORTY-FIVE

Jo pushed down her frustration and tried to put her faith in canvassing the strip mall. The grocery store had a video of Helen's car driving past the front of their store, the camera didn't extend far enough to show where she eventually parked, but Panda Express's had no video of her.

"She must never have made it into the restaurant," Arnett said.

"That suggests our killer was waiting for her rather than following her," Jo said. "He must have known her schedule, which makes sense—her boyfriend said she picked up the food every Wednesday, it was their special treat. Chelsea said the guy she thought was watching them was in a dark sedan, so I say we go back an hour before she was due and pull plates for any dark sedans that drive through the parking lot."

Four cars matched that description, and Jo was able to capture visible plate numbers for each. They self-eliminated almost immediately—one was driven by a seventy-five-year-old woman, another by an eighty-year-old man who walked with a cane, and the last belonged to a woman who showed up with her three children on the grocery store's interior footage just minutes after her car parked.

Eyewitnesses didn't fare much better. Nobody saw anything suspicious—no lurking men, or even multiple people walking through the parking lot at the same time. The only eyewitness who even remembered seeing a light-skinned black woman reported she wasn't alone, but was walking and talking happily with a friend.

Just before midnight, Lopez appeared at their desk, eyes bloodshot and weary. "I'm heading out before my eyes fall out of my head. Just wanted to update you that I found zero-zip-zilch that was helpful on Helen's phone. No contact with Chelsea, Madison, Julia, or Naomie directly, although she does have past calls to Beautiful Bouncing Babies. Her location tracking confirms she went to Triple-B each Monday and Wednesday from five to six, and then on to Panda Express every Wednesday. Nothing to connect her to The Velvet Volcano, including location tracking. Unless she left her phone behind when she worked, she's got nothing to do with the place. And I've got two people on the paper puzzle, but it's slow going."

"Thanks. I appreciate it. Hopefully piecing them together isn't just a huge waste of everyone's time." Jo rubbed her face with both hands, as though she could rub away her frustration. "It's looking more and more like a serial killer who has nothing to do with the stolen money or with The Volcano, except maybe as a place where he first caught sight of Madison."

Lopez's head tilted, and she plopped herself on the corner of Jo's desk. "You okay? It's not like you to give up on any lead, however small."

Jo forced a smile. "I'm okay, I just can't shake the feeling we're missing something important, and the more I try to figure out what, the more my brain shuts down. And since there could be another dead woman by sun up, I've been pushing myself as hard as I can."

She stood and grabbed her blazer. "But, it's clearly to the point now where it's counterproductive, so I'm going to follow your lead by going home, getting some sleep, and allowing my subconscious time to connect whatever dots it's trying to string together."

Lopez held out her fist for a bump. "And we'll come back in the morning and dive into everything, and we won't stop until we've got ourselves a killer."

———

Deep sleep pulled Jo under the moment her head hit the pillow. But when she woke the next morning, her subconscious hadn't come to any new conclusions—the voice from the back of her head was agonizingly silent as she showered and yawned over her Moka pot.

Her phone chimed a notification as she pulled open the door to HQ, causing her to wince—Hayes would be calling at some point to chew her out, and she wasn't sure she could face it without more coffee. Tempted as she was to ignore it, she paused to check it as Arnett appeared behind her.

"Oh, thank God," she said. "It's just Lopez asking us to come to the lab."

Arnett smiled and shook his head, well aware why she was relieved.

Lopez greeted them with a broad smile, practically bouncing with excitement.

"Either you have good news, or someone left you a free case of Rockstars." Jo laughed.

"You owe me one after this." Lopez jumped out of her chair, snatched a narrow piece of yellow paper off her desk with her gloved hand, and held it up for them to view. "It's not a full sheet yet, but it's enough for a go-directly-to-jail card."

Jo stepped closer, careful not to touch. As she did, she realized it wasn't a single piece of paper, but a number of strips that had been matched up and taped together. Not one of the white documents as she'd been hoping for, but rather one of the yellow legal-pad sheets.

Madison Coelho's signature was scrawled repeatedly across the page.

"Well, well, well," Arnett said. "Looks like Julia's learning a new skill."

"We have the beginnings of several other sheets as well, and while it's too early to tell, they look like they're signatures, too. My guess is that the other documents in the bag are related. Probably whatever she used to prep the forged docs."

"I *knew* she was hiding something." Hope surged back up through Jo. "Nurse Julia lied to us, repeatedly. That ends now."

CHAPTER FORTY-SIX

As they pulled into Julia's driveway, she appeared through the door, carrying a satchel and a travel mug. She stopped dead in her tracks when she spotted them, her face leaking fear before she pulled on a concerned expression.

"Detectives," she said when they stepped out of the car. "I'd ask you in, but I'm on my way to class. I heard there was another murder last night. Helen Jackson?"

Jo nodded solemnly. "Yes. Did you know her?"

She nodded and drew in a sad breath. "She was a student in a few of my classes. Lamaze and prenatal."

"Were you friendly with her?"

"As friendly as I am with any student."

"But not outside of class," Arnett said.

"No." Her eyes narrowed slightly. "Do you need to know my alibi?"

"Yes." Jo made no effort to soften the request, or her expression.

Julia's eyes widened in surprise as Jo's tone landed. She stiffened. "For what time?"

"After your five o'clock exercise class last night."

"After class I grabbed some of the leftover food we have from the memorial for my dinner, then took care of emails at Triple-B until my seven o'clock class. After that class, I left around eight-thirty and went to a client meeting, which lasted until about ten-thirty. Then I came home."

"We'll need the name and address of the client," Jo said.

Julia's eyes flashed, and her lips tightened into a fierce line. "Is it really necessary to bother her?"

"Yes. We also need to know if anyone can verify you stayed at Triple-B between six and seven," Arnett said.

Julia's eyes flicked between them. "I—I took the food back into the classroom. But someone may have seen me in the break room. I can ask around."

"We'll take care of that. In the meantime, we have something we need to show you." Jo lifted her phone so Julia could see the display, a picture of the pieced-together signatures.

Julia's gaze shot out to the street, left and right, then she met Jo's eyes. "You'd better come inside."

————

Jo scanned the interior as Julia led them to the living room. Stacked moving boxes lined the wall of the entryway, and more lurked in the corner of the living room. The walls were undecorated but the spaces were orderly, with none of the transitory chaos Jo hated about moving into a new home—except for the new paper shredder sitting in the center of the living room, next to its newly opened box.

No wonder Julia hadn't wanted to invite them in.

She also didn't invite them to sit down. She turned, arms crossed over her chest. "You went through my trash."

"*Went through* is strong—you left the bag on top of your trash," Jo said.

"Ironic." Julia dropped the satchel from her shoulder to the floor. "I didn't have the money to rent the place I wanted, which had a fireplace. If I'd had a fireplace, we wouldn't be having this conversation right now."

"So you admit the paper is yours?" Arnett asked. "That you were practicing forging signatures of Triple-B clients on fraudulent grant applications?"

She gestured toward Jo's phone. "I don't see the point in denying it. Are you going to arrest me?"

"We may. But at the moment, we need to hear why you did it and what lengths you took to cover it up," Jo said.

Julia dropped into a tan armchair, arms still tucked tightly around her. "You know I'm getting divorced. You know it's not amicable. I'm sure you've looked into all of my financial records, so you know how little I make working for a non-profit and with clients who usually can't afford to pay me. What you don't know is I was too stupid to see the divorce coming, and started stashing money away far later than I should have."

"You make enough to survive," Arnett said.

She nodded, and held his eyes. "Living in squalor, yes. But I've spent the last twenty years of my life living a certain type of lifestyle, and while I don't expect to maintain designer dresses and vacations in Turks and Caicos, I'm not willing to go back to roach-infested apartments and ramen noodles. I just want a warm house in a safe neighborhood with a car that doesn't break down every other week. And the ability to retire somewhere down the road." She threw a hand up to stop what he was about to say. "And, yes, I could go work for another company or with wealthy clients, but I don't want to do that and I shouldn't have to. I just want what I'm entitled to for the work I put into helping build the Gagnon empire. But until the court settles that alimony, I need to survive."

"You want to help these women, but you have no problem stealing from them?"

Julia sat forward and threw up a single finger. "Wait just a minute. First of all, I fully intend to pay back every cent, in some form. Second, it isn't stealing from *them*. That grant runs from January first to December thirty-first and if the money isn't all used, it goes back to NIH. It's a use-it-or-lose-it situation, and we're almost to the end of the year."

"Doesn't the money returned to NIH go back into next year's pot?" Jo asked. "So you're just delaying the impact."

"That depends. Next year it may go to fund research investigating the mating habits of the midwestern iguana. And, yes, I'm really okay with diverting money away from *that*."

"Until your alimony is settled," Jo said. "When will that be?"

"You can't ever know how these things are going to go." Julia stared off toward her kitchen.

Jo's mind flew back to Julia's glance up and down the street, and her sudden willingness to let them inside. "Your husband's investigating you. He's looking for grounds to get out of spousal support."

Julia nodded, face blank, and didn't speak.

Certain she'd hit on something important, Jo pushed. "He wouldn't spend that sort of money without reason. What's he hoping to find?"

"Ask him." She crossed her hands in her lap.

But Jo was now familiar with this version of Julia—she was deflecting. "I'm asking *you*. And not so much *asking* as giving you a chance to come clean. Because from where we're standing, it's highly probably that the person who forged those forms tried to cover it up by murdering Madison, Naomie, and Helen."

"I could never—" Julia's face and neck went white, and her brow knit. "How would killing Helen cover it up?"

Part of what had been bothering Jo came together in a rush. "Helen's murder was different in important ways. We believe it was conceived and executed *after the fact* to distract attention away from the real motive for the first two murders."

Julia's eyes flicked frantically from Jo's face to Arnett's, who did a masterful job of not showing surprise at Jo's novel pronouncement. "For fuck's sake, it was only *six thousand* dollars. Why would I murder someone over that?"

"Six thousand dollars that could land you in jail. And apart from the fact we've just established you're not crazy about the idea of downgrading your lifestyle, that would severely undermine your reputation, end your career, and give your husband excellent character evidence to take into a divorce court."

Julia's eyes dropped, and her voice came out barely above a whisper. "I would never have hurt Naomie. I'd rather go to jail for the rest of my life. I'd rather somebody murder *me*."

Jo squatted down in front of her, trying to reestablish eye contact. "Then I need you to tell me the truth. All of it. What is your husband trying to get on you?"

Julia's head bobbed in an involuntary nod. "Adultery. He's looking for proof I cheated, because that would violate our prenuptial agreement."

Jo knew the answer before she asked the question. "Did you?"

Julia hesitated a moment, then nodded.

A few more pieces fell into place. "And you're still seeing him. That's why you didn't want the policeman assigned to you, because what you were doing would come out."

She nodded again. "And that's where I really was last night. With my boyfriend. But I didn't kill anybody. And if I were going to kill someone to cover it up, I'd've—" Her jaw snapped shut.

"You would have what?"

She pulled her arms tighter around her, and shook her head. "I'd have killed Rhea, too. Because she knew what I was doing."

CHAPTER FORTY-SEVEN

"Rhea knew you were forging the grant disbursements?"

"Of course. Nothing happens to a penny of Triple-B money without her knowing about it."

"She said Janelle handled the disbursements, and she just signed off."

Julia choked out a laugh, and some color returned to her face. "You think with only ten eligible clients she wasn't aware of every single application and every single approval? She could spout off everything each of our clients have been approved for and how much of our funding was involved, probably with exact dates attached."

There was a ring of truth to her words. "Why would she allow you to steal?"

Without a word, Julia stood up and left the room. Jo shot a look at Arnett—should they follow her?—but the footsteps U-turned before Jo could start down the hall.

Julia thrust a folder of papers at them. Jo took it and opened it—receipts and reimbursement requests.

"She was padding her expense account. Submitting requests with supposedly lost and altered receipts. And while

Rhea signed off on everyone else's requests, for obvious reasons, Naomie was supposed to sign off on Rhea's—but Rhea was forging the signatures. I found out by accident, when I borrowed one of her legal pads to write a quick note. I noticed there was ghosting from the last thing she wrote, and I could see enough to see some sort of repeating pattern. So I did that thing, you know, where you shade the paper with pencil to make the indentation stand out? It was Naomie's signature, over and over and over."

"So you blackmailed her," Jo said.

"*Blackmail* is strong," she said, mimicking Jo's earlier wording. "She begged me not to tell. Claimed that with the current inflation she was struggling, especially because her mother is on a fixed income. Claimed she'd pay it back when she could. I told her that was fine, but that I needed money right now, too, and that if it was okay for her in the short term, it needed to be okay for me, too."

"And she agreed to look the other way on the applications you sent through," Jo said.

Julia stared down at the floor, and nodded. "And she removed the initial applications from the files."

"So when Naomie called you about the fraud, what did you say?"

She continued to stare at the floor, and her voice came out as a whisper. "I had no idea what to say. Looking back, I wish I'd just come clean to her. But since Madison was already dead..."

"You told her Madison must have been stealing the money," Jo finished for her. "And then you warned Rhea that Naomie was looking into it all."

Julia's head snapped up, and her eyes pleaded with Jo. "I know how it sounds. Yes, I cheated on my husband, and, yes, I took money that wasn't mine. But I would never, ever kill anyone over any of it. Naomie was closer to me than anyone in the world except Rick—like my best friend, my sister, and my daughter rolled into one." Tears overflowed her eyes, and she dissolved into jerks of fierce sobs. "She and that baby were the only family I had left."

———

Above Julia's sobbing head, Jo signaled to Arnett that she needed to talk to him outside.

"What's up?" Arnett asked once out of earshot. "I'm surprised you don't want to just bring her in."

"I'm not sure there's any point right now, since an attorney will have her out on bail within hours for the embezzlement. If she's our killer, that's not going to stop her."

"So you like her for it?"

"I'm not sure." Jo's hand flew to her necklace. "Her emotions seemed genuine, and I wasn't picking up that same sense that she was lying at the end. But she did lie to us right up until we shoved proof of the forgery right under her nose, and that sort of liar only admits what they have to."

"Agreed. And if she's our killer, that answers a lot of questions. All of the women would have trusted her, not one would've thought twice about following her into the forest for whatever reason she made up. And she has the medical knowledge to kill them quickly and efficiently."

That reminded Jo of the satchel Julia was carrying. "Don't certified nurse midwives administer pain medications and such during home births? That would explain how she knocked them out."

"She'd have access to them, at least." Arnett scratched his chin. "Nice call you made about Helen's murder being a distraction, by the way. Makes sense why it was so hurried and incomplete."

Jo nodded acknowledgment. "So if her only alibi is a

boyfriend, she doesn't have a solid alibi for any of the three murders. And it wouldn't have been hard to kill Helen and be back at Triple-B in an hour if she followed her after class."

"Easy enough to make some excuse to get her over behind the buildings," Arnett said. "Claim her car was broken down or something, then push her over into the ravine."

"Two issues. One, I have no problem picturing her killing an adult, but I do struggle to imagine her killing a baby. Or even stabbing one that's already dead, frankly," Jo said. "Second, we don't have any proof. We should be able to get a search warrant based on the embezzling evidence, but I'm not convinced we'll find anything. That may be why Helen's scene was so different —she may not have anticipated needing the candles and such if it was a last-minute decision."

"No reason not to try," Arnett said.

"Absolutely. But I also think we should hedge our bets. I think the best shot we have at connecting her to the murders is to put her under surveillance. I think given the sensitive nature of the victims and all the pressure Hayes is getting from Barbieri and the public, she shouldn't have a problem approving it given the embezzlement evidence."

"Agreed. I'll call right now."

As Jo listened to the conversation over speakerphone, a text came through her own phone. Once Arnett verified the arrangements would be in place by the evening, she checked it. "Lopez wants us to come see her as soon as we can."

"No time like the present." Arnett climbed into the car and fired up the engine.

———

Almost before they crossed the threshold into Lopez's office, she jumped up to greet them, buzzing with manic energy.

"I'm sensing good news," Jo said.

"My system is overcompensating for sleep deprivation. I hope it's good news, though." Lopez flicked a hand at her desk. "You know how we said we were going to start fresh today, go back over everything and hope something we've learned in the meantime will make something pop out?"

Jo's hopes bumped up a notch. "Something popped out?"

"A whole big load of nothing, nada, zip. So I figured I'd try looking at it all a new way. I reorganized everything chronologically, and looked at everything I had about everyone hour by hour over the last week."

"I'm not sure what you mean," Arnett said.

"I pulled everything up, either on my monitors, phone, or via printouts, and laid it all out. Then, starting exactly one week before Madison was found murdered, I went over everything hour by hour. So, I looked at the emails Madison sent in that hour, the calls she made, the emails Naomie sent, etc. That way I had a picture of what exactly was going on with everyone at the same time, and I wrote out a summary for each hour as I went."

Jo leaned forward. "Can I get a copy?"

"Of course you can, but hold your damned horses," Lopez said.

Jo held up her hands and laughed. "Sorry. I should have known better."

"One of the things I included was the cell phone pings for both Madison and Naomie." She slid forward two stacks of papers, stapled and folded to her target page, where a line was highlighted. "This cell phone tower is the one closest to Naomie's house, here." She pointed to a map on the side of her main desk. "Then, at quarter to five, the phone starts pinging off this tower, here."

"On the east side of the park. So she was far enough in the park by that point for her phone to use another tower." Jo's brows creased. "You said it switched at four forty-five? But she hadn't left for the park by that time."

Lopez smiled triumphantly, then pointed at the second stack of papers. "Her cell phone feels differently. According to the pings, she didn't text her husband that she was going for a walk until she was already *well into the park*."

CHAPTER FORTY-EIGHT

Julia prided herself on always being ready for life to turn on a dime. But after finally spending an evening hidden away in the emotional fall-out shelter of Rick's sister's apartment, curled up in his arms, having the detectives show up at her door the next morning was like being plunged into an ice-filled lake.

She tried to go on with her day as though their visit hadn't happened, a trick she'd always used when life threw massive piles of shit at her. When her father died, when her mother died, when she couldn't afford to support herself, when the preeclampsia with Ethan had almost killed her; each and every time she'd picked herself up and just pretended it never happened. Shoved the inconvenient emotions into a mental deep freeze and did whatever she would have done otherwise. Completed the next task, took the next step, got the next job done. Naomie once told her it sounded an awful lot like denial. Julia had laughed and told her to call it whatever she wanted, because it'd worked extremely well her whole life.

Until now.

She taught her morning class, and while the exercises normally cleared her mind, today it only opened up a vacant space where Detective Fournier's face loomed in front of her. *They're coming for you*, her mother's voice kept telling her. *It's only a matter of time*. It took all her focus to ignore the voice and scrape her anxiety and anguish back into their sealed box.

Then, after class, she got another text.

> *Disappointed you haven't called when you know I want to see you. We need to talk.*

The emotions roared out of that sealed box and knocked through her like a tidal wave. Not just the emotions from the last few days, but from all the difficult, ugly situations she'd had to face in her life. And all the consequences of every choice she'd made, along with everything she currently had to lose. Which really boiled down to Rick, the first man to really love her. She'd give anything to go back and change those decisions, make all of this go away. But it was way too late for that. A reckoning was coming, and for once in her life she had no idea how to handle it.

She stared down at the text, at his whiny ass making demands of her just like he used to do, caring only about himself, with no regard for everything she was going through, and no sense of proportion about what was real. He was a fucking bacterium that no antibiotic could kick.

She grabbed one of the classroom pillows and screamed into it, at the top of her lungs, until she couldn't scream anymore. It didn't help, not in any real way, but it took the edge off, enough that she could put back a veneer of self-control.

She picked the phone up and texted him back. *I have the police on my back, Pete on my back, and clients I have to think of. If I step one foot out of line, I'm done. You need to understand that.*

His response came quickly. *Why are the police on your back?*

For a moment she wanted to scream again. Then, something inside of her released, like a popping balloon, and fatigue seeped into every cell and system of her body. She didn't have the energy to explain it all to him. She didn't have the energy to tiptoe around his volatile ego.

She glanced at the clock—she didn't have the time, either. She needed to leave immediately if she was going to make her scheduled client check-up. On another day she might have just canceled it, but if she didn't keep putting one foot in front of the other and doing what she needed to do, she'd lose her last, tenuous grasp on order and reality and she'd spiral completely out of control.

She forced her thumbs to type out a simple response: *I'll call you when I can.*

Then she hefted up her bag and trudged to the door. If that response wasn't enough for him—tough shit.

CHAPTER FORTY-NINE

"Are you sure there's not a mistake?" Jo asked. "Some fault in the cell tower system that relayed the signal over there rather than the tower closest to Naomie's house?"

"It's possible, but unlikely." Lopez tapped on the map again. "Especially since if something like that happened, this tower here would've been the one to take over based on proximity."

"Maybe Naomie just forgot to text him before she left for the walk," Arnett said.

"God knows I forget to text Matt all the time," Jo agreed.

"Except look at the wording," Lopez said.

Jo studied the text again. *Had a stressful day, can't seem to shake it. Gonna go for a walk to re-center. Shepherd's pie needs an hour in the oven, pull it out if I'm not back.*

"No, you're right, she wouldn't have worded it this way if she were already in the park," Jo said. "It says she's *gonna go* for a walk, not that she *went* for a walk to help her re-center."

"But the ping shows she *was* already in the park at that point." Lopez stroked her ponytail.

Jo's hand flew to her necklace. "You don't think she sent the text."

Lopez shook her head. "I do not."

"That's a leap," Arnett said. "Simpler explanation is she didn't want him to realize she forgot to text before she left. Maybe that's an issue they had in their marriage, her forgetting things like that. She might not have wanted to deal with the fight if so."

Jo shook her head. "Except that doesn't fit with the timing of the dinner. A standard-sized shepherd's pie takes half an hour in the oven when fresh, an hour when frozen. So it had to have been frozen, and there's no way she'd tell him to cook it longer than that. If she was trying to mislead, she would have cut the cooking time down."

Arnett held up a hand in surrender. "Not gonna argue with the cooking expert. So, what, we think the killer sent the text?"

"Or he could have forced her to send it," Jo said. "Either way, it means she was in the park half an hour before the earliest time we thought she could have been killed."

"We'll need to go back over everyone's alibis," Arnett said.

"And if the killer sent it or forced her to send it, that means the killer is somebody who knew she was cooking a shepherd's pie," Lopez said.

"If they were watching her through her kitchen window, they might have seen her put it in," Arnett said.

"True." Lopez's brows pursed, and she took a pull from her Rockstar.

"But why bother to even mention that in a text?" Jo said. "That's a strange detail to add in, and you have to know something about cooking to get it right. Why bother?" Jo asked.

"Authenticity?" Lopez said.

Jo shook her head. "It strikes me as risky, unless the person involved knew Naomie well enough to know she was careful about those things, and that she'd text Chris about it."

"So, a friend or a co-worker?" Arnett asked.

"Or family member. And something else about that text

isn't sitting quite right with me, but I'm not sure what." Jo reached out her hand. "Is that a printout of all her texts?"

Lopez passed it to her. "Yep. Why?"

"I'm not sure, but something's bothering me. Do you mind if I borrow this?"

"Let me print out copies for you." Lopez tapped on her keyboard. The printer came to life, whirring out white sheets. "Here you go."

"Thanks, Christine. This is amazing."

Lopez smiled. "I do what I can. Let me get back to it and see what else I can find."

Jo and Arnett quickly refilled their coffee on the way back to their desks.

"While you look over those transcripts, I'll start looking at the alibis," Arnett said as he veered off into his chair.

"Perfect." Jo grabbed a handful of highlighters in a variety of colors, then dove into the text transcripts. Starting with Naomie's exchanges with Julia, she highlighted as she went along, yellow for Naomie, pink for Julia. She moved chronologically, through exchanges about Julia's divorce, a variety of issues involving Triple-B, and then, shock about Madison's murder and navigation of details for the memorial. Jo read through them a second time, paying close attention to the content, searching for something that matched the concern lurking in the back of her brain. When she found nothing she started again, this time focusing on voice rather than content—*how* they phrased their texts. Julia's texts were shorter and more direct, edged with sarcasm, while Naomie's were more casual, with a friendlier tone.

But whatever it was her brain was trying to tell her, nothing in the texts brought it forward.

"This isn't looking helpful so far," Arnett said. "Brad, Kiernan, Chelsea, and Sandra are all in the same position—they didn't really have alibis for the afternoon or evening of

Naomie's death, regardless. It may make a difference for Rhea, but that's hard to say."

"Keep the faith," Jo said. "There's no reason to send a fake text unless you're setting up a fake alibi."

"Yep," Arnett grunted.

Jo turned to Naomie's exchanges with Rhea. A few were friendly and personal, but most were about administrative details for Triple-B. Nothing in the content spoke to her, and Rhea's texting style fell somewhere in between Naomie's and Julia's. Next she went over the conversations with Chelsea, which focused far more on pregnancy, shopping, and gossip. Chelsea's texts leaned toward slang, laced profusely with LMKs and AFs, acronyms anywhere she could use them. Naomie rarely used any shortcuts, preferring complete sentences.

Pushing down her growing frustration, Jo flipped over the final page of Chelsea's texts. Next up were Naomie's conversations with Chris, the thickest section of the printout. She dove in, gulping coffee as she read through the predictably domestic texts. Messages navigating errands, meal choices, timings of events, all typical of a marriage long out of the newlywed phase —affectionate despite small spats here and there. She smiled at a series of texts that turned snipey about the money Naomie was spending—they could be word-for-word exchanges between Sophie and David.

Halfway through her second reading, what had been nagging at her brain hit her full force. Naomie's voice didn't match the text sent from the park—in very specific ways.

She flipped back and stared at the text sent from inside the park: *Had a stressful day, can't seem to shake it. Gonna go for a walk to re-center. Shepherd's pie needs an hour in the oven, pull it out if I'm not back.*

Naomie normally spoke in full thoughts, as though typing out a business letter. But this text dropped out subjects, saying 'had a stressful day' rather than '*I* had a stressful day.' And, 'gonna go' rather than 'going to go.'

Jo flipped through the pages again, checking every yellow-highlighted utterance. Not one of them dropped the subject, nor did she ever use the contraction 'gonna.'

But everywhere she looked, Chris did.

———

"Chris," Jo and Arnett blurted out simultaneously.

Jo's head snapped around to Arnett. "Did you just say 'Chris?'"

"I did." He pointed down at his notes. "Chris has an alibi for the time after six, but no alibi for the time just before that. He claims he was out on an insurance call, but he could have finished that with plenty of time left over. He could have gone home, talked Naomie into a walk—which would explain why she was willing to go out for one when her friend had just been murdered walking alone—then hurried back to work after killing her. Why did you say his name?"

Jo showed him the texts and explained what she'd discovered. "The text is in Chris's voice, not Naomie's."

Arnett nodded. "The problem is, he has no motive to kill her."

"Do we know that? We never bothered to find out what the state of their marriage was like. And there's evidence right here that Chris wasn't happy about the money Naomie spent. They remind me in tone of Sophie and David's, which at first I thought was cute, but the more I think about it frankly isn't the best indicator of relationship health."

"Fine, maybe, but what about Madison and Helen?"

Jo squeezed her eyes shut and her hands flew to her temples. Arnett was right—he barely knew Madison, and he didn't know Helen at all.

Or did he?

"Hang on. We've said that Triple-B is the connective tissue here. Chris is a part of that. He spent time there, and he knew the people there. He could have run into Helen there, and we know Madison and Chelsea visited Naomie's house."

"Sure, but what possible motive could he have to kill them?"

His words caused Julia's to echo in her head: *Why would I kill Helen?*

Jo had answered with a Hail-Mary pass thrown out by her subconscious—that maybe Helen had been a decoy, to deflect attention and confuse the police. "What if both Helen and Madison were decoys? What if Naomie really was the intended victim all along, and he just bookended her murder with two others to make it look like a serial killer was at work, one obsessed with Lucifer Lost, to make sure we paid attention and the public got riled up? You even said on the scene it felt like some sort of three-part ritual the killer had to see through for some reason."

"But Chelsea saw the strange man outside the juice bar, in the dark sedan. Chris drives a white Chevy SUV," Arnett said.

"He might have more than one car." Jo whirled around to her monitor and attacked her keyboard. But there were only two cars registered to Chris Alexander—his SUV, and Naomie's champagne Lexus. She sagged back against her chair. "Dammit."

But almost immediately, another thought hit her. "Maybe, since Chris had to travel to his insurance calls, his job provided him with a car?"

Arnett swiveled back to his monitor and pulled up the insurance company's information. After several phone trans-fers, he found the person he needed—who told him the company routinely provided cars to the employees. There was a fleet of three that the employees shared as needed—one of which was a black Toyota Camry.

"Okay, I'm listening," Arnett said. "But I'm still struggling with the notion he'd kill both his unborn child as well as his wife because she was a spendthrift."

"No, I agree, that doesn't feel right. If there was a problem in their marriage, Julia would know." She snatched up her phone, but Julia's line went directly to voice mail. "Either she's with a client or she's ducking us. I'll try Chelsea."

The phone rang several times. Just when Jo thought it would go to voice mail, Chelsea picked up. "Hello?"

"Chelsea, I don't have time to explain, but I need to ask you about Naomie and Chris's relationship. Were they having problems?"

"Problems? I don't think problems exactly," Chelsea said. "No relationship is perfect."

Jo mentally gritted her teeth. "What wasn't perfect about theirs?"

"Well, I mean, there was always going to be some tension, wasn't there? When one person comes from money and the other doesn't. And he's one of those men who gets his nose all out of joint if he's not the main provider for his family."

Jo nodded. "So they fought over money?"

"I mean, not *fight* exactly, at least not that I know of. But when we'd be out shopping, Naomie would always say things like how she'd better not buy such and such because Chris would lose it if she did. Like when we were at Maman et Bebé, they had *the* most amazing crib, and Naomie loved it so much she was actually stroking it. I told her she should get it, and she waved me off and laughed. She said Chris would have a fit, and she had to pick her battles because he was freaking out about how much a baby was going to cost."

Jo met Arnett's eyes. "But Chris was happy about having a baby, right?"

"I mean, I'm sure he *was*. But it's always an adjustment, isn't it? Like when David found out. He was *not* happy."

Jo clenched her hands into fists, trying not to let Chelsea's cluelessness rip through her self-control. "So you don't know how Chris felt about the pregnancy?"

"I mean, I never talked directly to him about it. When I was over there, he stayed in the other room playing video games or whatever. But Naomie told us a couple of things, like that he'd become distant and grumpier since they found out."

"Did that upset her?" Jo asked.

"A little. But she also said he went through something like that about a year ago and it passed eventually, so she figured the same thing would happen this time."

"How did the two of them interact?"

"From the little I saw, he was sweet. But he gave us our space and hung out in the other room like I said, so I didn't really see them interact much."

Jo thanked her for her help and hung up, then stood and grabbed her blazer. "If Chris wasn't happy about impending fatherhood, that's a definite motive. We need to find him as soon as possible."

CHAPTER FIFTY

Chris's car was nowhere to be seen when Jo and Arnett pulled up to the Alexander house. Hoping it was parked in the garage, they strode to the door and rang the bell. Nobody answered, and they couldn't hear any sounds coming from the inside. Their luck was no better when they tried his workplace—his boss informed them he was out on bereavement leave and wasn't expected in until the following week.

"Maybe we should just call him?" Arnett asked.

Jo grimaced, her mouth a tense line. "I think the element of surprise is going to be crucial for this. He's not stupid, and if we say we need to talk to him in person, that'll tip him off to our suspicions. I want to be able to see his face when he makes that connection."

Arnett nodded. "Makes sense. So stake out his house until he comes home?"

"Let's try his in-laws. If he's taking care of the funeral arrangements, it makes sense he'd be there."

But he wasn't there, either.

"He was here, but he's gone now." Cecile Gagnon's dark-brown eyes were puffy, and she looked like she hadn't slept.

"He left about an hour and a half ago to deal with some issues at the mortuary."

"Do you expect him back?" Jo asked.

"I don't think he said." She turned to her husband to verify; he shook his head. "Is it important? We can call him and ask."

"Oh, there's no need." Jo scrambled to downplay the visit. "We have a couple of loose ends we wanted to check on and figured we'd try here since we were in the neighborhood." She made a quick decision. "It seems like you and your husband have a good relationship with Chris. That must be very helpful right now."

Cecile's smile quivered. "Chris has always been a sweet boy. He made Naomie happy." She choked, and tears welled in her eyes.

"I'm so sorry." Jo backed off. "We hope to have news for you soon. We'll be back in touch as soon as we know more."

"Naomie's parents like him," Jo said when they were back at the car. "And I didn't pick anything up from him. Am I jumping the gun?"

"Psychopaths can be very charismatic." Arnett shook his head. "I remember they said something about Helms' Brothers mortuary during the memorial. Should we swing by there?"

"Let's do it."

Jo and Arnett had met Richard and Robert Helms multiple times in the course of their investigations, but it never ceased to amaze Jo how perfectly funerary the twins were. Both were excessively tall, slender, and had shocks of gray hair closely cropped into traditional 1950s businessman haircuts. Their demeanors were unfailingly sedate, and they'd both mastered the standard mortician tone, the one meant to soothe, but that usually disconcerted. She tried—and failed—to push away an image of Lurch from *The Addams Family* as she explained what they needed.

"He was here earlier, but just to deal with some quick

paperwork. He left over an hour ago," either Richard or Robert Helms told them. "Is there any way we can be of help?"

After assuring them there wasn't, Jo and Arnett hurried out to the car again.

"That's plenty of time for him to have made it back home when we checked," Arnett said. "Maybe he's out running errands?"

Jo's teeth raked her lower lip. "Possibly. Since we have no idea where else to look, our best bet is to go back there. But if he doesn't come home within the next hour, I say we put an APB out on him."

CHAPTER FIFTY-ONE

Julia made it through her client consultation by sheer force of will, and a large, highly sweetened triple espresso. Normally, despite not having much patience with most human beings, she had almost infinite patience with expectant mothers because she understood the fears that came along with pregnancy, and wanted to ease them for others the way nobody had been there to ease hers. But today she caught herself snapping when her client asked questions she'd already answered several times during previous sessions.

Dropping her medical kit by the side of the door, she slid onto her couch still wearing her coat and her trainers. She'd never been a napper—once she began the day inertia took over—but she'd never experienced anything like the last week, and never in her entire life had she needed sleep more. Not just sleep, but the escape a few hours of unconsciousness would give her from it all. She pulled a pillow under her head and tugged her coat tightly around her.

But sleep wouldn't come. Maybe it was the caffeine; she'd had more today than she normally drank in a week. Maybe it was the hellish limbo that took over with sleep deprivation, when your body flooded with cortisol to deal with stress and ended up suspending you in a strange, zombie-like state. Whatever it was, she was in it now, and her thoughts dipped and circled like vultures attacking roadkill. Taunting her with how stupid she'd been to take the risk with the grant money, how the police were certain she was a killer, how the actual killer was still out there possibly coming for her or Chelsea next.

But most of all, her thoughts kept returning to Naomie.

Naomie, who she'd loved since Naomie was a child. Naomie, who'd come into Julia's life just as Julia's mother died, allowing Julia to channel her own need to be mothered into mothering someone else. Naomie, who she'd betrayed, justifying that betrayal to herself as being an unimportant throwaway thing when she knew full well Naomie's heart would be broken by it, and how her own selfish needs allowed her to justify it all. And now Naomie was gone and Julia would change every decision she made along the way if it meant she could have Naomie back. At least there was some solace in the fact she'd never discovered Julia's betrayal before she died.

The tears came again, even stronger than they had when the detectives were there, wracking her violently, like her body was trying to expel some toxin through the saline of her tears and phlegm and even the vibrations of her larynx.

When, finally, the tears subsided, leaving her head throbbing and her heart empty, she slipped into the still darkness of sleep.

Until someone pounded on her front door.

CHAPTER FIFTY-TWO

As Jo and Arnett waited, hidden behind a set of towering bushes down the road from Chris Alexander's house, they continued what investigation they could do from the car.

"Paperwork for a warrant to search the Alexander house has been submitted," Arnett said.

"I've done some more digging on Chris. I still can't find any sort of trouble in his past. He and Naomie were definitely living paycheck to paycheck, however. All of their credit cards are running heavy balances, and their savings is non-existent. And, there's an insurance policy on Naomie."

Arnett's head popped up. "How much?"

"Pretty standard: fifty thousand, and he's insured for the same should he have died first. Not nearly enough to pay off all their debt."

"But it'd go a long way, that's for sure—"

Jo's phone buzzed, and she checked the number. "Lopez." She tapped, and answered. "Christine. What's up?"

"Jo. The judge signed off on a warrant for Julia's records. Not surprising given the overwhelming evidence of embezzlement."

"Glad to hear it."

"But what is surprising is Julia has *three* cell phones. One personal, one business, and one other. And on that third, she's been receiving some *very* personal texts."

"Right. She has a lover. She cheated on her husband with him," Jo said.

Lopez paused for a beat. "You already knew she was having an affair?"

"She told us earlier when she confessed to stealing the money," Jo said.

"Not cool keeping that from me, Jo," Lopez chastised. "Not cool at all."

"You're just annoyed she cut the legs out from under your surprise revelation," Arnett said.

"Harumph," Lopez said. "Luckily, I have a backup bombshell hiding out in my pocket. You said *lover*, right? Not lovers, plural? 'Cause there's two of them. Sounds like she left that out."

A prickling cold shot down Jo's neck to her arms. "She sure did leave that out. Do you know who they are?"

"I do not. There are two numbers, both from burners whose origins I can't trace. And she's very careful not to mention either one by name."

"So how do you know there are two? Just because there are two numbers?" Arnett asked.

"No. The texts overlap, and the tones are different—they're not the same person. One she's very lovey-dovey with, and the other she's standoffish. It sounds like up until a few days ago she hadn't heard from him in a while, and she's been putting him off."

Jo's face screwed up in concentration. That made no sense, unless—

Lopez continued, interrupting her thoughts. "Lucky for you, I may be able to get more info on that for you shortly. Both numbers texted her today, both within the last few hours. That makes me think they're still active, and if so, I should be able to get some location pings for you shortly."

"You're brilliant and amazing," Jo said, and ended the call, then pulled up Julia's contact. "But in the meantime, I've had enough of Julia's BS."

CHAPTER FIFTY-THREE

Julia bolted up out of her sleep, disoriented—who the hell could be pounding at her door? She grabbed her phone, afraid she'd missed something important. But no, she'd been home for less than forty minutes, asleep for maybe ten, and who would come looking for her here anyway? None of her clients knew she'd—

More pounding.

She jumped up and winced at the pain in her head, then pulled open the door without looking to see who was outside.

Chris strode in without waiting to be invited. He closed the door behind him, then glanced around the room. "Smaller than I expected. But homey. Nice."

She rubbed her eyes and shook her head, trying to make sense of what was happening. But everything was fuzzy except for the sense of danger screaming at her to be careful. "Chris? What are you doing here?"

"I needed to see you."

"I told you I'd call you when I could."

He crossed to the window and closed the interior drapes. "The last few days have been hell, and I love you and couldn't wait anymore." He crossed back to her, took her into his arms, and kissed her.

She pressed on his chest, still too groggy to fully understand what was happening. They'd ended their affair mutually, *both* agreed it was for the best. His ego had been bruised, yes, but they hadn't been in love—

But for some people, ego and love were one and the same. They certainly had been for Pete.

Her phone buzzed softly, still in her purse where she'd dropped her things by the door. She mentally pushed away the sound like a gnat circling her head.

As his lips pressed against hers, the situation came into focus, and her brain started to fire. She pulled gently away and forced a weak smile onto her face. "I'm sorry, I have a migraine. You woke me." She dropped into her armchair and pressed her hand to her forehead. "Could you get me a glass of water and some Excedrin Migraine, please?"

As he fumbled around the new kitchen locating glasses and medicine, she tried desperately to pull herself together. When he returned she swallowed the pills with the water, then spoke. "You have to go, Chris. You can't be here. Pete has someone watching me and I don't know where or when. But Pete knows your car."

He took the water from her and set it on the coffee table, then sat on the closest edge of the sofa. He grabbed her hand and stared into her eyes with a dangerous intensity. "We've just had a death in the family. There are a thousand legitimate reasons for me to be here. If he sees us, I'll just tell him I wanted to ask you about funeral details."

She wanted to scream at him, tell him he was being insane. Instead, she softened her tone and put an edge of fear into it she didn't have to struggle to manufacture. "He's not stupid, Chris. He knows there's no reason for you to come rather than call.

And when he puts two and two together, he'll find a way to look into your call records, and I'll be left with nothing."

"No, you won't. You have me. I can't give you what Pete could, but we can live here, we can afford this no problem." He gestured around the room. "You're not like Naomie, you don't expect the fucking world and all its trimmings, you came from a poor family like me. It's time to tell Pete to go to hell and stop living in constant fear."

She grabbed the glass of water again, scrambling for a way to buy a few moments. She'd been stupid, she realized. Unforgivably overconfident to think that her brain was any match for his insecurity complex, to think that putting him off, hoping another shiny object would catch his attention, would work. She'd played it wrong and she needed to come up with a way to deal with this, because that look in his eyes—it terrified her. When she was a little girl she'd had a dog who loved to play fetch so much that when he saw the ball he'd get a gleam in his eye and start snapping and jumping, so crazy she was always afraid he'd bite her to get it. The look in Chris's eyes made her feel the same way. She needed to keep him balanced, but get him gone.

"But, honey, think about it. Pete isn't the only problem. The police are watching me, too—"

"That freaked me out when you said it this morning. Why are the police watching *you*?" he asked.

His response gave her hope, and an idea. "It's a long story, but they think I might have killed Naomie. If they see us together, if they put two and two together, they'll find out we had an affair. And if they find out about that, they'll think we killed her so we could be together. I can't have you pulled into this."

A smug, triumphant smile slid over his face. "Don't worry, darling. I made sure they can't prove anything."

CHAPTER FIFTY-FOUR

Julia's stomach clenched, nearly regurgitating the water and pills. "What do you mean they can't prove— Chris, what are you talking about? Did you hurt Naomie?"

The smile dropped off. "Oh, no. I made sure she didn't feel any pain."

The room spun and retreated, like Julia was looking through some sort of kaleidoscope with Chris at the center. "What did you do?"

"I gave her a roofie. Madison, too."

She gripped the arms of her chair, trying to fight back the dizziness. "You killed them? Both of them?"

"Of course. But *humanely*. I knew you would have wanted that, but it made it easier, too." He leaned forward and grabbed her hand, clearly wanting her approval.

Julia snatched her hand away and struggled to draw breath. "Why? Why would you hurt Naomie?"

Chris's smile shifted to confusion. "What do you mean, why? You know why. So we could be together."

"I—I don't—We broke up. We agreed it was over— What—" she gasped, reaching for words that wouldn't come.

"We broke up because we were both married and it was only a matter of time before we got caught, and it was all too complicated. But now you and Pete are getting divorced, so you're free. That changes everything, but I needed to be free, too."

Julia shrank back. "Free? Why didn't you just divorce her if you wanted to be free?"

He stiffened, his confusion now turning hard. "How could I be free once we had a baby? As it was I couldn't afford to support *her* with the way she spends, let alone support a *child* on top of that. You saw the lists of things she was putting together that we supposedly *had to have*. Even if I could have gotten out of paying alimony, there would've been child support. But when I heard you were divorcing Pete right at the right time, I knew you were throwing me a lifeline."

Her stomach clenched again, this time sending its contents up into her throat. Her breathing sped, so fast now she struggled to get oxygen. She tried to speak, but nothing came out.

Naomie's face loomed up before her—Naomie, who'd devoted her life to helping other people—Naomie, who she'd watched grow from a little girl. Then Madison's face appeared beside Naomie's, so young and so full of promise, who'd fought so much injustice already in her life. The lost scholarship and ending up pregnant, but she was fighting to make her life better only to— And Helen— Oh, God, Helen—

"Why are you acting like this? You don't seem happy." His eyes hardened as he watched her.

She'd seen that particular look in his eyes before. Only once, because he didn't lose his temper often. It was the look that convinced her she had to break things off with him, and looking at it now, any doubt he could kill faded far away. And if he'd turned on Naomie, he'd turn on her, in no time flat. If she didn't pull herself together, buy herself some time to get out of this, she was sunk.

She forced a smile on her face, and took his hand again. "My love, I'm just trying to understand. The last few days have been beyond hard and I'm barely hanging on. You didn't tell me you were going to do this, so of course I'm surprised and trying to take it all in. I can't believe you'd—do this for me."

His expression softened—slightly. "I'd do anything for you, darling. I wouldn't just kill three people, I'd kill a hundred if I had to."

His chest puffed with pride as he said it, and electric needles jabbed through her limbs. He was proud—actually *proud* of what he'd done. She faked a cough and grabbed the water glass, pretending to drink as she struggled to keep her true reactions off her face. *Keep him talking,* her mother's voice told her. *Keep him talking so you can think.*

"But why did you kill the other two?" she choked out.

He preened. "It's brilliant—that's why they'll never figure it out. They think it's some random killer, someone who has some sick obsession with pregnant women and Satanic cults. There's no connection between me and the other two women."

Madison's and Helen's faces filled Julia's mind. She squeezed her eyes shut, forcing them away—she couldn't think about that now, she had to get him out of the house and get to the police. Or at least distract him long enough to call the police. Her gaze flicked to her purse—it was too far away, there was no way she'd be able to get her phone out without him seeing.

She cleared her throat. "So what do we do now? We can't let the police see us together."

He shook his head. "They can see us together, but we have to be careful. What we'll do is console one another. A husband and aunt-in-law, both heartbroken by Naomie's death. You'll come make sure I'm eating, all that stuff, and then, in the course of it all, we'll slowly let everyone see us falling in love. It happens all the time—"

A loud knock on the door interrupted him.

He whipped toward the door, then looked back at her. "Who's that?" he mouthed.

She shook her head: *I don't know.*

A second knock came, louder this time. "Julia? Are you in there? Are you okay?"

Julia's heart sank.

Rick.

CHAPTER FIFTY-FIVE

Jo twisted in her seat, surveying the landscape around Chris Alexander's house.

"Something's wrong," she said.

"What?" Arnett asked.

"I don't know. It's just—something feels off. With the multiple text chains and Julia not answering her phone, and Chris off doing God knows what when his wife just died—something's not right."

"Julia's probably with a client," Arnett said.

"Maybe. Except then I would have expected the call to go straight to voice mail, or after a ring or two. But it rang, what, five times before voice mail picked up? And I left the message five minutes before the hour. Whatever appointment or class she was in should be over, and she should've gotten the message by now."

Jo's phone rang again. She snatched it up and instantly answered it.

"Jo," Lopez's voice came over the phone. "I was able to get current location towers for both burner phones."

"How did you manage that so quickly?"

"Ask me no questions and I'll tell you no lies," Lopez said. "Both of them are pinging the tower down off of Varness."

"Varness? The one in the outskirts, over by Julia's house?" Arnett asked.

"That'd be the one."

"What the— Is she texting herself?" Jo asked.

"I'd've thought that, too, except up until about half an hour ago, they were both in completely different locations," Lopez said. "My guess is something's going down."

"We're on it." Jo hung up the phone and fired up the engine of the Crown Vic. "Whatever's happening, I hope to hell we aren't too late."

CHAPTER FIFTY-SIX

Chris turned to her, posture taut. "Who is that?" he whispered.

Julia froze. What the hell was Rick doing here? Hadn't she made it clear to him he couldn't be seen? If Chris figured out what was going on, he'd lose his shit.

"A friend from work checking on me," she whispered back.

His eyes narrowed at her. "Open it."

She mentally flailed for a way out. "He can't know you're here," she whispered furiously.

His face turned to steel. "Open it or I will."

Her limbs went numb as she crossed to the door, her mind still frantically searching for any way out of the situation. Could she just open the door a crack and send him away somehow? But he'd want to know why she wasn't letting him in—

She partially opened the door. Rick stood right in front of it, a toolbox in one hand and a clipboard in the other.

As soon as he saw her, he pushed in. "I know I'm not supposed to be here, but I dressed up like I'm a repair guy so it looks like you hired me to come fix something. I've been trying to reach you all morning and when I couldn't get through I was worried you were this psycho's next victim—" He stopped in his tracks when he spotted Chris. "Who's this?"

Julia cleared her throat. "This is Naomie's husband. My nephew-in-law."

Rick's face shifted as he calculated the relationship to Julia's husband. He glanced from Julia, to Chris, and back. "I—"

Chris threw up a hand. "Don't bother." He turned to Julia. "You're fucking this guy?"

Rick's face shifted again. He was smart enough to know there was no point in denying it. He set the toolbox down and pulled himself up to his full, considerable height. "Julia and Pete are getting divorced. What she does and who she sees is no longer any of his business."

Julia's last shred of hope imploded. He was brave, and it was a gallant thing to do. He had no way of knowing it was exactly the worst thing he could've said.

Chris turned to her. Time slowed as she tried to read his emotions: his face flexed and twitched, and his fists squeezed open and shut.

"Son of a bitch," he finally said. "Turns out, I'm a pathetic moron. You told me you loved me, and I believed you. You told me Pete was the reason we couldn't be together, and that you'd never leave him. And all the time you were out whoring around with this joker."

"Hold on right there, asshole," Rick said, and stepped forward. "I don't care who you are, you can't talk to her like—"

Chris's hand flew into his pocket and back out with a gun. He swung it up, pointed it at Rick, and shot him in the face.

CHAPTER FIFTY-SEVEN

Jo rounded the turn to Julia's street at full speed, then slowed as they approached the duplex. "Isn't that Chris's SUV?"

"I think so," Arnett said. "But who's blue Civic is that by the curb?"

"No idea," Jo said. "But I don't have a good feeling about it."

They climbed out of the car, carefully surveying the house and environs.

A gunshot rang out, followed by a scream.

Jo dropped back behind the car, then reached inside for the radio. As she called in for backup, Arnett unholstered his weapon, and started toward the house.

Jo pulled out her Beretta, and hurried to catch up. They climbed the few stairs up the porch as quietly as they could.

"What did you do?" Julia's voice cried out. "He didn't mean anything to me!"

"Then it won't be a problem that I killed him," Chris answered.

Arnett met Jo's eyes, and, positioning himself by the door, reached for the knob. Jo nodded. He turned the knob and swung the door in.

Jo rushed into the room, Arnett covering her. Chris stood, gun pointed at Julia. A man Jo didn't recognize lay dead and bleeding on the floor.

"Drop your weapon," Jo yelled.

Chris's head snapped toward her, and the arm with the gun stiffened. "Come any closer and I'll kill her."

"It's over, Chris," Arnett said. "We know you killed those women."

"Then you know I don't have anything left to lose, and I'll have no problem killing another one." He raised the gun still higher, now pointing directly to Julia's head.

Julia stared at Chris, tears streaming down her face. "You're going to kill *me*, too, Chris? The woman you supposedly love?" Her voice rose, escalating to hysteria. "You used your love for me to justify killing Naomie, who loved you with all of her heart, and Madison and Helen and three babies who hadn't even had a chance to live because you supposedly love me, but now you're going to kill *me*?"

Chris's face twisted with rage. "You betrayed me—"

But Julia wasn't listening anymore. Suddenly, she flew at Chris. "You better kill me, motherfucker, because if you don't I'm going to send you right to hell—"

A shot rang through the air as Julia landed on Chris and they tumbled to the floor. The gun dropped from between them.

Jo and Arnett jumped forward. Jo pointed her gun at Chris's head. "Don't move."

Arnett kicked the gun out of reach, safetied and holstered his weapon, then pulled out handcuffs.

"Both of you, raise your arms slowly to where I can see them," Jo barked.

Chris tugged his arms out from under Julia.

Julia didn't move.

Arnett slid the handcuffs onto Chris. Once Chris was secured, Arnett reached for Julia, and pushed her off Chris. She rolled over, onto her back.

A gaping red hole poured blood from her forehead down and over her open, staring eyes.

CHAPTER FIFTY-EIGHT

Jo watched as Chris settled himself into the gray plastic chair across the interrogation table, amazed that the meek, seemingly gentle person in front of her was the same man who'd registered as a raging colossus over Julia. She'd have sworn he was at least three inches taller, weighed twenty pounds more, and had completely different facial features—and she had two decades of experience taking in scenes accurately. Matt would tell her memories were fallible, influenced by context and emotion, and he was right. But this was more than that. Chris had transformed, maybe not his height and weight, but his ability to psychologically fill a room.

He leaned forward, clumsily navigating his cup of water between cuffed hands. Arnett shifted impatiently as he drank.

Backup had arrived shortly after Arnett secured Chris. Julia had been pronounced dead at the scene by the paramedics, as had the man who turned out to be Rick Moranto, proprietor of a small café downtown. Chris had been arrested and processed, and as soon as Jo and Arnett had been able, they pulled him into the interrogation room.

When he set the cup back down, she Mirandized him. "With these rights in mind, do you wish to speak to us?"

He sat back in the chair, expression and posture tight. "Will the judge go easy on me if I do?"

Jo held his eyes. "I can't promise what the district attorney, or, should it come to that, the judge will do."

He sighed, and slumped down. "There's not really much point in denying any of it. You saw what you saw, and you have the texts. What do you need me to tell you?"

"We need a statement from you for the record," Jo said. "Just start at the beginning."

He started with the first days of his marriage to Naomie. He'd loved her and thought she loved him, but she was used to a lifestyle he couldn't give her, and refused to scale down her expectations. Worse, she went behind his back to get what she wanted from her parents, which emasculated him. Made him a joke to his father-in-law.

"Julia understood. She was an outsider, too, although nobody expected her to be a bread-winner. She was expected to look good and help charm people into business deals with The Mighty Gagnons, and raise the next generation. And she was good at it, but there was still a disconnect, one that only she and I understood, and it brought us together. We laughed at the family's foibles behind their backs, and got closer over time. Then, one night when we'd both had a little too much to drink and had taken a little too much shit from the Gagnons and Naomie was out of town at some conference, she ended up in my bed. And we realized that night that we were in loveless marriages and needed to get out."

"But you didn't ask for a divorce."

"It was complicated for Julia." A sneer flashed across his face, and for a moment, the raging colossus returned. "At least that's what she *said*. Between her son Ethan being in his final year in high school and the expense of a separation it just didn't make any sense, yadda yadda yadda."

"And you've been seeing each other since?"

"No. We had a couple of close calls where we almost got caught, and she was afraid it would blow up her life. She felt guilty about what she was doing to Naomie and couldn't bear that anymore. That was about a year ago."

"And the other guy, Rick. When did they start dating?"

The rage flashed across his face again. "No idea."

"Julia said you used her as an excuse to kill Naomie. What did she mean by that?"

He stared off to the side of the room. "You have to understand, I never wanted to be a father. When Naomie got pregnant, I just saw us plummeting down an endless black hole of debt. That was going to be the rest of my life—trying to live up to the expectations of two princesses who I'd never be able to satisfy. Then I found out Julia and Pete were divorcing, and I knew it was a sign. Julia would be free, but she'd never be willing to take me away from Naomie, so I knew I had to take things into my own hands."

"And divorce wouldn't get rid of the baby," Arnett said.

Chris nodded.

"And you killed Madison and Helen to make it look like Naomie wasn't the real target."

He nodded.

"But if you wanted to distance yourself from the killing, why did you pick one of Naomie's friends?"

"I didn't realize they were that close, I just thought Madison was someone from Triple-B. Lots of people from there came around."

"But why use Triple-B at all?" Arnett asked.

"That's how the whole idea came to me in the first place. Naomie talked about Triple-B endlessly, about all these women out there having babies nobody wanted."

"She said that? That nobody wanted the babies?" Jo asked.

"No, she'd never say that, but it was the truth. She was always talking about their situations under the guise of how our social system fails women. Some of the women were married and excited about their babies, yeah. But most of them were going to be single mothers because the fathers didn't want anything to do with the children. I'd bet you anything they begged the women to have abortions. In some cases the women themselves don't even want the kids, but for religious reasons or whatever they don't want to abort."

Jo nodded, careful to keep her disgust hidden.

"Then Naomie had a couple of the women over for some sort of get-together with Julia. I listened to their chatter from the other room while I played Borderlands. And I realized—all three of the pregnant women in that room, the fathers didn't want the babies. Three babies that were going to come into the world unwanted." He pointed to Jo with an intimate gesture of understanding. "I don't have to tell *you* how Chelsea got herself knocked up by a married man who doesn't want to have anything to do with her. Yeah, he shouldn't have cheated, but everyone makes mistakes. He shouldn't be tethered to a child for the rest of his life because *she alone* gets to make a decision about having the baby. So when I was figuring out how to get rid of Naomie, I knew I'd be doing him a huge favor by getting rid of that child. And, it turns out, doing your sister a favor, too."

Jo shoved the horrible layers aside to deal with later and tried to tug him back on track. "But you didn't kill Chelsea, you killed Madison."

"Originally I wasn't sure which one of them would be better. So I followed both Madison and Chelsea to find out more about them and their schedules, and what I found out stunned me. Chelsea at least had the money to take care of the baby on her own. The kid could have had a decent life, even if his whole existence was one big manipulation tactic. But

Madison—when I followed her, I found out she was a stripper. No money, no nothing. How was she going to take care of that baby? She'd have been on public assistance for the rest of her life, and the kid would have been raised in the back of strip clubs surrounded by sex and drugs and God knows what else. She wasn't in a relationship, and I heard the women talking about it—they were sure she didn't even *know* who the father was. She added nothing to society, and had nobody to miss her or the child other than a mother who'll be dead herself within a few months. So I killed her first, and planned on killing Chelsea after Naomie."

"We believe Madison got pregnant by someone who forced themselves on her," Jo said, struggling to keep her voice above a whisper.

He narrowed his eyes at her. "Let me guess. By someone at the strip club?"

"What does that matter?" Her hands clenched at her chair under the table.

He stabbed a finger toward her. "Because if wouldn't have happened if she hadn't put herself in that situation in the first place."

"You said Chelsea's baby was a manipulation tactic. What did you mean by that?" Jo asked.

He shook his head and laughed. "When I first started following her, I was in my car waiting outside her house. She came out her front door talking on the phone, upset and loud, on speakerphone. She was talking to someone called Pierce, defending her decision to purposefully stop taking birth control so she'd get pregnant, begging him to understand her side of things because he was the only friend she'd ever had. He told her she'd crossed a line, and that as a guy he found it the ultimate betrayal to trick a man into having a responsibility like that." Chris shook his head and stared at the wall. "He's not wrong. It's not right that men don't get a say, especially when a woman can just trick them like that."

When Jo didn't speak, Arnett shot a quick look down at her clenching fists and took over. "And so you kept following Madison."

"I scoped out her and Chelsea's schedules for a couple of weeks, and overlaid them with Naomie's to find something they all had in common. They all took walks in parks, so that seemed like the most convenient way. Then all I had to do was 'run into' Madison at Crone Ridge, which wasn't hard to do. I followed her, let her get a little ahead of me, then ran up and pretended to be surprised to see her."

"And she just agreed to go into the woods with you?" Arnett's tone was skeptical.

Chris grimaced at him. "She may not have had morals, but she wasn't stupid. I walked with her for a bit, chatting with her about her pregnancy and pretending to be oh-so-happy about Naomie's. Scratched the dog's head and fussed over her so she was sure I was a friend. Right about the time we approached the target section of the path, I could tell she was starting to wish I'd go away, but my Smith & Wesson took over from there."

"So you led her into the woods at gunpoint," Jo said.

"Yep. Once we were out of earshot—or so I thought—I had her tie up the dog to a tree, then brought her farther into the woods, to the location I'd selected and set up."

"And you gave her a roofie so she wouldn't struggle," Jo said.

An odd look of triumph gleamed in his eyes. "I did, but I didn't even need to. From the moment I produced the gun, she was resigned, like a child who knew they'd done wrong. She knew what was happening and that it was for the best."

Jo shoved that delusion into her to-be-processed later compartment. "And then you staged the scene to throw suspicion on Lucifer Lost."

He shrugged. "I knew that wouldn't hold water for long. But I needed something to make sure you linked the two attacks, so I did all the staging and put the little babies into their hands knowing that would just tear at everyone's hearts. I also needed you to find them quickly, because I couldn't risk killing Naomie until you found Madison. So I left her phone on so you could track them. I still can't believe it took you almost a full day to find her—what do we pay taxes for if it takes you that long to track a phone?"

Jo refused to take the bait. "And that's why you left Helen's clothes up on the bank of the culvert. Because it took us too long to track the phones."

"Yep, exactly. You were all over the connection between Madison and Naomie, so I had to distract you as quickly as possible by killing someone who wasn't a personal friend of Naomie's. I needed you to find her before you started looking too closely toward me."

"And that's why you changed your mind from Chelsea as the third victim?" Jo asked.

He waved his hand like he was shooing a fly. "That, and because my initial research didn't uncover that Chelsea had a homicide detective on speed dial."

"And having someone particularly motivated to avenge her death was too risky," Arnett said.

Chris nodded. "So I brought Naomie some coffee at work, conveniently 'forgetting' she had a team meeting at that time. I went through her files and picked out another unwed mother from the wrong side of the tracks. Then I followed her, and the first chance I got after dark I killed her."

"How did you get her to go behind the strip mall with you?"

He shrugged. "Pretended to recognize her, and introduced myself as Naomie's husband. I asked her about her baby, and that was that—if I've learned one thing over the last few months, it's you can't shut pregnant women up about their damned babies. They all think theirs is special and amazing, like everything from elephants to rats don't manage to get themselves knocked up every day. Once I had her off guard I pulled the gun on her."

Jo's mind flew to the witness who'd reported a black woman talking happily with a friend. "You were taking quite a risk that she wouldn't just start screaming."

"Not really." He leaned forward like he was sharing a stock tip. "I told her I was going to rape her, and that she and her baby would be fine if she didn't put up a fuss, but that if she called any attention to us, I'd shoot her through the side of her stomach so her baby would die, but she'd live."

Jo stood abruptly, sending her plastic chair flying back to the wall. Both Chris and Arnett jumped—Chris back from her as far as the handcuffs allowed, and Arnett up to put himself between her and Chris.

Jo stared into the monster's eyes for a long moment, summoning every ounce of will she had.

Then she turned and walked out of the interrogation room.

CHAPTER FIFTY-NINE

Jo pulled up to Chelsea's street and parked two doors down. She sat in the car, staring up at Chelsea's brownstone, taking a moment to decide if this really was the best way to handle the situation.

Events had developed quickly after they captured Chris. He'd pleaded guilty to killing all four of the women and Rick Moranto, on the condition that Julia's murder be charged as manslaughter rather than murder.

"Saves the taxpayers the expense of a trial at least," Arnett had said. "Too bad we don't have the death penalty anymore. I'd flip the switch on the electric chair myself."

Jo found it hard to argue. "At least the families know what happened to their loved ones, and the pregnant women of Oakhurst County can rest easy again."

"Amen," Arnett said.

Then, three days later, Ben Silva from the Springfield PD called them with an update. "We got the bastard."

"Travis Hartley?"

"Yep. He was slick, but not slick enough. Some guy got rough with one of his girls, one of Travis's favorites apparently.

Travis personally took him out into the back of the parking lot to teach him a lesson, not realizing we had a night-vision camera stuck up in a tree. As soon as my guys saw what was up, they intercepted. That allowed them to search Travis, and the coke they found in his pocket got them a search of the premises. That's when they found two thugs in the back room with an assortment of pharmaceutical goodies and stacks of bills. Things escalated from there. Long story short, I got you your DNA sample."

She thanked him profusely, and made arrangements with Marzillo to have the DNA tested. "I'll pay for it personally," Jo had said. "It may not matter much to the case anymore, and even if the baby is his, I'll never be able to prove the relationship wasn't consensual. But I'd like to know, and I'd like him to know I know."

"Not a problem. I have a favor I can call in," Marzillo had said. "Because I couldn't agree with you more."

And she hadn't been kidding—she called in the favor so fast they had the results two days later: Travis Hartley was Madison's baby's father.

Jo smiled at the thought of Marzillo's face when she'd relayed the news. Sometimes—too often—she forgot how lucky she was. To have friends like Marzillo, and Lopez, and Arnett. And family who loved her, and a wonderful partner in Matt. She had zero doubt they'd go to the ends of the earth for her, as she would for them.

And, she reminded herself as she gazed up at Chelsea's house, not everybody was so lucky. After what Chris said he'd overheard, she'd done a little digging on Chelsea. No matter where she looked, she couldn't identify any close connections in Chelsea's life other than her sister, who David had said was essentially out of her life. Chelsea's parents had died tragically, and while her social media over the last ten years had countless photos of parties and sorority events, Chelsea was always surrounded by a crowd. There was never any particular person —other than the man named Pierce—who recurred regularly.

And that was the reason she'd waffled back and forth on what she was about to do.

With a deep intake of breath, she climbed out of the car and made her way up Chelsea's stairs. She rang the bell, then punctuated with a firm knock.

Chelsea's face when she opened the door was a strange mixture of fear and gratitude. Apparently, she wasn't much happier about their inadvertent relationship than Jo was.

"Oh, hello. I wasn't expecting you." She glanced up and down the street. "Is everything okay?"

"Everything's fine. I just wanted a word with you if you have a minute."

"Sure, of course." She stepped back, signaling that Jo should follow. "I was just about to make some tea. Would you like some?"

"That would be nice. Thank you."

Jo followed her down a long hall to a French-country kitchen.

"Please forgive the mess." Chelsea rubbed a hand over her belly. "It's hard for me to clean these days, and the maid doesn't come until tomorrow."

Jo glanced around, looking for crumbs on the counter or dust in a corner, but came up short—no small feat, since Jo was no slouch herself when it came to obsessive cleaning. She sat at the white kitchen table as Chelsea opened a cabinet.

"I'm doing peppermint since I can't have caffeine, but I'm guessing your tastes run more to Earl Grey?" she asked.

"That would be perfect."

Jo allowed silence to fall over them as Chelsea poured water from an electric kettle into two mugs, then carried them over on a tray. She handed one to Jo, then settled herself into a chair.

"Well. This is a surprise. I never thought in a million years you'd come pay me a visit."

Jo smiled wryly. "I thought we should talk."

Chelsea set her mug down. "Okay."

"Chris explained why he committed the murders." Jo summed up the motivations as succinctly as possible without telling her she'd come terrifyingly close to being his third victim.

Chelsea's hands flew to her belly. "All that just because he didn't want to be a father?"

Jo sipped her tea and weighed Chelsea over the lip of the mug. She still couldn't quite get a full handle on her. Was she self-centered or just naive and lonely? Was it some blend of both? "There's a lot to unpack in all of it," Jo said. "That's what I want to talk to you about."

"What do you mean?" Chelsea asked.

"Chris didn't want to be a father, but there was more to it than that. He believed he loved Julia, and couldn't deal with it when Julia didn't love him. Julia loved Pete, and lashed out by having an affair when she realized he didn't love her. Rick Moranto died protecting the woman he loved. And Madison gave up the thing she wanted most in the world, her education, to take care of the mother she loved so deeply. Love is a very powerful emotion, and it can drive people to do very unwise things."

Chelsea stiffened. "You said Chris *believed* he loved Julia. You don't think he did?"

"You don't kill someone you love. We all get our hearts broken, that's part of being human. And for all of us there's a point where we can choose to accept that heartbreak with grace, learn from it, and move on to find the love we're truly meant to have. Julia tried to do that, even if she made mistakes along the way. But she was stopped by someone who couldn't."

Chelsea sipped her tea, still silent.

"Do you understand what I'm trying to say?" Jo finally asked.

Her eyes narrowed. "You're warning me to stay away from David."

Jo shook her head. "I'm not. If you and David want to be together, you should be together. And if so, I'd rather you figure that out now than later."

Chelsea froze, cup midway to her mouth. "Then what *are* you saying?"

"I'm asking you to think deeply and honestly about the situation, and about whether the two of you really are meant to be together, or if this is something else." Jo paused to take a sip of tea. "You told my sister that you broke things off with David. But that wasn't true, was it?"

Chelsea swiped at an invisible spot on the table. "I don't understand what you're getting at."

"David broke things off with you, didn't he? But when you told Sophie *you* broke it off, he tried to show you a kindness by not stirring up trouble between you and Sophie. And you've been trying to keep him on a close leash ever since, thinking you can change his mind."

Chelsea pursed her brow. "I'm the mother of his child. Everyone has agreed he needs to be involved in the child's life."

Jo took another deep breath—she'd been hoping to avoid this. "Chris overheard you saying you tricked David into getting you pregnant by stopping your birth control."

The brows wavered, then defiance burst in her eyes. "He loves *me*. He wasn't happy with *her*."

Jo grasped her mug with both hands. "At the memorial, when you fainted, you didn't want me to call him. I hoped at that point you'd given up. But you'd just changed tactics, hadn't you? You pretended to faint, didn't you?"

Chelsea's mouth twisted, like she was chewing on words before spitting them out. "If I call him, I'm trying to get him back. If I don't call him, I'm trying to get him back. There's no winning, so why should I even bother to answer your ridiculous accusations?"

With that show of pointless petulance, the last string of hope Jo had been holding stretched and broke, and the darker possibilities she'd been trying to deny snapped into focus. "I need you to hear me. This situation is at a dangerous crossroads —a very dangerous crossroads. The kind where it's easy to slip into the kind of bad choices like the ones Julia and Chris made. I don't want to see anybody hurt, including you. If you're going to be a part of our lives—and that's inevitable at this point—I'd like it to be in the healthiest, most honest way possible, so we can all be on your side. So I'm going to ask you again to think carefully about what you want, and what course of action is going to bring you happiness."

Chelsea's chin lifted. "Is that a threat?"

Jo chose her words carefully. There was next to no chance that anything she'd said was going to penetrate, and that left her only one course. "Your actions have consequences without any intervention from me. I'm just here giving you the advice I'd give to my sister or any of my friends if they were in your situation. The advice I hope they'd give me. Do some thinking. Choose carefully."

Chelsea's eyes flashed and a plastic smile creased her face. "I can't tell you how much I appreciate you checking in on me, Jo. Thank you so much for your visit." She stood. "But I have a thousand tasks I need to attend to, so I'll see you out now."

CHAPTER SIXTY

"Ugh." Jo extracted a handful of flesh and seeds from the pumpkin on the table in front of her, and sent a teasing glare at Isabelle. "How do I get roped into doing your dirty work every year?"

"Because you understand the importance of tradition," Matt said as he watched Emily draw a lopsided triangle on her pumpkin's squat face.

"Here, try this out." Sophie pulled a hand mixer out of her cabinet, attached the beaters, and gave it to Jo.

Jo took the mixer like she was handling a venomous snake. "What am I supposed to do with this?"

"I saw a video on YouTube that said if you run it around the insides, it pulls all the stringy insides out lickety-split."

"Have you tried it?" Jo asked.

"That's your job." Sophie laughed. "I stay in my lane."

Jo stuck the beaters into the pumpkin and, with one eye squeezed shut, slid the power button to medium. When the pumpkin didn't explode, she reopened the eye. "I'll be darned. It works."

"Did you carve *your* pumpkin already, Aunty Jo?" Emily asked.

Jo rolled her eyes. "A pumpkin that large would take a month to carve. So we just drew a scary face on it."

Emily thrust her hands onto her hips. "That's cheating!"

Jo wagged a teasing finger at her. "Hey, you take care of your pumpkin and I'll take care of mine."

Keys clanked in the door, and Emily sprung up. "Daddy!"

Isabelle, temporarily forgetting she was too old to get excited about things, ran after her sister.

Jo glanced over at Sophie with a question in her eye.

"He's here to take them trick-or-treating. I'm going to stay here and hand out candy."

"But he's using his keys again," Jo said, putting a sing-song lilt into the words.

Sophie grabbed the cookie sheet filled with pumpkin seeds and took them to the counter, but not before Jo spotted the blush on her cheeks.

"Mama, we're going to go put our costumes on!" Emily cried from the hallway.

"Finish your jack-o'-lanterns first," Sophie called, separating out pumpkin seeds onto another cookie sheet.

Emily ran in, and grabbed Matt's hand. "I finished drawing. Can you cut it even though it's so small?"

"Of course." Matt fired up the electric pumpkin carver and headed toward one of the drawn eyes.

"You're not gonna mess it up, right?" Emily doubtfully eyed the pumpkin's small, squashed sides.

"That all depends on how nervous you make me." Matt widened his eyes in mock terror.

"He's a surgeon, *cherie*," Jo said. "Hands steady as a rock."

"Ooh." Emily stared up at him like he was Elsa from *Frozen*.

Jo finished cleaning Isabelle's pumpkin, then passed it over.

With deft strokes, Isabelle drew on a cute, funny face and slid it toward Matt.

"Done." Matt set Emily's jack-o'-lantern in front of her and picked up Isabelle's. Jo watched the blade slide around the fine lines; as promised, his hands were steady and sure.

When he finished, the girls ran off to light the pumpkins and put them on the porch.

Sophie watched them go, then turned to Jo. "I owe you an apology."

Caught off guard, Jo's tone came out in a squeak. "What for?"

"For calling you up while you were dealing with those murders, complaining about Chelsea. I overreacted right when you didn't need it."

Jo shifted in her seat, uncertain how to respond. She didn't like leaving Sophie with an impression that caused her to doubt her own instincts, especially when it turned out she'd been disturbingly close to the truth. "I'd have been just as worried as you were."

"No, you wouldn't have been." Her hand shot up in the air like a tent revivalist giving testimony. "I actually started to wonder if she was murdering those other women just so David would be worried about someone harming *her*. How convoluted is that?"

Jo didn't think it was a good idea to mention what she'd found out about Chelsea—Sophie was worried enough as things were. She reached for a diplomatic, noncommittal response. "I told you you'd make a good detective. Everyone has to be a suspect."

"Yes, well. That may be all well and good for a detective, but in real life if you want to avoid going insane, you can't see murderers behind every tree." She glanced out of the kitchen toward the stairs, checking to see if anyone was around. "Any-way. We haven't heard hide nor hair from her in days, not since you brought in that horrible killer. I suppose she really was just stressed about the killings after all."

Guilt tugged at Jo. Maybe she should tell Sophie about her conversation. It was one thing to play it all down, but another to leave Sophie with a deluded sense of security.

Under the table, Matt reached over and squeezed her hand. Surprised, she looked up at him. She'd told him about it all, including her certainty that the conversation with Chelsea had fallen on deaf ears. He must have read the expression on her face, because he gave a subtle, almost-not-there shake of his head. *No.*

"And," Sophie continued, "I'm going to tell David tonight that he should move back in."

She watched her sister seasoning the cleaned pumpkin seeds with a flush of happiness again on her cheeks, and an invisible hand clenched around Jo's heart. Matt was right. Sophie deserved a little peace of mind, and if she knew Chelsea was in fact out to capture David, she'd never be able to sleep at night. And, if Chelsea wasn't calling David, maybe she *had* taken what Jo said to heart—maybe she'd given some thought to what would truly ease her loneliness and realized David wasn't it. There was no reason to think that wasn't the case, and no good would come from Sophie obsessing about a problem that might never surface with respect to a woman she had no choice but to interact with.

Jo squeezed Matt's hand back. *You're right. I'll let her relax.*

Because whatever Chelsea decided to do, Jo would be watching.

A LETTER FROM M.M. CHOUINARD

Thank you so, so much for reading *Little Lost Dolls*! Whether this is your first time reading one of my books or you're a long-time friend of Jo and her team, I'm deeply grateful to you for spending time with us. If you enjoyed the book and have time to leave me a short, honest review on Amazon, Goodreads, or wherever you purchased the book, I'd very much appreciate it. Reviews help me reach new readers, and that means I get to bring you more books! Also, word of mouth means everything to authors, so if you have a friend or family member who'd enjoy the book, I'd be so grateful if you'd mention it to them.

If you have a moment to say hi on social media, please do—I love hearing from you! You can also sign up for my personal newsletter at www.mmchouinard.com for news directly from me about all my activities, new releases, and updates; I will never share your email.

SPOILER ALERT: Don't read further unless you want to risk me spoiling the book for you!

As is usually the case, this book was the result of two issues coming together in my head. The first had to do with a case I read about where a pregnant woman was killed—and the murderer targeted her because she was pregnant. Murder is horrible no matter what, but there's something about someone committing murder fully knowing an unborn baby will also die that hits a very sensitive core in me, and sent me thinking about what possible motives would lead to that, and what has to be missing in a person to make them willing to commit such an act.

The second is very different—it's been brewing ever since, when I was a youngling, the movie *Indecent Proposal* came out. If you've never heard of it, the premise is simple: a millionaire offers a struggling couple a million dollars—if the wife spends the night with him. I remember countless conversations sparked by the movie—would you do it? And if not, how much would it take? Would you do it for ten million? A billion?

I found that question intriguing on a broader level. Money can buy a lot—sometimes even people—and the lack of money can cause great desperation. Even if we're not at the extremes of that continuum, every day we make choices about what we're willing to exchange for money—it determines what jobs we're willing to take, how much we'll pay for a given object, everything from what foods we can afford to eat to what clothing we wear. And, just like in *Indecent Proposal*, the choices we make around money have implications and consequences for our personal relationships. Would we take a million dollars for spending a night with a billionaire? What if we knew it would destroy our marriage and our self-esteem? What if it was the only way we could save the life of a loved one who had emphysema? Would we be willing to work at a strip club if it meant saving that loved one? Do we shop at certain stores knowing they don't treat their employees well because doing so allows us to make our paycheck stretch? And there are a parallel set of questions on the other side of that equation—do we spend our money to get not just things we want, but to buy people? Respect? Friendship? Are we willing to give up that money and lifestyle for love or other priorities? And what happens when our wallets can't back up our egos? These are the dilemmas I wanted to explore in this book—the lines people draw with respect to money and relationships, and what the consequences of those lines are. Hopefully the choices my characters made will spur some interesting discussions!

Thank you so much for reading!

Michelle

facebook.com/mmchouinardauthor

twitter.com/m_m_chouinard

instagram.com/mmchouinard

goodreads.com/mishka824m

ACKNOWLEDGMENTS

You, dear reader, are the wind beneath my wings. That sounds cheesy, right, like I'm trying to be funny, but I'm really not—every time someone tells me they enjoy one of my books or that they love Jo, it lifts me up and makes my day. Reading (and writing) has always been an escape for me, and I've made so many fictional friends over the years—it fills my heart to know I've done that for another reader and makes me want to run to my computer and start the next book. So, thank YOU for reading my books, and if you've reviewed them, told someone else about them, blogged about them, or requested them from your local library, double thank you! All of those things help me continue bringing Jo Fournier to you, and mean the world to me.

None of it would be possible without my team at Bookouture. Rhianna Louise guided the early stages of editing, and Maisie Lawrence took it from there. Alexandra Holmes, Billi-Dee Jones, Jane Eastgate, and Nicky Gyopari all helped edit and produce it. Kim Nash, Noelle Holten, Sarah Hardy, and Jess Readett did an amazing job promoting it; Melanie Price, Occy Carr, and Ciara Rosney helped market it; Alba Proko made the audiobook a reality; and Jenny Geras, Jessie Botterill, Laura Deacon and Natalie Butlin oversaw it all. So many amazing hands making it all happen!

I couldn't do what I do without the help of experts to guide me along the way. Thank you to the NWDA Hampshire County Detective Unit, to Leonard Von Flatern, and to Detective Adam Hill for their invaluable expertise and patience answering questions about police procedure and strange scenarios. Thanks also to Dr. Jen Prosser for her expert toxicology guidance. Thank you all so much for taking your valuable time to answer my many questions and guide me in the right direction. Any errors/inaccuracies that exist are my fault entirely.

Thanks to both my agent, Lynnette Novak, and Nicole Resciniti for your advice, guidance, and support.

Thanks also to my writing tribe, who encourage me, educate me, write with me, critique me, lift me up, and make me laugh. This includes my fellow SinC brothers and sisters (especially Ellen Kirschman, George Kramer, Ana Manwaring, T.E. MacArthur and Heidi Noroozy), my fellow MWA members (especially the Monday & Wednesday write-in crew), D.K. Dailey, Karen McCoy, M.M.'s Murder Mob, Katy Corbeil, and my fellow Bookouture authors. Writing can be so solitary, I am truly thankful to have friends like you.

Where would I be without my furbabies? Cold and lonely and completely bereft of the fur that always covers my clothes and the shredded sides that keep my sofa from feeling uninvitingly perfect. They make me laugh, help me keep perspective, and love me unconditionally.

Speaking of which, without my husband my books would not exist. Not only because he said "go for it" when I said I wanted to quit my day job to write, but because he nods in all the appropriate places when I talk to him about my plots and characters so I can figure out how to plug my story's holes. He's a pretty cool guy.

Made in the USA
Las Vegas, NV
27 July 2023

75325891R00194